# The Heart of Lies
## A Paradise Valley Mystery: Book Two

## DEBRA BURROUGHS

# THE HEART OF LIES

Copyright © 2012 Debra Burroughs

All rights reserved.

ISBN: 1480107506
ISBN-13: 978- 1480107502

All rights reserved as permitted under the U.S. Copyright Act of 1976, no part of this publication may be reproduced, distributed, or transmitted in any form or by any means, or stored in a database or retrieval system, without the prior permission of the publisher.

This is a work of fiction. Names, characters, places and incidents either are the product of the author's imagination or are used fictitiously. Any resemblance to actual persons, living, dead (or in any other form), business establishments, events, or locales is entirely coincidental.

Lake House Books
Boise, Idaho

First eBook Edition: 2012
First Paperback Edition: 2012

THE HEART OF LIES by Debra Burroughs, 1$^{st}$. ed. p.cm.

Visit My Blog: www.DebraBurroughsBooks.com

Contact Me: Debra@DebraBurroughsBooks.com

# DEDICATION

*This book is dedicated to my amazing husband, Tim, who loves me and encourages me every day to do what I love – writing.*

*I also dedicate this book to my awesome Beta Readers, Buffy Drewett, Cathy Tomlinson, and Janet Lewis, who inspire me and help me with their words of encouragement and critique.*

*Finally, this book would not be what it is today without my amazing editor, Lisa Dawn Martínez, The Finicky Editor.*

# THE HEART OF LIES

## TABLE OF CONTENTS

|    | Prologue                    | Page 1   |
|----|-----------------------------|----------|
| 1  | Rocky Mountain Oysters      | Page 5   |
| 2  | Welcome Party               | Page 23  |
| 3  | Lunch with the Girls        | Page 31  |
| 4  | The Art of Persuasion       | Page 41  |
| 5  | The Hotel Job               | Page 49  |
| 6  | Emily's Break-In            | Page 63  |
| 7  | The Presentation            | Page 71  |
| 8  | Engagement Party Invitation | Page 83  |
| 9  | Engagement Party Surprise   | Page 93  |
| 10 | Sully's Regrets             | Page 105 |
| 11 | Josh's Confrontation        | Page 113 |
| 12 | A Grizzly Discovery         | Page 121 |
| 13 | Colin's Return              | Page 131 |
| 14 | The Arrest                  | Page 143 |
| 15 | A Conversation with Josh    | Page 151 |
| 16 | The Crystal Paperweight     | Page 161 |
| 17 | Sully's Admission           | Page 169 |

| | | |
|---|---|---|
| 18 | Taking Care of Maggie | Page 181 |
| 19 | Evan's Identity | Page 193 |
| 20 | The Hospital Visit | Page 203 |
| 21 | The Short List | Page 213 |
| 22 | Searching Maggie's House | Page 223 |
| 23 | Date at DaVinci's | Page 237 |
| 24 | Trust No One | Page 249 |
| 25 | A Surprising Discovery | Page 261 |
| 26 | The Set Up | Page 271 |
| 27 | The Game of Love and Trust | Page 281 |
| | The Scent of Lies Excerpt | Page 297 |
| | Three Days in Seattle Excerpt | Page 321 |
| | Author Biography | Page 335 |

*"Oh, what a tangled web we weave when first we practice to deceive."*

~ *Sir Walter Scott*

# PROLOGUE

*Lies are deceptive little things. Whether they are innocent white lies or the evil midnight black ones, they all have a way of coming back to expose us at the most inopportune moments.*

~*~

The unsuspecting young woman approached the doorway of the dimly-lit private office. She jerked to a halt, catching sight of the man sprawled on the floor next to his desk, his body motionless, his face bloody and battered. Her hand flew over her mouth. Her other seized hold of the door frame for support, feeling her knees begin to give out.

A plethora of painful emotions roiled in her chest as she stared, eyes wide, fighting to stuff down the overwhelming urge to scream. Perhaps the attacker was still within earshot.

*Who did this? Who?*

The list of people who might want him dead was long—that much she knew. The only question to be asked was which one actually followed through. She needn't ask why, though, she already knew that answer.

Hot tears stung her eyes. She fought against the powerful desire to run into the office, to fling herself down and put her arms around him. Under different circumstances, she would have caressed him one last time and kissed him a final good-bye—but not now.

With her heart thudding loudly in her ears, she could hardly think, she remained frozen to the safety of the door jamb. Self-preservation dictated that she could not risk running to him. Someone could discover her there and she would be found out. And if she got his blood on her, she might even be blamed for his murder.

She struggled to hold herself back and cling to the safety of the solid frame, torn between grief, terror, and rage. Nearly choking on the knot in her throat, she whispered a raspy and tearful good-bye. "I'm sorry, James, but I can't go to prison. Not even for you. Good-bye."

Her attention was pulled away as she picked up the sound of a car door slamming in the parking lot. Her thoughts flew to the police, who would certainly be coming. Images of them flashed through her mind—finding her there, digging into her background, arresting her. She couldn't have that.

Her mother always told her that men would come and go, but no matter what, her top priority had to be to look out for number one.

Her instincts to save herself won out.

# THE HEART OF LIES

# CHAPTER 1
## Rocky Mountain Oysters

"WHO'S UP FOR THE ROCKY MOUNTAIN Oyster Feed?" Emily Parker asked her cluster of friends as they stood on the sun-drenched sidewalk, watching the end of the Founders Day Parade. The music from the high school marching band began to die down as the last musicians rounded the corner, drifting out of sight.

Emily loved the parade and small town festivities in Paradise Valley, but most of all she loved the interesting women that made up her close circle of friends. After recently taking over her husband's private investigation business after his murder, no one was more important to her than these three girlfriends.

They had helped her through her devastating loss, not to mention her transition from real estate agent to lady PI.

A chorus of "count me in" and "me too" rang out from the group, with the exception of one loud dissenter.

"Eeew, fried bull testicles?" Maggie's face screwed up in a look of disgust. She tucked a strand of long blonde hair behind her ear and rolled her big blue eyes like a teenager half her age.

"Oh Maggie. You're such a drama queen." Isabel shook her head. Isabel Martínez was a no-nonsense FBI financial analyst who had seen it all. She and her attorney husband, Alex, had been looking forward to the Rocky Mountain Oyster Feed for months and they clearly weren't going to let Maggie Sullivan, the Southern belle fitness queen, put a damper on their fun. "They're delicious, Maggs. You have to put it out of your head what they really are."

"But they're fried bull testicles, Isabel." Maggie frowned. "How can y'all ever get *that* out of your head?"

"They're a delicacy, Maggie," redheaded Camille Hawthorne piped in. As a caterer and event planner, sometimes the spiky-haired diva had to put an enticing spin on some of her unique specialty dishes. "Think of them simply as Rocky Mountain Oysters—that's what I keep reminding my Jonathan."

"But the thought, Camille—" Her tall, lanky husband, Jonathan, wore a wincing look on his face. "I feel for those poor bulls—ouch."

"All right, all right." Emily waved her hands and shook her head, making her honey-blonde curls dance around her neck. "Enough talk. Whoever wants to go to the Oyster Feed, follow me."

"All y'all can go on without me. I'll meet up with y'all later," Maggie called out as the group left her standing her ground.

The small crowd of friends chatted and laughed their way to the city park, where a large open-air tent was set up to serve the Oyster Feed. People had already begun lining up at the serving station to grab a plateful of the "oysters" along with a piece of buttered corn on the cob and a juicy wedge of ripe, red watermelon.

Emily, along with her girlfriends, Camille and Isabel, and their husbands, Jonathan and Alex, descended on a long folding table, balancing their oyster-laden plates and cold drinks.

"I wish Colin could have been here," Emily remarked.

Six months after her husband, Evan, had been killed, Emily began dating the town's new police detective, Colin Andrews. Within a few short months, he had been called back to San Francisco to help his mother take care of his father, following a debilitating stroke. He wasn't sure how long he'd be gone, but had said he felt duty-bound to help out.

Ex-Marines were like that, Emily reminded herself.

She and Colin tried to keep in contact long distance by way of emails, phone calls, and Face Time on the computer, but it wasn't the same as having him there in person. She was lonely for him, especially when she saw her friends enjoying life with their men. Her only solace was that Maggie was single too and they could commiserate together.

"How is Colin doing?" Alex asked. They had been basketball buddies, and as an attorney, Alex found himself working the opposing side of some of the cases Colin investigated.

"He misses you all." Emily's hair hung in loose tousled curls, brushing her shoulders, as she looked down at her plate, bravely cutting into an oyster.

"But he misses you the most, I'm sure." Camille patted Emily's hand.

Emily sighed. "I'm sure you're—"

"Hey, y'all." Maggie burst in and stood next to their table. "I told y'all I'd catch up sooner or later."

"Have a seat." Isabel motioned to the folding chair next to her.

"I have someone I want all y'all to meet." Maggie gestured to a young brunette standing next to her in the crowded tent. Maggie stood behind the empty chair and put an arm on the shoulder of the young woman. "Everybody, this is Fiona. She's new to Paradise Valley, and I offered to introduce her 'round."

"Hello, Fiona." Emily was first to greet her, but the others quickly followed.

Isabel's training in the FBI caused her to always be the first to question and be suspicious. "Where did you two meet?" she asked. Isabel sounded interested, but wore a far-too-analytical look for mere small talk.

"Fiona was in one of my aerobics classes at the Y," Maggie replied.

"Yes, in aerobics class." Fiona nodded. "I don't know anyone here yet, so I figured there might be people I could get to know in an exercise class."

"Why don't you two grab some food and come and eat with us?" Emily suggested.

"I already told y'all, no fried bull's testicles for me," Maggie shot back.

"What?" Fiona's eyes widened with surprise as she looked down at the half-eaten food on the plates. "What are you eating?"

"Bull's testicles," Maggie repeated, linking her arm through Fiona's and pulling her away from the tent.

The friends at the table burst out in laughter at Maggie's over-the-top disgust with their dining choice. Soon conversation began to flow again and the meal was quickly devoured.

Camille was seated across the table from Isabel and Emily, and she leaned in toward them as if she was about to say something of great importance. In response, they inclined forward as well.

"Did Maggie tell you yet about the man she met?" Camille asked, dipping her chin and raising an eyebrow for emphasis. She glanced over at the husbands, who were thick in conversation about the latest baseball scores and rankings.

"No. What man?" Emily asked.

"Yeah, what man?" Isabel repeated with typical concern.

"Well, I thought she would have spilled the beans by now, so don't tell her I told you girls, but she met a man on one of those online dating sites." Camille sat back in her chair, running her hands through her short spiky red hair, an intentional pause, as if to let that information sink in.

"I don't like the sound of that." Isabel pushed her long black waves over her shoulder. "You never know what kind of kook or pervert is lurking on those sites."

"They seem to be getting more popular," Emily remarked. "I think the reputable ones might be safe, don't you think?" She looked from Isabel to Camille.

"I don't want to sound paranoid," Isabel crossed her arms on the table, "but no site is totally safe from scam artists and perverts."

"Any details, Camille?" Emily inquired.

"All I know is," she leaned forward again, "his name is Lucas and he has money."

"Is that what Maggie said?" Emily asked.

It was well known among these close friends that Maggie had always hoped to snag a man with money. She had grown up poor in Texas, escaping that life as a young single mother with a small son, making her way to Hollywood in hopes of becoming a movie star. When her ship never came in, she left her deadbeat husband and moved north to Idaho where her brother and his family lived.

Over the years, her son, Josh, grew up into a fine young man and joined the Navy two years earlier. Her brother, Clifford "Sully" Sullivan, co-owned and ran the local golf course and had been elected Mayor of Paradise Valley a couple of years before.

When Maggie had arrived in Paradise Valley, she'd brought little more than her young son, but she learned all she could about fitness training and she'd opened her own studio, which gave her a decent living. Still, she always said it was her dream to find herself a man of means who would love her and treat her like a queen. Maybe now her dreams were coming true.

"What does she know about this man?" Isabel asked.

"All she's told me is that he lives in Colorado, his name is Lucas Wakefield, and he's an investor," Camille reported.

"Investor? What does he invest in?" Isabel questioned.

"You'll have to ask Maggie if you want any more facts," Camille said. "But, please, wait until she brings him up. Otherwise, she'll know I told you."

"Maybe I should run a background check on him," Isabel suggested, tapping her finger on her chin.

"Oh, Isabel, I don't think Maggie would like that," Emily warned. Being a private investigator made Emily as skeptical as Isabel's FBI training had made her, but Emily knew Maggie wouldn't see it that way. "Why don't you wait on that one?"

"All right—for now," Isabel agreed. "But as soon as she tells us about this Lucas character and she starts talking like they're getting serious, I'm doing a background check."

"Enough talk about Maggie, what about you, Em?" Camille asked. "Have you found out anything more about Evan's mysterious past?"

Emily's late husband, Evan Parker, had been a private investigator in Paradise Valley. He'd been murdered while working late in his office one night about a year ago. Eventually, Emily was able to start putting her tragic loss behind her. Hoping to move on to a new relationship at her friends' urging, she began to pack Evan's things away.

While going through his closet, she had come upon a slender silver key that turned out to belong to a safe deposit box at a local bank. She had been shocked that he had kept secrets from her and angry that he had lied about his past.

Gaining access to the safe deposit box, she'd examined the contents and found three passports with three different names—Alexi Krishenko, Michael Boerner, and Sean McDonough. She'd also discovered a large bundle of cash, some Euros, a mysterious brass key, a gun, and an old photo of Evan with a pretty, young, dark-haired woman. He had his arm intimately around her shoulders and they were smiling into the camera.

Of all the things she'd found in the box, the photo had packed the biggest wallop. Emily had removed the key and the photo from the metal box and left the rest at the bank for safe keeping.

"I still haven't been able to find out who the woman in the photo is or what the key unlocks," Emily replied.

Months after Evan's death, Emily had been pulled into one of his old cases and had taken over as the investigator. She'd worked the case, but it had dragged her deeper into her own puzzling mystery. The items in Evan's safe deposit box clearly spoke of another life, a life he had kept from her, leaving her to wonder who he really was and if their marriage had been one big lie.

"You know, I did offer to help you with that." Isabel had suggested that on numerous occasions, but Emily always put her off, telling Isabel she didn't want her to get involved, that she would take care of it herself. Still, Emily hadn't been able to solve the puzzle by herself—perhaps now she should accept the offer.

"What do you have in mind?" Emily stared seriously into Isabel's eyes.

"See, I knew you'd come around. I could see it in those blue eyes—"

"They're green," Camille interrupted.

"They're both," Isabel corrected. "Anyway, I have a friend who just retired after thirty-five years with the FBI. He's living over in Boise and he may have some contacts that could identify the woman. If I can give him a copy of that photo you found, the one with Evan and the woman, he may be able to find something out about Evan's past life for you."

"Assuming Evan Parker was his real name," Emily added.

"Whatever his name was, my friend may be able to dig something up."

"What do you have to lose, Em?" Camille encouraged.

"Okay, I'll scan the photo and email it to you, Isabel. Then you can forward it to your FBI friend."

"Retired FBI friend," she corrected.

"So, what's your *retired* friend's name?" Emily questioned. "That is, if you don't mind my asking."

"No," she waved her hand. "If I told you, I'd have to kill you." Isabel said it with a straight face, but then she snickered and Emily and Camille laughed, too. "Let's just call him Jethro."

"What are you girls laughing about?" Jonathan asked from the other end of the table. He and Alex gawked suspiciously at the women.

"Just girl talk." Emily flashed a quick smile to her girlfriends. "Hey, I heard there was a pie baking contest somewhere around here." She changed the subject and rose to her feet. "And afterwards, they're selling the entries. Tell me. Who's ready for pie?"

~*~

Emily and her friends had a ritual of meeting together on Thursday nights for a potluck dinner at one of their homes—girls only. This Thursday it was Emily's turn to host the dinner and the theme was Italian. Since Emily was the worst cook of the four of them, she decided her contribution would be a big green salad and fresh sourdough bread from the local bakery.

She was setting the table for dinner when her cell phone rang. A big smile spread across her face and her heart began to beat a little faster when she saw it was Colin.

"Hello." She answered in her sweetest tone—the one she reserved for Colin.

"Hi, Emily. I've missed hearing your voice," he said.

She missed hearing his, too. It always reminded her of warm, dark chocolate—smooth, sweet, and sensual. "Me too. How's your dad?"

"He's doing better, but Mom's not able to take care of him all on her own yet."

"Any idea when you'll be back?" Soon, she hoped.

"No, but I'm as anxious to come back to Paradise Valley as you are to have me." He chuckled.

"What's so funny?"

"Me. I can't believe I'm actually missing that small town. I never thought I'd say that."

Colin had been a San Francisco policeman, then a detective there. He loved the big city—until his fiancée was killed. He had taken the job in the small picturesque town of Paradise Valley to escape her memory. That's when he and Emily met, and when, according to him, he was captivated by her.

"I thought it was me you were anxious to return to, not this town," Emily replied, feeling a little deflated.

"Absolutely—but I do have to admit that I was becoming attached to that place and the people in it. Before you know it, I'll be back."

"You better be, mister. I'll admit it. I'm so lonely for you I can hardly stand it."

"I'm glad to hear you say that. I feel the same way."

"Oh you do, huh?"

"Yes, I do." Colin cleared his throat. "Emily, I, I—"

Emily's attention was jerked away. "Knock, knock! Where are you, Emily?"

Camille and Isabel entered the house, calling for their host.

"I'm back here!" Emily shouted from the kitchen. "I'm sorry, Colin, the girls are here for our weekly girls' night. You were saying something?"

"Well, I was but...you go have fun with the girls."

"All right, Colin. Let's talk again soon. I miss you."

"I miss you, too—love you." He quickly hung up, leaving Emily staring at her phone.

*What? Did he just say he loved me?*

There had always been a mutual attraction, a strong desire to be together, but neither of them had ventured into the deep waters of "I love you" yet. Before she had time to decide if she'd been hearing things or not, Camille and Isabel strolled into the kitchen.

"You look like someone just slapped you, Em." Camille set her hot pan of lasagna down on the stovetop.

Emily shook her head and put a broad smile on her face. "Uh, no. I was saying good-bye to Colin on the phone."

"How's he doing? I'll bet he misses you as much as you miss him." Camille smiled as she rifled through the utensil drawer.

"I think you're right." Emily gave her friend a hug.

"I brought homemade meatballs," Isabel proudly announced as she set her crockpot on the counter, lifting the lid to show Emily. She had been taking cooking lessons from Camille and was becoming quite accomplished. Camille was proud of her, but Maggie, the fitness queen, often gave her grief for the extra pounds she carried with her new love of cooking.

"They smell divine," Emily complimented. "I can't wait to taste them."

"*Grazie,*" Isabel replied.

"Where's Maggie?" Camille took the foil off her lasagna.

"Late, as usual." Isabel stirred her meatballs and fresh marinara sauce around with a large spoon. That was Maggie's one downfall, being notoriously late for just about everything. "She'll probably be late for her own funeral."

"Hey, I heard that!" Maggie shouted as she came through the door. All heads turned in her direction and the girls giggled. Emily hugged her and took her dinner contributions—a container of strawberry Gelato in a plastic grocery bag hanging from her arm and a bottle of red wine in each hand. "So, what did I miss?"

"Emily was on the phone with Colin when we walked in," Camille reported. "She hasn't said if there was anything new."

"Was there? Anythin' new, I mean?" Maggie asked.

Emily felt herself blush, and it did not go unnoticed. She hadn't planned on saying anything, but being put on the spot as she was, she decided to just come out with it. "Well, nothing big."

"Go on, Em, spit it out." Camille's bright blue eyes were wide with anticipation.

Emily could feel the heat of all their eyes on her. "Well, just as Colin was saying good-bye—"

"Out with it, Em!" Camille insisted.

"He said, 'Love you,' and then hung up." Emily eyed her friends, waiting for a response. "It took me by surprise."

"Did he actually say, I love you, or just a quick, love you?" Isabel questioned.

"What difference does it make, Isabel? He said the L word." Maggie gave Emily a big hug.

"It makes a big difference—at least it would to me," Isabel replied.

"I've decided I'm going to let it slide. I'm going to wait for the real, I love you, Emily, before I say it back."

"That's wise, Em," Camille agreed. "Just make sure you let us know the second he says it. I'm going to be waiting on pins and needles, my friend."

"Maybe not the second he says it," Isabel added, grinning at Camille.

"Well, y'all, speakin' of bein' in love," Maggie interjected, all eyes turning on her, "I have some news of my own."

"What news, Maggs?" Emily asked.

"I met a wonderful man online through one of those datin' services that match you up, and we've been talkin' on the phone and emailin' for a couple of months now. We've even had a few video chats on the computer with that Face Time *thang*."

"How come you never said anything before?" Isabel asked pointedly.

"I guess I wanted to see if it was goin' anywhere before I did. I didn't want to jinx it, y'know? I haven't had the best luck with men."

Maggie had had her share of relationships with men, but none of them seemed to stick. She was a force to be reckoned with, and as a single mother she held the bar high.

"Ooh, give us some details, Maggie," Camille encouraged.

"His name is Lucas Wakefield, and he's an investor and land developer. He lives in Colorado and he's been lookin' into doin' a project in this area."

"What kind of project?" Isabel questioned.

"Somethin' up in the mountains, like a resort," Maggie replied.

"That sounds exciting. Does that mean he's coming here?" Emily asked.

"As a matter of fact, he is, in the next week or so."

"Let us know and we'll throw a big party to welcome him," Camille offered.

"Oh, Cam, that would be fabulous!" Maggie beamed.

"This is all very exciting, ladies, but the food is getting cold," Isabel noted. "Why don't we serve ourselves and we can sit down and talk more while we eat?"

They happily agreed to Isabel's suggestion and spent the next hour eating, talking, and laughing. Wine flowed, dessert was relished, and conversation of Lucas Wakefield was thoroughly exhausted.

"You've been very quiet about your work, Em," Camille noted, licking the last bit of Gelato from her spoon and wagging it at Emily. "Working on any exciting cases?"

"Ever since I solved the Delia McCall murder case a few months ago, it's been pretty uneventful."

Emily had taken over the McCall case after Evan was killed, and it quickly went from tracking Ms. McCall's philandering husband to solving his murder. Emily had exposed the murderer, almost losing her own life in the process.

"That was an excitin' case." Maggie poured herself more wine.

"Since then, it's just been a handful of suspicious wives hiring me to follow their wayward husbands. Seems like not much happens in this sleepy little town—except maybe adultery." Emily gave the girls a playful grin.

"Oh, my," Camille gasped as a little giggle escaped her. She stood and began to clear the plates from the table.

"How can y'all say that?" Maggie asked. "We had two murders in the same year."

"You're right," Camille agreed. "And if Jonathan cheated on me, there'd be another murder in this town, for sure," she quipped, winking at Emily.

"Don't get me wrong," Emily explained, pouring herself another half glass of wine. "I'm not complaining. Believe me I'm not out looking and hoping for another murder to solve. That would be pretty ghoulish, don't you think?" she asked with a little chuckle. "I'm just ready for a case with a little more meat that I can sink my teeth into."

"Well, I, for one, am glad Paradise Valley has remained so crime-free," Isabel weighed in. "I get enough of investigating criminals for the FBI in other cities."

"Okay, okay, enough talk about me and my business," Emily said, changing the subject as she turned to Maggie. "How's your new friend doing? Sorry, I forgot her name."

"Fiona," Isabel offered.

"Yes, Fiona," Emily repeated. "How's she doing?" Emily picked up her glass to finish the last swallow of wine.

Camille stuck the dishes in the sink and hurried back to the table, dropping down in her seat as if she didn't want to miss a word.

Maggie explained that her new friend was still looking for a job. "Fiona didn't think that she'd have any trouble finding one with all her experience as an administrative assistant, but no luck so far."

"Well, hon, if we hear of anything, we'll let you know and you can pass the word on to Fiona," Camille promised, glancing around the table to the others, who nodded their agreement.

"I'd surely appreciate that. I know Fiona would, too," Maggie said. "She's gettin' a little discouraged, I think."

"When we have the party for Lucas, why don't you invite her, too?" Camille suggested. "She'll have a chance to meet some new people, maybe make some connections. Perhaps that'll lift her spirits."

"I think she'd like that," Maggie replied. "Y'all are just the best."

"Enough talk, I need more wine." Isabel scooted her chair out and went to the counter. "Anybody else?" she offered, holding up the bottle.

"I guess I'll be driving," Camille laughed.

# THE HEART OF LIES

## CHAPTER 2
## Welcome Party

MAGGIE LET CAMILLE AND THE REST of her friends know that she had spoken with Lucas and found out when he was coming for his first visit to Paradise Valley. As promised, Camille planned a lavish party at Isabel and Alex's beautiful home in the upscale neighborhood of River Woods.

The next time Maggie spoke to Lucas, he told her once more how much he looked forward to meeting her friends and her brother, and that he hoped she would also invite some others who might like to hear about the new resort.

"But this is a party to introduce you to my friends," Maggie moaned.

"I know, sweetheart, but I'm coming to Paradise Valley to start a new business, and I could use all the help

I can get. Don't you want to see this resort succeed? Then I could buy you all the nice things you deserve."

She did like nice things, she had told him so on several occasions. So, Maggie added a few more people to Camille's guest list, people she knew had money and influence and could be helpful to Lucas's success. She even spoke to her brother about inviting a few of his friends and business associates, and Emily reminded her to add Fiona to the list, as well.

~*~

The warm weather in late June was perfect for the outdoor party, and Camille had outdone herself with the hors d'oeuvres, drinks, and decorations. She strung little white lights wherever she could so the ambience was enhanced as the sun sank below the horizon. Maggie paid for a local DJ to keep the music playing throughout the evening, encouraging people to dance on the expansive slate patio. She even asked Isabel and Alex to invite their neighbors, also people of means, hoping to avoid complaints of the loud music while adding to Lucas's circle of influence.

Maggie had originally wanted a small intimate affair where her friends and brother could get to know Lucas and he could get acquainted with them. The party, however, turned out to be the event of the year, she overhead a number of guests say.

She introduced Lucas to her friends and her brother first, and then she took him around to meet others. He was tall and handsome with sandy brown hair, highlighted by the summer sun, a strong angular jaw line, and a distinguished cleft in his chin.

He seemed right at home meeting new people, holding a friendly smile, and shaking hand after hand. They would inquire how he liked their town and he would reply how it was a beautiful place, in great proximity to the new ski and golf resort he was building.

Maggie watched as most people's eyes lit up at his detailed description of his endeavor. Even her brother, Sully, seemed captivated by the idea of a new resort nearby.

In the middle of Lucas's portrayal of the resort, he paused and flashed a quick smile at her, then went back to the people hanging on his every word.

As the night wore down, Maggie left Lucas to his conversations and took a chair next to Isabel at one of the round tables Camille had set up around the meticulously landscaped yard.

An exhausted Emily plopped down on the seat next to them. "Great party, don't you think?" She ran her hands through her loose curls.

"Yes, great." Maggie sat, leaning an elbow on the table, staring at Lucas across the lawn.

"What's wrong?" Emily looked into her friend's pensive blue eyes.

"Nothin'. Just not what I expected. I wanted to introduce Lucas to my friends and family, but all these other people are takin' his attention."

"He is charming," Isabel commented, "and it sounds like this get-together is a good thing for his new resort."

"You're right. I'm just tired, I guess." Maggie propped her head up on one hand.

"He'll be here for a while, won't he?" Emily asked.

"Yes, and I'll have him all to myself tomorrow when we drive up to Sun Valley. He said he wants to check out the competition."

"I saw your brother is here, Maggs, but I didn't see his wife with him," Emily commented.

"No, Carolyn wasn't well. She's got MS, you know," Maggie said.

"MS? How awful." Isabel had a tone of sadness in her voice.

"Their daughters are off to college. And with Carolyn so sick, my poor brother must be buried under a pile of debt." Maggie shook her head at the thought, then she shot up straight and put her hand to her lips. "Oh, girls, please don't tell him I said that."

"Hello, Maggie." Fiona approached their table.

"Hi, Fiona," Maggie responded warmly. "I wasn't sure you were goin' to make it. You remember my friends, Emily and Isabel?"

"Yes. Hello, Emily, Isabel. So sorry I'm late. I had a flat tire on the way, but all's well now."

"Flat tire? Oh, how miserable. Well, I'm glad you finally made it." Maggie reached out and gave Fiona's hand a light squeeze. "I'm sure there's still some food left. Camille made enough to feed an army."

"I'm not really hungry." Fiona looked over at Lucas as the small crowd around him began to dissipate. "Is that him?"

"Yes, that's my Lucas. Let me introduce you," Maggie offered.

"I don't want to be a bother," Fiona said.

"Look, here he comes. His ears must have been burnin' with us talkin' about him." Maggie laughed.

"Hello, ladies," Lucas greeted as he approached them.

"Lucas, I'd like to introduce you to one of my friends, Fiona Merlino," Maggie said.

Lucas stuck out his hand and smiled cordially as he shook hers. "It's nice to meet you, Miss Merlino. Have you lived in Paradise Valley long?"

"No, only a month or so. I'm still looking for a job, actually."

"What kind of work do you do?" he asked.

"I have an extensive background as an administrative assistant," Fiona replied.

"Really," he responded, looking into her deep brown eyes. That was one thing Maggie had noticed about Lucas, he always looked a person in the eye when he spoke to them. She liked that. Her daddy used to tell her that was the sign of a person who could be trusted. "Well, if you're still looking for a job when I set up my business here," Lucas went on, "I'll have to give you a call for an interview."

"You're moving here?" Isabel asked, sounding surprised by the news.

"Yes, didn't Maggie tell you? I've decided to set up my office here as soon as possible to start selling the condo units. I'm going to be starting construction soon, once the dirt gets leveled, and I'd like to get the capital coming in to keep the construction moving forward."

Isabel and Emily exchanged questioning glances.

"I'm sorry, I completely forgot to mention it." Maggie shrugged her shoulders apologetically.

"You'd like to set up an interview?" Fiona smiled sweetly at Lucas. "Sure, that would be terrific. Maggie has my number."

"Now," Lucas held his hand out to Maggie, "I would like to ask the most beautiful woman at this party to dance. I have ignored her far too long."

Maggie's face lit up as she took his hand. He helped her to her feet and led her to the dance area.

Emily, Isabel, and Fiona watched as Lucas and Maggie joined the other handful of couples swaying to the beat of a slow song the DJ had just begun to play.

"Boy, Fiona, that was a lucky connection," Isabel said.

Emily nodded her agreement.

"I couldn't agree more," Fiona said. "That Maggie Sullivan is a lucky woman." She turned sharply and went inside the house, leaving Isabel and Emily wearing puzzled expressions on their faces.

~*~

The evening was winding down and most of the guests had left. Camille and Jonathan were busy cleaning up with Emily and Isabel's help. Alex had been out front for a while directing traffic, making sure the multitude of cars made it away without a scratch.

Maggie and Lucas were standing on the front steps of the Martínez home, saying good-bye to the last of their guests. Mayor Sullivan was one of the last to leave, and he hugged his sister good-night. He shook Lucas's hand and promised to make time to meet with him about his exciting new project.

"I think the resort will be a good thing for this valley. What are you calling it?" he asked.

"Whitetail," Lucas replied. "Whitetail Ski and Golf Resort."

"I like the sound of that. Whitetail," Sully said as he stepped off the porch. "It has a nice ring to it."

"I'll call you," Lucas shouted out as he waved good-bye. "Let's go inside, Maggie. Maybe they need help cleaning up."

# THE HEART OF LIES

# CHAPTER 3
## Lunch with the Girls

UPON THEIR RETURN FROM A QUICK TRIP up to Sun Valley, Maggie reported to the girls over lunch at Bar deNay's one day that she and Lucas had explored what they could of the ski resort there. It being summer, there were no snow activities to observe, but Lucas had scrutinized the other activities, studying the layout of the resort and condos, as well taking a tour of the massive Sun Valley Lodge.

Maggie also mentioned that Lucas was ready to start setting up his business and that he'd been able to secure a lease in the old Graystone Building where Emily had her private investigation office. Maggie had thanked Emily for the referral.

She told them how Lucas followed through on his promise to Fiona and had hired her to help him set up his files and his office.

Emily wanted to be happy for Maggie, so she was willing to welcome Lucas into their tight circle of friends, but Isabel, with her suspicious nature, remained somewhat aloof and watchful.

A few days later Emily and Isabel had lunch together at The Blue Moon Café. As they sat on the sun-drenched patio under a big blue umbrella, looking out over the rushing Boise River, Isabel shared her misgivings about Maggie's relationship with Lucas.

"I think I need to do that background check now. They're moving too fast, getting serious too soon. Don't you think, Em?"

"It does seem pretty quick, but it's not like they're kids. They're both mid-thirties. Some relationships just move faster than others," Emily replied.

"But he just seems…" Isabel tapped her finger on her chin and rolled her eyes upward, as if she was searching her brain for the right word.

"Seems what?"

"Seems too nice, too slick. I don't know, I can't put my finger on it," Isabel said, frowning and pursing her lips.

"Too perfect?"

"Yes, and too sweet, like pure honey. He always seems to have just the right thing to say—an answer for everything. Maybe I'm too suspicious, but I think for Maggie's own protection we need to make sure this guy is legit."

"Isabel, you know if she finds out you're checking him out, she'll hit the roof," Emily warned.

"How's she going to find out if you don't tell her? I know I'm not going to mention it."

"Fortunately for you, Camille isn't here. Otherwise, you certainly would have something to worry about." Emily laughed.

"Here we go." The young waiter set their food down, then refilled their water glasses, and moved on to the next table.

"Oh, before I forget, my retired FBI friend, you know *Jethro*," Isabel made air quotes with her fingers when she said his fake name, "he's going to be in town this week. He said he could meet with us day after tomorrow."

"What time?"

"I thought we could come by your house about seven," Isabel suggested. "He's anxious to see if he recognizes Evan or the woman, and I figured it would be best if he could see the original photo."

"No more anxious than I am. That nagging doubt is eating me up. I can't help but wonder if she was his wife before me. Or was she his lover? Did she die? Is she still alive?"

"Whoa!" Isabel waved her hand. "Save the questions for our meeting."

"Sorry, I got a little carried away there," Emily apologized, picking up her turkey sandwich, "but that's what keeps running through my mind. Some nights I can hardly sleep wondering who my husband really was."

"I'm hoping Jethro can identify both of them" Isabel picked at her fries.

"Wouldn't it be something if he recognized Evan right off? I'd love it if he said, I know that guy, his name is something or other," Emily remarked, speaking in a deep manly voice, waving her hand for emphasis.

Isabel chuckled at Emily's impression of Jethro, then her expression became deeply serious. "Are you sure you wouldn't be satisfied to tell yourself you had five wonderful years with a great guy named Evan who made you feel loved... and just leave it at that?"

"No, my friend, that train has definitely left the station. I'm dying to hear what Jethro has to say. If he's been working in DC for over thirty years, it's possible he came in contact with Evan—or whatever his name turns out to be—at some point, don't you think?"

"Yeah, maybe, but you might find out something you don't want to know, Em." Isabel's expression grew even more serious, as did her tone.

"Like what?" Emily lowered her voice. Her brow wrinkled as she leaned closer to Isabel.

"What if Evan was a hit man for the CIA or something like that?" Isabel glanced around to make sure no one could overhear their conversation. "And maybe that woman was his partner. You need to prepare yourself for the worst."

"Evan? A hit man for the CIA?" Emily's voice rose in disbelief.

"Shhh, keep your voice down."

Emily sat back in her chair, shaking her head. "I don't know."

"It may not be as bad as all that. I'm just saying, prepare yourself—it could be ugly."

"Ugh! You're right." Emily leaned forward once more and kept her volume low. "I don't want to believe he was something horrible, like an assassin, but one way or the other, my husband was obviously not who he said he was. The proof is in those fake passports I found, all that cash, and the mysterious gun."

Isabel nodded sympathetically.

"That gun has to be the key to *something*. Evan had several guns at the house, so why would he have stuck that one away in a safe deposit box if there was nothing to hide? There had to be a reason."

"If you leave it lying in the safe deposit box, you'll never know what that reason was," Isabel said.

"Are you saying I should turn it over to the authorities and have it tested, see if it's connected to any open murder cases?"

"Perhaps. Why don't you mention it to Jethro—hypothetically, of course," Isabel suggested, raising her eyebrows at Emily, as if asking if she understood.

"Oh, yes, of course, hypothetically, right." Emily caught on. "I appreciate your setting up the meeting." She patted Isabel's hand. "I'll owe you."

"I'll remember you said that." Isabel flashed a wide grin as she picked up her burger. "Now let's eat. I'm starved."

"Hey, y'all," Maggie's lilting Southern drawl sang out as she and Lucas approached the table.

"Maggie," Emily responded as she and Isabel looked up from their plates.

Maggie's hand was threaded through the crook of Lucas's arm.

"Hello, ladies," he said. "You both are looking beautiful today."

"That's slick," Isabel mumbled to Emily as she wiped a napkin across her mouth.

"What's that?" Maggie asked, batting her big blue eyes.

"Nice lipstick, I said to Emily," Isabel covered. "I love the color."

"Oh, thank you so much," Maggie gushed. "We were just havin' lunch over there with my brother and Lucas's new assistant," she pointed to the other side of the spacious patio. "You know Fiona."

Emily and Isabel nodded.

"I happened to see you girls across the deck, and Lucas suggested we come over and say hello. Wasn't that sweet?" Maggie looked up at him with adoring eyes.

"Yes, like pure honey," Isabel said with a straight face.

"Yes, very sweet." Emily gave Isabel a kick under the table.

"Ouch!"

"Oh sorry, was that you? My foot must have slipped," Emily apologized.

"Well, we won't keep you." Maggie seemed to be clueless, but Lucas shot Isabel an almost imperceptible frown for a fraction of a second, then it was gone. "We need to get back to our party, I mean, our business lunch. Talkin' about the Whitetail Resort and all," Maggie said, beaming.

"So nice to see you ladies again." Lucas plastered a polite smile across his face as they turned and began to make their way back to their table. Maggie stopped short and hurried back to the girls' table with Lucas close behind.

Emily thought she caught a glimpse of a quick rolling of his eyes, then the polite smile again.

"I almost forgot," Maggie said, "I wanted to remind y'all about the presentation Tuesday night for the Whitetail Resort. The Hilton Hotel at seven o'clock. You'll get to see all the gorgeous images of the whole project—the lodge, the condos, the lake, the golf course—all those beautiful places. Say y'all are gonna come, *please*."

"Yes, I'd love to come," Emily told her, thinking it would be a good opportunity to observe Lucas in action.

"Isabel?" Maggie inquired.

"Yeah, I'm sure I can drag Alex there after a long day at the office. Why not."

"Great! Y'all are gonna love it, I promise!" Maggie took Lucas's arm again.

He cast Isabel a suspicious glance over his shoulder as they cut their way through the crowded patio.

Once Maggie and Lucas were out of earshot, Isabel bent and rubbed her calf. "Why did you kick me?"

Emily glared at her. "Are you kidding me? I can't believe you're asking me that. If we're going to investigate this character you can't be giving him clues that you don't like him. You, better than anyone, should know we can't tip our hand."

"I do know that, but—"

"No buts." Emily looked across the patio and watched the couple rejoin their party. "Promise me you'll be nothing but kind to Lucas, until you have something concrete on him—for Maggie's sake." Emily's gaze returned to her own table and she looked into Isabel's face for reply.

"All right, all right." Isabel raised her hands in surrender, grinning at her friend. "But don't you ever kick me again. I'm warning you, I have a gun and I'm not afraid to use it."

~*~

Maggie and Lucas returned to their table, where the mayor and Fiona were thick in conversation.

"I hope y'all didn't miss us too much," Maggie apologized as she sat in the chair Lucas had pulled out for her.

"No," her brother replied, "I was just getting to know Lucas's charming assistant."

"Yes, she is terrific, isn't she?" Lucas said, catching her gaze for a moment before returning his attention to Maggie.

Their waiter approached the table, asking if they were ready to order and they all made their selections. He wrote them down and nodded. "I'll have those right out."

"You know, I never would have found Fiona if it hadn't been for Maggie," Lucas added. "She introduced us."

He leaned over and kissed Maggie on the cheek. She lowered her eyes for a moment and her lips curled into a shy smile, a slight giggle escaping. When she raised her eyes, they were sparkling and happy.

"Mayor, your sister is a remarkable woman. She is capturing my heart like no other woman I have ever met." Maggie's beauty and sweetness made it easy to be with her—she was gorgeous with her flowing blonde hair and intense blue eyes. Her deep magenta dress was fitted and accentuated the slender, toned body she had worked so hard to achieve.

"You seem to make her very happy, Lucas. I wish my Carolyn was here to see you two together."

"How is your wife?" Lucas asked.

"She's in a lot of pain most days, in and out of the hospital," Sully replied.

"Sorry to hear that. I know when my mother was in the hospital with heart problems, the hospital bills were overwhelming," Lucas said, noting Sully's financial situation as a possible leverage opportunity.

"Yes, they're enormous," he nodded, "but let's not talk about that now. Tell me more about this resort you're building."

"Here we are." The waiter arrived, setting the plates before each person. "Is there anything else I can get you?"

"No, I think we're good," Lucas responded, gazing at each person around the table.

"Then I'll be back to check on you in a bit," the waiter said and stepped to another table.

Lucas regained Sully's attention and proceeded to explain the concept and the plan, describing all of the luxurious amenities in animated detail, complete with hand gestures.

Lucas watched Maggie out of the corner of his eye as he spoke, hoping to draw her in. Fiona stepped in to add details, too, when Lucas appeared to be searching for the words.

"That sounds like a spectacular resort, Lucas. Sounds like a place I could take Carolyn to get away once in a while. How much are the condos going for?"

"Depending on the size, from two hundred to five hundred thousand," Lucas replied, watching Sully's expression.

"Geez," Sully grimaced, "that's kind of steep for my blood."

"If you really want one, we could work something out, you being Maggie's brother and all. Why don't we talk about it privately sometime?" Lucas began to salivate, everything was coming together as planned. This was the connection on which their entire project would hinge.

"I'd like that," Sully said. "Why don't you come by my office Monday afternoon and we'll talk."

*Yes!* Lucas was reeling in the big fish and loving it. He shot a quick glance over at Fiona, who flickered a momentary grin. "Certainly, Mayor. I'd love to stop by."

# CHAPTER 4
## The Art of Persuasion

FIRST THING MONDAY MORNING, Lucas was on the phone to Mayor Sully Sullivan, setting up a time to meet later that afternoon. He collected his spreadsheets and renderings, ready to impress and hook the mayor to help him persuade the prosperous people of Paradise Valley to invest in the new ski and golf resort.

Showing up a few minutes early for his appointment, Lucas took the opportunity to introduce himself around the city offices and ingratiate himself with the employees. He knew his charm was sizeable and often irresistible. It was one of his many talents that helped him accomplish the things he did.

"The mayor is ready for you, Mr. Wakefield," Sully's frumpy, middle-aged assistant announced with a friendly smile. "Please, follow me." She led him down a hallway, knocked lightly, and opened the door to the office.

"It was such a pleasure meeting you," Lucas said, giving her hand a light squeeze, before walking into the Mayor's office.

"Lucas, it's good to see you again." Sully stepped from behind his desk, buttoned his suit jacket, and extended his hand to Lucas as he entered. Sully had blonde hair, like his sister, but without the salon highlights. His blue eyes were warm and welcoming. "Have a seat, please," he said, gesturing toward the two leather club chairs that sat across from his desk.

"I'd rather stand, Mr. Mayor," Lucas said, holding out the renderings.

"Oh, yes, of course. Why don't you spread those out on the conference table over here?"

Lucas followed his directions, spreading the artwork out on the table and made a sweeping motion toward them. "Have a look. I think you'll like what you see."

Sully hunched over and looked down at each drawing, placing his hands on the edge of the table. "You've done a superb job, Lucas. People around here will be lining up to get in on this project." He looked up at Lucas with a big smile, showing his excitement for what this would mean for Paradise Valley's economy as well.

"That's what I was hoping you'd say." Lucas grinned widely. "What about you, Mayor? Would you be interested in one of these condos?"

"Oh, please, call me Sully. And as for the condos…I would, if it wasn't for the huge mountain of medical bills I have."

Sully's excitement dulled.

"I'd love to do that for my wife, but I don't see how right now."

Lucas laid his hand on Sully's shoulder and looked him in the eye with absolute sincerity. "I tell you what, *Sully*, since you're Maggie's brother, you're like family."

Sully chuckled.

It was a bit of a leap. After all, Maggie and Lucas had not been dating that long. Still, Lucas would work the angle.

"I'd be happy to work a special deal with you," Lucas offered. Turning back to the table, he opened his briefcase and pulled out his spreadsheets.

"What kind of special deal?"

Lucas stopped and smiled to himself, hearing the interest in Sully's voice. "What would you say if I sell you two of the condos at a greatly reduced price?" Lucas spread the papers out on the table, then straightened his posture and faced Sully. "That way you could resell them and make a healthy chunk of change to put toward your hospital bills."

He turned back to his spreadsheets. "Here's my calculations." He tapped his finger on a column of numbers, watching Sully's face for a reaction. "What do you think of that?"

"What exactly are we talking, Lucas?" Sully's eyes lit up as his gaze hovered over the numbers.

"What if I sell you two of the three-hundred-thousand-dollar condos for two hundred each, then you can turn around and resell them for three hundred. That would give you a two-hundred-thousand-dollar profit. That should make a pretty sizeable dent in your hospital bills, wouldn't it?"

"Sounds like a screaming deal. Only problem is I don't have that kind of money to put down. Aren't you asking for twenty-five percent?" Sully's voice began to deflate.

"Yes."

"That could be a problem."

"I'd really hate to see you miss out on this opportunity, Sully, being Maggie's brother and all. Is there any way you could borrow it from someone?" Lucas asked. "Or take an equity loan against your house?"

"I've already mortgaged my house to the hilt. I probably shouldn't tell you this, but a few more bad months at the golf course I own and I may be in danger of losing that."

"Maybe you could take it from the retirement account or something?"

"The retirement account? You mean the city's or mine personally?" Sully's eyebrow quirked with suspicion.

"I mean yours personally," Lucas replied. The truth was, though, he didn't really care which account it came from, as long as it came. *But since you mentioned the city retirement account...*

"I don't have that much in there anymore, not since my wife got sick."

"Well then, since you brought up the city retirement account, perhaps you could borrow from it without anyone knowing. I could help you resell your condos quickly, even before they're finished, and put the money back in. No one would be the wiser," Lucas suggested, "and you'd make a tidy profit."

If Sully got the money from city funds, it would actually give Lucas more leverage. He liked that.

"No, I couldn't do that," Sully said, shaking his head. "I'd be breaking the law and I could wind up in jail."

"Not if you were careful and got the money back into the accounts before anyone noticed it was missing." Lucas used a warm even tone, putting his hand on Sully's shoulder. His studies in the art of persuasion over the years had taught him that placing a gentle but firm hand on someone's shoulder created an atmosphere of confidence and care. Lucas gave a gentle pat, then shrugged his shoulders as if it didn't matter to him. "It's something to consider, Sully."

Sully gazed at the artist's conception of the beautiful condos once more and shook his head. "I don't think I could do that," he said in a small voice.

"Yes," Lucas said, nodding his head rhythmically, "I think you can."

*Come on, stay with me, Sully.*

"It would help you tremendously." Lucas continued to nod. His hand still rested on Sully's shoulder and he controlled his voice to sound warm and caring. Was he succeeding in turning him?

He sensed that if he pushed too hard at this point, Sully might put up his defenses, so he backed off. "You don't need to decide right now. Take a day or two to make up your mind and let me know. Consider what it could mean for you, Sully," Lucas began to gather up his presentation, "and your sweet wife, Carolyn." He was hitting where Sully was most vulnerable—his wife.

*Now play the fear-of-loss card.* "We have a presentation at the Hilton Hotel tomorrow night. I expect these condo units to sell out quickly, so let me know before then. I'm warning you, Sully, the window on this opportunity will be closing fast."

"Okay."

As Lucas stacked the papers, Sully was still eyeing the renderings, as if he was under their spell.

"I'll let you know."

Lucas slipped the spreadsheets into his briefcase, then slid the renderings into a large leather portfolio. "I wouldn't have suggested this special deal to you if you weren't Maggie's brother. She means the world to me, Sully. She's worried about you. So I'm just trying to be the good guy here and help you out. You understand that, don't you?" Lucas nodded and tried to catch the mayor's gaze, but he turned and walked back to his desk.

"I know," Sully muttered. His eyes were lowered and he fidgeted, rearranging papers and pens on his desk. "I could really use that money—it's just that I could get in a boatload of trouble if I got caught."

"No pressure," Lucas said evenly. *Now give him the I-know-what-you're-going-through line.* "I know what it feels like to be drowning in debt, that's why I'm offering you a lifeline, to help you get out from under it."

"It is a tempting offer." Sully sat down, still nervously moving a few more things around on his desk.

"Close your eyes, Sully."

"What?" He looked at Lucas, noticeably surprised at the request.

"Work with me here, Sully."

Sully rolled his eyes, then complied with Lucas's request.

"Now imagine how free you'll feel when you've taken your windfall and cleared your debts—gone, paid off, free," Lucas chanted. "Go ahead, do it."

With his eyes still shut, Sully leaned back in his leather chair and laced his hands across his stomach. He remained silent for a few moments. A smile spread across his face, then a rush of air escaped his lips as he released a long sigh.

"Feels pretty good, doesn't it?" Lucas asked.

Sully opened his eyes and grinned widely at Lucas.

"Now remember that feeling. That's what it's going to feel like as soon as you sell those condos." *Gotcha!*

# THE HEART OF LIES

# CHAPTER 5
# The Hotel Job

EMILY HAD TOSSED AND TURNED throughout the night. She'd fought off a barrage of questions about Evan's secret life that her subconscious had mercilessly thrown at her. Over and over in her mind, visions played out, possible scenarios, like a series of movies running in her head—spy movies, conspiracy theory movies, witness protection movies.

After several cups of coffee in the morning, she was wired and looking for a way to release her pent-up anxiety. Emily spent much of that day scrubbing and cleaning anything that got in her way. She tried to keep her mind focused on other things, working out her stress, but she kept returning to the old photo of Evan and the mystery woman, as well as the other suspicious finds in the secret safe deposit box.

Colin called her shortly before seven o'clock that evening—just checking in, he said.

She told him about her upcoming meeting with Isabel and her FBI friend and about her hopes for some real answers to who had killed Evan, and why.

"Sounds like an incredible opportunity, Emily. This Jethro character may open some new doors you haven't had access to before."

"I know." She paced the bedroom floor in her bare feet. "I owe Isabel, but I'm going nuts just waiting for them to get here."

"Just breathe, they'll be there soon. Call me as soon as they leave—I want to hear everything."

"I promise," she agreed, resting against the edge of her bed. "I have a stakeout later tonight—"

"Corporate espionage?"

"Ha, ha. No. Another philandering husband, but I'll call you as soon as I can. Maybe you can keep me company on the phone."

"It's a date. I so enjoy being near you, in your Bluetooth, I mean. Bye, love." Colin hung up.

*Bye, Colin.* She sighed. *I love you, too.*

Emily checked her watch again and went to the living room window to peek out. No one yet. She paced from her living room to the kitchen and back as seven o'clock approached. Any minute, Isabel would be bringing the man she could only refer to as "Jethro" to her little bungalow for a hush-hush meeting. It all felt so clandestine. Emily knew a bit about clandestine actions, but this felt different somehow—it felt national, maybe even international—and it felt personal.

With a pair of black leather flats by the door, she was prepared to sling them on before letting her guests in. Dressed in jeans and a stretchy black top, she was more comfortable when her feet were bare, so she left her shoes for the last second. *What kind of impression would that make if I greeted this seasoned federal agent in my bare feet?* She figured Isabel would be mortified with embarrassment and she would owe her doubly.

To prepare for her meeting, she had set out a tray of cheese and crackers, with beer and wine chilling in the refrigerator. The infamous photo lay on the coffee table next to the food, along with a copy Jethro could take with him, if he chose to.

*What else will Jethro want?* She tried to anticipate. Something with Evan's fingerprints or DNA maybe.

Emily went to her bedroom and rifled through the top drawer of the highboy. Though she had packed away Evan's things from the closet months ago, she still had not cleared out the top drawer of this chest. It was too intimate. He kept things like his brush, comb, and other personal items here. It was where he threw his keys, change from his pockets, and his wallet before coming to bed.

Lifting the brush out of the drawer by the bristles, she slid it into a new plastic baggie and took it to the living room to set it next to the photo.

As she set the brush down, the doorbell rang and Emily dashed to the door. She saw it was them through the small row of windows across the top and she opened it to welcome her guests.

"Hello," she greeted. "Please, come in."

Isabel stepped in first, followed by an older gentleman. His hair was an attractive silvery gray and he had eyes the color of black coffee. For a man in his early sixties, he had kept his body in good shape. Emily gave Isabel a quick hug and offered her hand to Jethro.

"It's so nice to meet you," Emily said. "I appreciate your coming, more than you know. I'm sure Isabel has told you—"

She noticed he was looking down at her feet.

"Would you like us to remove our shoes?"

Emily looked at him, then to Isabel, as her cheeks flushed red. She had forgotten to slip her flats on as planned.

Isabel glared disapprovingly at her.

"Oh, please, no. I just forgot to put mine on." She turned to slip them on.

"Don't put them on, on my account. I'm just a country boy. I'd go around barefoot all the time if I could." He chuckled and Isabel relaxed.

"That's kind of you to say," Emily responded. "Let's go in the living room."

Isabel led the way and motioned to the sofa.

"Can I get you something to drink? I have Dr. Pepper, beer, and wine."

"I'll take a beer," Jethro replied.

Isabel asked for a small glass of wine.

Emily hurried to the kitchen and brought the drinks back, finding Jethro already studying the photo.

"Either of them look familiar to you?" Emily asked, kneeling on the floor next to the table.

"He does look vaguely familiar," Jethro noted. "I can't say exactly how I know him just yet. I'm flying back to DC next week. I can take the photo and ask a few long-timers if they know him."

"I'd appreciate it," Emily said.

"I wonder where this was taken." He held the photo at arm's length, scrutinizing. "The building in the background looks very old—like Europe somewhere."

"Funny, I thought that, too," Emily agreed. "What about the woman?"

"No, I don't think I've ever seen her. She's a looker, I'd remember." He smiled as he held the photo closer. "Yeah, she's a beauty. Reminds me of my third wife."

"Your third wife? How many times have you been married?" Isabel asked with a chuckle.

"Four—well, no, five if you count Lola. I married her in Vegas one night when I got real drunk. I was working undercover, getting close to a mob guy. He was having a big party and I had to keep up with him so I didn't blow my cover. Lola was one of the girls at the party and we connected somehow. Woke up the next morning married, but we had it annulled a few weeks later."

Emily's eyes widened as he spoke, her gaze shooting to the beer in his hand.

He followed her gaze. "Don't worry, I don't have a drinking problem. That was in my early days, before I learned some tricks to only look like I was drinking."

Both Emily and Isabel sighed in relief.

"If we could run Evan's fingerprints or DNA, maybe that would help to identify him," Jethro suggested.

"I had the same idea, so I put his hairbrush in a baggie. I was careful not to touch it and smudge his prints."

"Good thinking." Jethro tucked the baggie in his coat pocket. "I'm not promising anything, but I'm happy to check with my friends at the CIA, see what I can turn up. Maybe the FBI had him in witness protection or something, too. Did you consider that? Fits the facts."

Emily ran her fingers through her hair as she sat cross-legged on the floor. "Could be."

After a few more minutes of playing *what-ifs*, Jethro stood, so Isabel and Emily followed suit.

"You have no idea how much it would mean to me to finally know the truth," Emily said, facing the retired federal agent.

"Yes, my friend, your help is huge," Isabel agreed, patting his shoulder.

"Before you go, I have one more question—a hypothetical question." Emily looked at Isabel, who nodded for her to proceed.

Jethro's eyes fixed on Emily's with a serious stare. "Okay." He drew out the word as he crossed his arms across his chest. "What's your question—hypothetically?"

She paused for a moment and swallowed hard before speaking. "What if Evan had been involved in something where a gun was used and he hid the gun so it wouldn't be found?"

"Go on," Jethro encouraged.

"And let's say, *hypothetically*, the gun was found by a friend. What should that *friend* do with the gun? Give it to the police?"

Jethro frowned. He turned and glanced at Isabel, then back to Emily. "Hypothetically?" he asked, raising his brows.

Emily nodded.

"Hypothetically, the *friend* should give it to the FBI. If the friend gave it to Isabel, for example, she could make sure it's checked against any federal investigations first."

"I agree—hypothetically, of course," Isabel concurred.

Jethro explained that Isabel could also check with the CIA to see if the gun was used in any cases they were involved with. Then, if it was cleared by the FBI and CIA, the gun could then be turned over to the police to search for a match in any of their investigations.

"I see," Emily replied, feeling overwhelmed.

"So, one could start with the federal agencies, then go local, or vice versa—either way," Isabel said.

"Good to know," Emily replied, "if I ever run across something like that."

"So," Jethro grinned, "can I get a look at this hypothetical gun?"

~*~

After Isabel and her friend left, Emily cleared the food and drinks, then raced back to her bedroom to change into her black jeans and thin black sweater. She pulled her hair up into a stretchy skull cap and tugged a curly dark brown wig on over it—just a girl getting ready to go to work. She stuck a pair of black framed glasses on and admired her handiwork in the bathroom mirror. Grabbing her purse and camera, she headed out.

Emily stuck her Bluetooth earpiece on as she drove to the Hilton Hotel to catch her mark in the act. The wife, her client, had found credit card charges to this hotel dated every Monday for the last month, when her husband claimed he was working late.

Emily had a friend, named Trudi, who worked the evening front desk at the hotel. Trudi had experience with a cheating husband, and she happily agreed to help Emily and temporarily loan out a hotel uniform jacket to catch the *scumbag*, as her friend put it.

On the drive over, Emily called Colin and told him all about her meeting with Isabel and Jethro.

"And then he asked to see the gun," Emily said with a hint of disbelief.

"You didn't really think he'd buy the hypothetical thing, did you?" Colin asked. "I wouldn't have either."

"No, it was more of a veil. I couldn't exactly admit I had a gun that could have been involved in a crime, but I wanted his advice." Emily pulled her car into the hotel's nearly empty parking lot and turned the engine off.

"Are you going to turn it in?" he asked.

"Probably, but I want to discuss it a little further with Isabel." Emily looked around for a silver Lexus SUV, as the wife had described, but it was nowhere to be seen. "I might as well. We're not going to find out the whole truth until I do."

Just then, the Lexus pulled in and parked. A middle-aged, balding man with a paunch climbed out and headed into the hotel, carrying a briefcase. Emily recognized him from the photo her client had provided.

*He didn't come with anyone. He must be meeting her at the room.*

"Sorry, Colin, but I need to go." Emily kept her eyes on the man.

She hung up, then stuck the small camera in her front jeans pocket. Emily glanced around the parking lot as she hurried to the hotel.

Entering the lobby, she saw Trudi standing behind the check-in counter, her red hair neatly pulled back in a French twist, dressed in her forest green hotel uniform. Catching her eye, Trudi nodded her head toward the bar. Emily hung back and peeked in. The man was talking to the bartender, ordering drinks to be brought up to the room perhaps.

Emily eased backward, around the corner and out of sight, before the man turned to come out of the bar. She inconspicuously waited for him to get on the elevator. Then she glanced around the lobby before ducking into the hotel bar to wait, giving the man time to get to his room and become involved in whatever questionable activity he had planned.

Standing in the doorway, she took a quick look around the dimly-lit room, searching for a small table where she could sit alone and wait. Her breath stopped as she caught a glimpse of Lucas, sitting at a table in the corner, with a dark-haired woman. The woman's back was to Emily, and she couldn't tell who she was, a potential investor maybe.

Lucas leaned over and whispered something in the woman's ear and she looked to the side and laughed. It was Fiona.

Surprise mixed with anger sizzled just below the surface, sending heat to Emily's face. Should she go and confront them? Were they carrying on behind Maggie's back? Maybe it was just an innocent drink after work with a co-worker. Either way, she didn't have time to deal with it right now, especially with the wig and glasses, but it would not be overlooked.

She checked her watch, then peeked again in Lucas and Fiona's direction. She figured she should wait at least twenty minutes for her mark to settle in and his guest to arrive, so she had a few minutes to do a little reconnaissance. Feeling her wig and glasses to make sure her disguise was in place, she nonchalantly moved to a table next to theirs.

"Can I get you anything, ma'am?" a young waiter asked, taking Emily by surprise and putting her on the spot. Now she'd have to speak, which may expose her.

"No thanks, I'm waiting for a friend." Emily raised her voice a few decibels and answered sweetly. She watched out of the corner of her eye for any hint of recognition by Lucas or Fiona, but there was none. The pair was speaking to each other in low tones, and Emily's conversation with the waiter obliterated any chance of overhearing what they might have said.

The waiter left her alone as Lucas and Fiona stood. Lucas threw a fifty on the table and they walked out. *Either Lucas is a big tipper or they've been here awhile.*

Maggie taught an aerobics class at the Y on Monday evenings, so she'd never suspect Lucas would be with anyone else. Emily shook her head, trying to focus. Maybe it was all these wayward men she'd been tailing that made her hypersensitive to the situation.

Checking her watch again, she decided she'd left the man upstairs long enough—it was time to pay him a visit. She went to the front desk.

"Room three-ten," Trudi muttered, looking around as she discreetly handed the hotel jacket to Emily.

"Did you see anyone come in who may have gone up to his room? A woman perhaps?" Emily asked, keeping her voice down.

"No, but that doesn't mean he couldn't have let someone in through the side door," Trudi uttered lowly.

"All right. Thanks." Emily turned toward the elevator.

"Go get him, girl."

"Will do." Emily smiled, grateful for the help, and moved to the elevator, waiting until she was inside to put the coat on.

Stepping off the elevator, dressed in the dark green hotel worker's jacket, she walked down the hallway, the camera in her hand, reading the room numbers as she went. Emily noticed a room service tray outside of one of the other rooms with an empty champagne bottle and two glass flutes. She picked them up as a prop to get the perp to open his door.

Emily knocked on the door and called out, "Room service."

She put her eye up to the peephole and saw the man walking toward her. She stepped back and gasped, trying to stifle a giggle. *Oh, my gosh, what is going on in there?*

"Room service already delivered," the man shouted back.

"This is champagne—on the house," Emily replied, holding the full tray close up to the peephole where the man could only read the label.

Emily heard the door unlock, so she rushed to set the tray down on the floor. She whipped the camera out of her pocket and hit the *On* button. He opened the door a crack, which gave Emily the opportunity to shoulder it open all the way. He stumbled back a couple of steps.

There stood Harry Wykoski, attorney-at-law, father of six, married to the same woman for twenty years, wearing a sheer red negligee and matching high-heeled slippers with little fuzzy pom-poms on them.

Emily took the shot, the light flashing in his eyes, capturing his look of shock and terror. She struggled to contain the laughter that was bubbling up inside her.

"Are you alone in there, Harry?" She looked past him but didn't see any movement.

"Who are you?" he demanded, as he snatched a white hotel robe from the back of a chair. "Why are you taking my picture? Gimme that." He lunged forward and reached out to grab for her camera, but she stepped back and slipped it into the waistband of her jeans. She felt safe in assuming he wouldn't come out into the hall after her.

"Uh-uh, Harry." Emily chuckled and shook her head. "Your wife hired me to find out what you were doing at this hotel every Monday night. She thought you were having an affair. She'll be happy to learn that isn't the case." Emily chuckled again.

"Please, lady, don't show that to her," he hollered.

"Look, Harry, your wife already paid me for this job—I have to. How about you come clean with her tonight? Before I give her the picture. Believe me, she'll be thrilled you weren't with another woman—you just like wearing women's clothing."

"I can't do that, she won't understand."

"Enough of the lies, Harry. Don't keep secrets—they'll eat you up. Trust me, I know."

"Please…" he begged.

"Do you love her, Harry?"

"Yes."

"Then be honest with her. Tell her you love her, but tell her why you do this." Emily gestured toward his outfit. "Work it out, because you can't keep doing this and trying to hide it from her. The lies will destroy your family."

Emily turned and ambled down the hallway. "I'll give you forty-eight hours before I give her the photo," she said over her shoulder.

# THE HEART OF LIES

## CHAPTER 6
## Emily's Break-In

ON THE DRIVE HOME from the Hilton, Emily phoned Isabel, describing what she'd witnessed in the hotel bar and her concerns for Maggie.

"I'm definitely going to do a background check first thing tomorrow," Isabel asserted. "Just something in my gut tells me this guy is not what he seems."

"You might be right. Let me know what you dig up. Until then, not a peep to Maggie."

"Better not mention it to Camille either," Isabel warned. "That resort presentation tomorrow night will give us an opportunity to watch him and Fiona in action."

"Hey, were you able to talk your husband into going?"

"Alex actually was happy to go—said some of the partners at his firm were excited about going. He even suggested maybe we should buy one of the condos for ourselves, as a nice weekend retreat."

"It would be nice for you two to be able to get away from your work once in a while. Perhaps you could even loan it out to a friend now and then," Emily hinted.

"As much as I don't trust Lucas," Isabel said, "the thought of a weekend retreat does sound enticing."

"It does, doesn't it? Skiing and snowboarding in the winter, sipping hot cocoa by the big stone fireplace in the Lodge. Golf, tennis, swimming and boating the rest of the year," Emily suggested.

"And don't forget the hiking, biking, and picnics. Oh, and the upscale restaurant they're planning to build up there," Isabel added.

"Listen to us! We sound like we're making a commercial to promote this resort," Emily chided.

"I can see why this project could be a huge hit around here. There are a lot of people with money in this town just burning a hole in their pockets. No doubt they'll be lining up to plunk down their twenty-five percent for a piece of that mountain, just as fast as Lucas can rake it in."

"We'll see tomorrow night, won't we?"

"Say, how did your stakeout go tonight?"

Emily giggled.

"What happened?"

Just then Emily noticed another call coming in on her cell phone. "Hey, Colin's calling me. Can I get back to you later?"

"No fair, you can't leave me hanging like that!"

~*~

"Hello, Colin," Emily answered, the lilt in her voice giving away how happy she was to hear from him.

"Hello, my hot lady PI."

Colin's deep, sexy voice always made Emily sigh. "What happened to smokin' hot?" she joked.

Colin's police detective buddy in New York City had dubbed her the *smokin' hot lady PI* when they had flown there to interrogate a suspect a few months before. Somehow the nickname stuck for a while, until Colin's departure to San Francisco.

"Well, I didn't want to go overboard, give you a big head or anything," Colin replied.

"I'm hurt."

"I bet you're pouting, aren't you?"

She giggled.

"Doesn't mean I don't still think of you as *smokin' hot*, Emily." He laughed, then his voice turned sensually serious. "If I was there with you, you couldn't stop me from showing you how hot I think you are. I ache for you, woman."

"Okay, okay. You're making me blush."

"Glad to know I can do that even from a long distance. All joking aside…I do ache for you, Emily. I'm hoping I'll be able to come and visit before too long."

"I would love that. This long-distance relationship is excruciating."

"Agreed. I'll let you know when I can work things out. But until then, tell me how your gig went tonight?"

"You wouldn't believe it if I told you."

"Try me."

She explained the case of the suspected philanderer and how she discovered the truth, including her disguise.

Between laughs and giggles, she did her best to describe the man's red negligee and slippers, as well as the advice she gave him to come clean with his wife.

Colin laughed deeply as she painted the visual image—the kind of thoroughly satisfying belly laugh that gave Emily pleasure just hearing it.

Then their conversation took a serious turn. Emily explained to Colin what she had observed in the hotel bar between Maggie's new man and his assistant, and how it seemed suspicious to her, even though it might have been completely innocent.

"I have a bad feeling about it," she said, pulling her car into her driveway. "Isabel is going to do a background check in the morning, see if we can dig anything up on him."

"I hope for Maggie's sake she doesn't find anything," Colin replied. "From what you've told me, she's been waiting for a good man for a long time."

"She has. Maggs raised Josh alone and now he's off to the Navy. Even though she's late for just about everything and she doesn't know how to keep a secret, she is one of the sweetest, kindest people I know. She'd do absolutely anything for a friend." Emily turned the engine off, set her Bluetooth in the console, and raised the phone to her ear.

"She's lucky to have you, Emily."

Emily climbed out of her car. "Not just me, Isabel and Camille, too."

With the wide front porch illuminated by the lamplights on either side of the front door, Emily stuck her key in the lock and went inside her bungalow.

"They were all there for me when Evan died, and we'll all be there for Maggie—however this thing turns out." She flipped on the inside foyer light and kicked her shoes off as she went to the kitchen.

"If there's anything I can do to help, just ask," Colin offered.

Emily turned on the kitchen light and pulled the wig and glasses off with her free hand. As she laid them on the breakfast bar, she noticed the back door was unlocked and partly open. Her heart began to beat hard at the realization.

"Colin, I think someone's been in my house." She closed and locked the door, then pulled her gun out of the back of her waistband.

"What makes you think that?"

"The back door was ajar. I'm sure I locked it before I left. I *always* lock it. I'm going to set the phone down and check the house. Stay on the line."

"Wait!" She heard Colin holler into the phone, but she had already set it on the counter.

Emily drew her gun and crept from room to room, peeking around corners, behind shower curtains, and into closets. After a thorough search, she felt confident whoever had been there was gone.

She picked up the phone. "All's clear."

"Emily! You should have stepped outside and called the police to come and search the house. The perp could still have been in the house and you'd be dead."

"You forget, Colin, I'm not just any helpless woman. Please don't treat me like I am." Emily knew Colin was just being protective, but she didn't appreciate it.

Even though he had lost a fiancée to gunshot wounds, and she had lost her husband to a bullet, Colin needed to remember that she was a gun-carrying private investigator who'd decided a long time ago not to shrink from danger.

Emily had read his over-the-top protectiveness early on in their relationship as a lack of respect. She had suggested to him that maybe they should both date other people—people with safe, boring jobs.

His response was to grab her and kiss her so deeply that her body melted against him and he had to support her as her knees went weak.

Even though they had both been in dangerous situations since that pivotal kiss, with him as a police detective and her as a private eye, they had never discussed fears about each other's safety again—until now. Perhaps it was the distance that made Colin feel so out of control, of no help to her at all.

Emily padded to the living room and sunk down the sofa. She laid her gun down on the coffee table before drawing her feet up under her.

"I know you're not just *any* woman—you're lovely and sweet and kind—but you're also stubborn and pigheaded and *ugh!* I care for you, Emily. I—"

"Hold that thought."

The photo of Evan and the mystery woman was missing from the coffee table. She glanced around the floor. Had it fallen? No.

She remembered clearing the food and drinks after her guests left. The photo was the only thing she purposely had not cleared away.

"It's gone!"
"What's gone?"
"The photo."

~*~

Distraught over the missing photo, Emily phoned Isabel once she'd hung up with Colin. Apologizing for the lateness of the hour, she told her friend about the break-in and the stolen photo.

"Oh, Emily! Are you all right?"

"I'm fine."

"Did you call the police?"

"Yes. I called Colin's friend, Ernie, after I checked to see if anything else was missing. Seems like the photo was all they took. I told Ernie just to file a report, no need to come over."

"I wonder why someone would want that old photo."

"Do you know if anyone besides Jethro knows about it?"

"Maybe he made a few calls or sent some emails about it already, trying to find something out for you," Isabel guessed.

"Yeah, maybe. Can you check with him? Because if that's the case, then someone he told didn't want me to have it."

"Perhaps they don't want you snooping around, uncovering their real identities. Do you want to spend the night here?" Isabel offered.

"No. I think they already got what they came for."

## THE HEART OF LIES

# CHAPTER 7
## The Presentation

SEVEN O'CLOCK WAS APPROACHING, and Emily arrived to see Lucas and his team busy setting up the large conference room at the Paradise Valley Hilton Hotel, preparing for the first of several sales presentations for the new Whitetail Ski and Golf Resort.

Fiona was busy setting out stacks of brochures and financing flyers on one of the green-skirted rectangular tables that sat at the front of the room.

Emily looked around for her friends, but they had not arrived yet. A few people were already milling around, though, talking in small groups, or watching the presentation being set up.

Lucas and the three real estate agents he had contracted with were setting up the renderings. They were positioning them across the front of the room on gleaming brass easels. The massive main lodge, the lush green golf course, and the breathtaking lake dotted with boats and swimmers was showcased alongside the snow-covered mountain, depicting skiers and snowboarders, and the tennis courts with families in white tennis outfits pictured on the courts. There were also drawings of the charming rustic condos with vignettes of the luxurious amenities inside.

Maggie walked in a side door, handed Lucas a red tie and helped him put it on. Emily watched her friend interact with Lucas. She hadn't seen Maggie this happy since—well, never. Lucas seemed to dote on Maggie, as well.

Emily peered over at Fiona and noticed her glancing at the happy couple from time to time, looking none too pleased. Was that jealousy she saw in Fiona's eyes? She wasn't sure, but it was something unsettling.

Emily took a seat on one of the back rows, saving a couple for Isabel and Alex. Camille had told her they might come, if Jonathan was back in town, but not to hold any seats for them.

Then Maggie left through the side door she had entered from. She must not have noticed Emily in the audience.

Sully Sullivan came in, shaking hands with everyone as he made his way to the front. Then he shook hands with Lucas and they spoke to each other, leaning in conspiratorially. What was that about?

"Hey, Emily."

Emily jumped, startled out of her conjecturing.

Camille greeted her, bending down to give her a hug. "Jonathan is stuck in Seattle, so I decided to come by myself. Are Isabel and Alex on their way?"

"Yes, but here, let me move over a couple of seats and we can leave the two on the end for them."

"You're a doll," Camille said as she squeezed past Emily, taking the next chair over. "This is so exciting, isn't it?"

"What do you mean? The new resort?"

"No, silly, Maggie and Lucas—I think she's in love."

"Did she tell you that?"

"Well, I don't know if she wants me spreading it around, so keep this between you and me—and Isabel, of course—but Maggie thinks Lucas is going to pop the question pretty soon." Camille grinned, digging around in her purse and pulling out a mirrored compact and a tube of lipstick. "I think she's finally snagged the handsome rich husband she's been dreaming about her whole life."

"Knowing what humble beginnings she came from…"

"Dirt poor," Camille added as she applied the color, snapping the compact shut. "Mayor Sully, too. I guess because he's older than Maggie, he escaped that life first and has done pretty well for himself."

"Yes, he has." Emily glanced around the room again, which was filling up fast, trying to catch a glimpse of her friends. She saw Alex first and waved them over. Isabel filed in and Alex took the seat on the aisle.

"Did we miss anything?" Isabel asked her friends.

"No, but I think they're about to begin," Camille answered, fidgeting with excitement.

Emily leaned toward Isabel and asked if she'd had any word from Jethro. Isabel looked her friend in the eyes, pursing her lips, and shook her head no. Grimacing, Emily sat up straight in her chair and turned her attention to Mayor Sullivan as he took the microphone.

The mayor gave a few words of greeting and told how thrilled he and the other council members were to have such a spectacular resort being built so close to their community.

As Sully was speaking, Maggie returned and took a seat on the front row, looking lovely in a chic electric-blue designer dress and heels, wearing a look of sheer bliss on her face. Emily assumed Lucas must have bought the dress for her, because it looked far more expensive than anything she'd ever seen Maggie wear.

Sully finished his short speech and turned the microphone over to Lucas to tell about this extensive new project. Lucas strode up to the microphone, looking dashing and powerful, his smile dripping with sincerity. He offered a few words of introduction, then he asked Maggie to join him. He held his hand out to her, and every eye in the room was instantly riveted on the handsome couple.

"I'm sure you're all wondering what's going on," Lucas began his announcement. "Most of you are probably familiar with Maggie Sullivan, the mayor's sister, and the love of my life. As a newcomer to your charming community, you have welcomed me with open arms and I am very grateful," he said, putting a hand over his heart. "That's why I want you all to be a part of what I'm doing here."

Lucas got down on one knee in front of Maggie and took her left hand. A collective gasp rose from the crowd, then a hush fell over the room. Everyone seemed to lean forward on the edge of their seats, including Emily and her friends. He pulled a diamond ring from his coat pocket, it sparkled under the spotlights, refracting the colors of the rainbow across Maggie's smiling face.

"Maggie, I am totally and completely in love with you. Will you do me the honor of making me the happiest man in the world? Will you marry me?"

The whole room seemed to hold its breath, waiting for her reply.

"Yes! Yes, I'll marry you," she exclaimed. She offered him her ring finger and he tenderly slipped the engagement ring on it.

He shot to his feet and took her in his arms, planting a serious kiss on her lips. The crowd applauded enthusiastically.

Emily clapped too, though she and Isabel applauded with less enthusiasm than the rest, while they observed the newly-engaged couple. Then Emily glanced over at Fiona, trying to read her reaction. Fiona was clapping along with the rest of the people, but Emily noted the unnatural smile plastered across her face and her unenthusiastic clap.

Was there something more that Fiona felt for Lucas that an employer-employee relationship? They had seemed rather cozy at the hotel bar the night before, but it wasn't like they had their hands on each other.

"Look at Fiona," Emily whispered to Isabel.

She shot a glance Fiona's way. "She doesn't look pleased, does she?" Isabel asked. "I wonder what's up."

Mayor Sullivan took the mic once more and asked everyone to be seated. He offered his congratulations to his sister and his future brother-in-law, wishing them every happiness, which elicited another round of applause.

"I wish we could go and congratulate Maggie," Camille leaned over and whispered to Emily, who nodded her agreement.

"Now, for the presentation we've all been waiting for, to get the details of the spectacular new Whitetail Ski and Golf Resort, here is the newest member of our community, Lucas Wakefield." The mayor led the crowd in another round of applause for Lucas and took a seat on the front row beside his sister.

"Thank you, Mayor Sullivan—one of my new favorite people in town. Not only is he going to be my brother-in-law, he is the first person to invest in the Whitetail Resort." Lucas looked over at Sully and gave him a few claps of his hands and pointed toward him. "You're the man, Sully. Thank you for believing in me and in the project."

A level of chatter rose as people in the room seemed to be commenting to each other on their mayor's investment in this new mountain resort. Emily and Isabel raised their eyebrows at each other.

Alex leaned over to his wife and friends. "If Sully's on board, maybe we should get in on it, too," he suggested, his face lit up with excitement.

"Whoa, slow down. We haven't even heard the presentation yet," Isabel reminded him. "We already talked about this, Alex. Take a deep breath and relax. You know I don't trust this guy."

"I'll try to just sit here and listen. But if the other partners in the office are buying into it, I don't want to look like I can't afford a condo too, you know?"

"You're going to give in to peer pressure?" Isabel raised her eyebrows and gave her head a shake.

"I don't exactly see it like that," he grumbled.

"I told you what I think, Alex. If you're willing to put a hundred thousand dollars at risk, in spite of my misgivings, what else is there to say." She crossed her arms and tightened her lips in opposition.

"Oh, let the guy have his fun," Camille reproved, leaning into her friends. "Besides, it might be nice for you two to have a getaway. We could all go up for a weekend sometime. Doesn't that sound fabulous? Oh, thoughts of the food I'd make are already filling my head."

"That's easy for you to say, Cam. It isn't your hundred grand," Isabel huffed.

"Shhh!" A middle-aged woman in the row in front of them craned her neck around and shushed them. "I can't hear the man."

The four of them acted like school children who had just been scolded, sitting back in their seats, listening in silence for the remainder of the presentation. Although, Emily noted that Alex's eyes lit up on several occasions, while Isabel frowned.

The price of the luxury condos ranged from two hundred to five hundred thousand dollars and a twenty-five percent deposit would be required to reserve them. The balance would be due, Lucas said, as soon as the unit was completed and ready for occupancy, giving them time to arrange their financing, if necessary. For those who did not want to own a condo but would like to have a membership in the resort, the price was five thousand dollars per year. He warned the crowd that only a certain number of memberships would be available to people who did not own a condo in the resort.

The presentation came to a close and Lucas invited all who were interested to come up and get a closer look at the drawings of the amenities the resort had to offer. "Then when you're ready, please make a line at the table over here." He pointed to the one where Fiona was sitting, with stacks of colorful brochures artfully fanned out across it. "My assistant, Fiona, will be happy to sign you up for membership in the resort."

She smiled and waved at the crowd.

"If you'd like to purchase one of the charming and luxurious condominiums, which includes a free membership, please step up to that table where the three sales associates are seated." Lucas motioned to the other side of the front of the room. "Please have your twenty-five percent deposit ready so we can get you through the lines quickly. And if you have questions first, please feel free to come and talk to Maggie and me here at the center table."

A steady stream of people made their way to the front, some studying the renderings first, others going straight to the tables. Alex glanced at the crowd gathering, then he nudged Isabel and nodded his head, gesturing toward a group of attorneys he knew. He put an arm around her and flashed his puppy dog eyes with an exaggerated pout, as if he was asking for her permission.

"Don't look at me like that. You know how I feel about this. But, if you must—"

He bolted from his seat before she could finish her sentence and sprinted down the aisle to join his colleagues in line.

"Yay!" Camille's deep blue eyes lit up, making her spiky red hair appear more vivid. She clapped her hands together exuberantly, obviously approving of their decision to purchase a condo. "We're going to have so much fun, girls!"

Emily folded her arms and gave Isabel as sideways look, which Isabel mirrored. "Why don't you go and get a look at those renderings, Camille? You can start planning our first weekend trip."

"Oh, that's a good idea, Emily." Camille shot up out of her chair. "Maggie and Lucas will probably have one, too. Aren't you girls coming?"

"We'll be there in a minute," Emily said. "We have some business to discuss first."

"All right." Camille climbed past her friends to get out to the aisle. "But don't be too long." She wagged her finger. "I'm just busting to congratulate Maggie." Camille's voice trailed off as she walked away.

Once Camille was gone, Emily felt she and Isabel could speak more freely. She looked around to make sure she would not be overheard. "Did you dig anything up with the background check on you know who?"

"Nothing yet. I've been buried, working on the Semanski case," Isabel replied. "It's going to trial soon."

"Better do it quick, looks like we're running out of time."

"Looks like it."

"I have to say, I'm surprised you let Alex invest with Lucas before we fully vet him."

"I didn't exactly let him. On the way over tonight, we had a doozie of an argument over this thing. I can't remember the last time we argued like that. For Alex, it's all about how he'll look at the office if the other partners have a luxury condo up there and we don't. You know how competitive those lawyers can be."

"Let's hope we're worrying about nothing." Emily squeezed Isabel's hand.

"We'd better go congratulate the happy couple."

Emily uttered a chorus of, "Excuse me, pardon me, sorry," as she and Isabel wormed their way through the crowd, pressing through to the front of the line.

"Hey, no cuts," a thirty-something, professional-looking man at the front of the line hollered. "Wait your turn."

"Sorry, mister, I'm not here to buy a condo," Emily apologized, grabbing hold of Isabel's arm and pulling her around the side of Maggie's table.

"Hey, y'all," Maggie exclaimed, jumping up from her seat with open arms, hugging Emily first, then Isabel.

"We just wanted to congratulate you," Isabel said graciously.

Maggie stuck her hand out, flashing a large single diamond in what looked like a platinum setting.

"That's gorgeous," Emily said.

"Yes, Maggie, stunning. You look so happy," Isabel added.

As Isabel was talking, Emily noticed Sully approach Lucas, who stood from the table and extended his hand. While Maggie and Isabel exchanged a few words, Emily diverted her attention to what Sully might be saying to Lucas. Straining to hear their conversation, she noticed Sully smile and grasp Lucas's hand with both of his, leaning again in to say something in private.

"This had better pan out or I'm going to be SOL." She overheard Sully say the words in a low, serious voice, still grasping Lucas's hand. That was all, no further conversation. Her observation undetected, she watched as the mayor walked away and Lucas plastered another charming smile on his face as he turned to help the next person in line.

That exchange prickled her. Something was not right, and for Maggie's sake, she was going to find out what.

"We'd better let Maggie get back to work," Emily said. "We'll talk tomorrow." She gave Maggie a quick hug good-bye right after Isabel hugged her, and they turned to leave.

Emily noticed the prospective investor who had scolded them earlier giving her the stink eye. "We're leaving—she's all yours," Emily quipped.

# THE HEART OF LIES

# CHAPTER 8
## Engagement Party Invitation

THE NEXT MORNING, EMILY WOKE with a splitting headache. She had endured another night of restless sleep, a jumble of thoughts about Evan, visions of Colin, and dreams about Maggie and Lucas that did not end well. Several times in the night she sat up, spooked and wide awake, checking the clock. Once she even checked for her gun in the nightstand.

She hardly remembered the details of the dreams, just the ominous, unnerving mood they left behind, especially the unsettledness about Maggie and Lucas. She and Isabel had had a bad feeling about Lucas from the start, but what she overheard Maggie's brother say, continued to prick her like a thorn in her side.

Emily glanced at the clock. Six thirty. The sun was just starting to come up as she padded barefoot down the hallway. The dawning light cast uneven shadows which gave her a chill that slithered up her back as she remembered that someone had recently invaded her quiet domain. She glanced around, then stepped into the kitchen, and turned on the coffee maker. She moved to the breakfast bar and perched on a stool to wait.

Tapping her nails on the counter while the coffee sputtered into the pot, she wondered what she could do to find out what Lucas was really up to. She'd make a point to talk to Isabel today.

Soon, a fully caffeinated Emily slipped into her jeans and t-shirt and decided to hit the shooting range to get in some practice. She half-wished she had a self-defense class that morning or a kick-boxing session to work out some of her tension.

~*~

As Emily left the shooting range, pleased with the close cropping of bullet holes on her paper targets, she received a call from Camille. Maggie had phoned Camille first thing in the morning, she said, and asked her to plan an engagement party for the coming weekend.

"It's going to be a casual affair, just close friends and family. Maggie wants a barbecue—chicken, ribs, the whole thing. I'm having the party at my house this Friday night at seven. You'll be there, won't you?"

"I'd love to come. I know I'm not the best cook, but is there anything I can bring?" Emily asked, trying to sound pleased.

"I think I have everything covered."

"Camille, can I ask you something?" Emily's voice grew serious.

"What is it, Em?"

"Don't you think this is kind of sudden?"

"It is rather fast, I have to admit, but Maggie's no spring chicken. She says she's met the man of her dreams and she's ready to take the plunge. Why do you ask?"

"Just seems awfully soon to me. We don't actually know Lucas very well. What if he's not what he seems?" Emily asked, trying not to expose all of her concerns.

"Do you think you might be feeling that way because you discovered your Evan was not who he said he was? Perhaps you're projecting your suspicions about Evan onto Lucas?"

Camille's question stung, but Emily had to consider that she might have a point. "You could be right. Maybe they'll have a long engagement."

"Oh, Em, hasn't Maggie told you?"

"Told me what?" Emily asked nervously.

"They're getting married two weeks from this Saturday."

"Oh, Camille, that's too fast. What's the rush? She's not pregnant, is she?" Emily asked, praying the answer was no.

"No, she's not pregnant," Camille chuckled.

"*Whew*! That's a relief," Emily sighed.

"It's funny you should say that, though. I asked her the same thing. She told me they haven't even slept together yet."

"Really?" Emily was glad for that bit of news.

"She said Lucas told her he was old fashioned and wanted to wait for the wedding night."

"Old fashioned?"

Camille ignored Emily's query, not offering further comment on it. "Oh, and the best part, I almost forgot to tell you—Maggie said she called Josh last night and told him about the engagement. He told her he'd already planned to be here in the next day or two, and he'll be able to stay for a couple of weeks or so. That might be why Maggie wants the wedding so soon, so her son can be there."

"Could be. It'll be great to see that kid again. I'm sure Maggie is thrilled."

"Over the moon is how she put it," Camille replied.

"What about Lucas's friends and family? Can they get here that quickly?"

"Don't know, Maggie didn't say. I guess we'll see."

~*~

As soon as she finished her conversation with Camille, Emily phoned Maggie.

"Hey, Em, I was just fixin' to call ya," Maggie said. "I wanted to invite y'all to my engagement party Friday night."

"I just got off the phone with Camille and she filled me in."

"Then y'all already heard that the weddin' is goin' to be two weeks from Saturday?"

"Yeah, Cam told me. Where are you holding it?" Emily asked.

"Well, that's another reason for my call. I was wonderin' if we could have it in y'all's backyard. You have such a beautiful garden, all the flowers and rose bushes, and that lovely white gazebo that Evan built would be perfect. It's goin' to be a small, intimate weddin' and I just thought…"

"Absolutely, Maggie, anything for my friends." Although Emily was happy to offer the garden, the truth was she hadn't been back there to enjoy the beauty of it for quite some time. She'd paid a local landscaper to keep it mowed and trimmed because it had been too painful to be out there after Evan's death. Together they had planned it out and planted all the flowers and trees, and he had built her the most beautiful white gazebo for their third anniversary.

In the spring months, when she dated Colin, before he left for San Francisco, she never once took him out to the garden. She had physically and emotionally shut the door to that place, and now she wondered how painful it might be to watch her friend get married in Evan's gazebo.

"Looked like Lucas was selling a lot of those resort condos last night after the presentation." Emily changed the subject.

"Yes, they were sellin' like hotcakes. Quite a few people put deposits down on their units. I'm so proud of my Lucas. Oh, and we have a special event set up next week where Lucas has chartered two luxury buses to take prospective Whitetail Resort members up to the mountain. He's gonna show them around so they can see the lake and where the golf course is gonna be and all that. I think the foundation may even be poured for the first set of condos."

"Wow, Maggie, that sounds exciting."

"Lucas did take a lot of deposits last night, about thirty I think, but there were some people who said they just couldn't visualize the resort from a drawin'. I think he'll sell more of the condos if people can actually see the gorgeous scenery and the project underway."

"Makes sense."

"Would y'all like to go?" Maggie asked.

"I might," Emily answered, thinking it may give her an opportunity to see what he's really selling. She wanted to believe he was a great guy, honest and sweet, but something wouldn't let her jump onboard. Maybe it was Isabel's suspicions—maybe it was her own.

"He's goin' to be very successful with this resort, Em, and I'll have the life I've always wanted."

"Sounds like it," Emily agreed. "Will all that money make you happy, Maggs?"

"Oh, it'll be nice not havin' to worry about payin' the bills for a change, but I'll be totally happy to have a wonderful man in my life, that loves me. I couldn't be happier if I was twins, as my daddy used to say."

"Then I'm happy for you, too." That wasn't a total lie. Emily was glad to see Maggie happy, but she hoped Lucas wasn't setting her up for a fall. She resolved to keep digging.

~*~

His mother and her new boyfriend picked Josh up at the airport on Thursday around noon. She'd been so excited. On the phone, she'd told Josh that she couldn't wait for her son to meet the man of her dreams.

Josh saw his mom and went to give her a big bear hug and then he politely shook Lucas's hand.

"I thought you'd be wearin' your uniform," his mother said.

He shrugged. "It's in my bag. I thought I'd go casual today and blend in."

They went to lunch at the Blue Moon Café, which gave Josh a chance to get to know his mother's future husband. The visit was pleasant and Josh could see his mom was happier than he'd seen her in a long time.

There had been other men, other boyfriends, but none she had committed to marry. He'd been surprised by the swiftness of their courtship and the rush to the altar, but if marrying this man was going to make her happy, he was going to be pleased for them and do his best to like her new man.

Once lunch was over, Lucas said he needed to get back to work. Josh thought he might drop by Lucas's office later and have a man-to-man talk with him, without his mother there. In private, he would be able to talk more freely with Lucas.

~*~

Late that afternoon, Lucas sat at the desk in his office going over the Excel spreadsheets he had spent hours designing to keep track of the condo units and the sales. Twenty-nine units sold that first night. He looked at the screen with a satisfied grin.

"Total sales of nine million, four hundred and fifty thousand," he said as Fiona walked into his office from the front area where she worked.

"So how much in deposits from Tuesday night's meeting?"

"Let's see…at twenty-five percent…that would be two million, three hundred sixty-two thousand and five hundred dollars."

"That's a lot of money, Lucas."

"I thought I'd have to hang out in this town and make friends with these people before they'd trust me enough to invest, but I guess we were right in picking Maggie and Sully as our connections."

"Maybe it's not Maggie or Sully at all. Maybe it's just that these people were ripe for a new resort nearby, somewhere new and exciting to spend their time and money."

"You could be right. I think we can get another forty or so under contract after our trip up the mountain next week, which should more than double our haul. At least a handful more by the time the wedding rolls around and then we're out of here."

"Have you heard from the boss lately?" Fiona asked.

"No, but I'm sure our progress reports are expected. Even though the boss came up with the initial idea, I'm doing most of the work."

"Hey! What am I? Chopped liver?"

"Sorry, babe, I just meant—"

"I know what you meant, that you're the top dog and I'm here to back you up, handle all the finances, and watch you romance another woman." She turned her face away.

"It's just a role I'm playing. You can't think I'm actually falling for Maggie."

"I don't know what to think," she snapped, turning back to face him, "but you're making it look awfully believable. It's hard for me to watch."

"Do you think we'd be raking in millions if I didn't make it look believable?" he shot back. "You think her brother would have invested in this project if he thought for a nanosecond that I was a fraud?" His voice rose with irritation at having to explain this all to her again.

"You're right," Fiona said, waving her hands in surrender. "I'm sorry." She walked around behind him and began to gently massage his shoulders. "I just love you so much."

"You shouldn't be doing that. Someone could walk in and see us."

"I know. I just need to touch you."

"Keep your eye on the prize. In two weeks, you and I will be sipping mojitos on the beach with millions in the bank, leaving Paradise Valley, and the boss, in the dust."

Fiona leaned her head down next to Lucas's.

"Lucas!" Josh hollered from the doorway. He had walked in on them, finding Fiona with her hands on him and the side of her jaw touching Lucas's sandy brown hair.

Lucas stood up and displaced Fiona's hands.

"Josh." Lucas's mouth went dry and a sheen of sweat covered his face. "It's not—"

"It's not what?" Josh cut in, asking through clenched teeth. The vein in his neck was bulging as his hands balled into fists.

Fiona backed away from Lucas, and sidestepped Josh, as she slinked out of the room.

"It's not what you think." Lucas's gaze went beyond Josh to Fiona standing in the outer office as he searched for a believable story. "Fiona and I were going over the numbers from the sales so far. I complained about my shoulders being stiff from sitting at this computer and she offered to massage them. That's all."

"That's not what it looked like to me." Josh's eyes narrowed as he stared into Lucas's face.

"That is what happened." Lucas's voice moved from shaky to calm. "You just misunderstood what you saw. I would never cheat on your mother."

"I want to believe you, but somehow I don't. I'm going to be watching you. If there's any funny business going on, I won't stand by and let it happen. You hurt my mom, you'll deal with me."

## CHAPTER 9
### Engagement Party Surprise

FRIDAY EVENING ROLLED AROUND and Emily made a dash to her favorite bookstore before heading over to Maggie and Lucas's engagement party. She had parked on Main Street in front of the shop, and as she was reaching for the handle of her car door, she heard someone call out.

"Miss?"

Emily turned to see the woman, maybe mid-sixties, with grayish blonde hair coiffed just above her shoulders. She was driving a late-model silver Mercedes that she had stopped in the middle of the street with her window rolled down. "Can you tell me where I can find the Graystone Building?"

"Sure, it's just down the block. My office is in that building," Emily replied. She noticed the woman was smartly dressed in a red suit and an abundance of gold jewelry.

"Oh, I'm looking for my son, Lucas Wakefield. Do you know him?" she asked.

Emily walked closer to the car and motioned to the three cars stacked up behind the Mercedes to squeeze around her. "Yes, I do. And you're his mother?" Emily was stunned. She hadn't heard Lucas's mother was coming to town.

"I am," she nodded. "Gloria Wakefield."

"It's nice to meet you, Mrs. Wakefield, but Lucas is not at his office right now."

"Oh no? Where can I find him?" the woman asked sweetly.

A car honked and Emily gestured for the driver to go around the Mercedes, too.

"I'm sure he's at his engagement party by now," Emily said, a little surprised the woman didn't know that. "You are coming to the party, too, aren't you?"

"Engagement party? Why, yes, of course, I'm going," Mrs. Wakefield replied. "I just thought we were meeting at his office first and then I'd go with him."

"I'm headed over there myself. Why don't you follow me?" Emily offered, thinking the elderly woman must have just gotten mixed up.

"Thank you, dear. That's so nice of you."

The party was in full swing when Emily arrived with Gloria Wakefield in tow. Everyone was out in the backyard with tiki torches blazing, conversation and laughter competing with the blaring country music emanating from a large black boom box.

Emily escorted Gloria from the front porch to the back of the house, and they stepped through the French doors leading to the expansive back deck. The lawn beyond the deck was set up with a ping pong table at one end and a fire pit with patio chairs at the other.

Lucas and Maggie stood on the deck, not far from the French doors, talking to Alex and Isabel.

"Look who I found?" Emily announced, watching Lucas's face for a reaction. His mouth dropped open, then a wide smile spread across it. Maggie turned to Emily with a quizzical expression.

"You must be Maggie," the woman said, putting her hand out. "I'm Lucas's mother."

At first Maggie looked stunned, but then she opened her arms and hugged the woman warmly. "Lucas, shame on you," she scolded with a bit of a frown, then her face blossomed into a smile. "Why didn't you tell me your momma was gonna be here?"

"Um, I, well, I wasn't sure she could make it," he mumbled. Emily noticed a flash of a frown and then it was gone. In its place Lucas plastered a polite smile. He stepped toward her, leaned down, and kissed her lightly on the cheek. "I'm glad to see you found the place, Mother."

"It is so nice to meet you, Mrs. Wakefield," Maggie declared.

"Please, call me Gloria."

"All right, Gloria." Maggie beamed.

Maggie took Gloria's arm and introduced her future mother-in-law to her friends, just as Fiona walked up to the group.

"Mother," Lucas said, "this is Fiona, my assistant. She's helping me with the Whitetail Resort project I told you about."

"Fiona, so nice to meet you," Gloria said, shaking Fiona's hand.

"And this is my brother, Sully," Maggie introduced. "He's the mayor of Paradise Valley."

"Well, this is an honor, Mr. Mayor," Gloria said, taking his hand in both of hers.

"Thank you, ma'am, but I'm just a regular guy," Sully replied, dressed down in jeans and a collared shirt. "Tonight, I'm just the brother of the bride."

"I'm sure you and my Lucas will become great friends," Gloria gushed.

"Like brothers," Lucas agreed with a grin.

Sully turned to Lucas. "Say, can we talk privately?"

"All right," he replied. "If you all will excuse us, we have a little business to discuss."

"No, Lucas, not tonight," Maggie pleaded.

"Just a few minutes, hon. We'll be right back."

Emily watched as Lucas and Sully stepped off the deck and moved to a private corner of the backyard.

~*~

"What's up?" Lucas asked.

"I hate to do this to you, but I need that hundred thousand back," Sully said in a low tone, glancing around.

"Why now? You'll make twice that when you sell the condos." Lucas's gaze darted around, as well.

"I just got a notice today that we're being audited in the next two weeks. I have to get that money back in the account right away." His voice revealed his desperation, as did the beads of sweat that formed on his forehead.

"I can't do that, Sully. Your money is being held in an escrow account. It's not like I just have it sitting in my office or something," Lucas replied coolly.

"I know you sold a lot of those condos this week, so I'm sure you have more than enough funds to repay what I gave you. I *have* to get the money back. If I don't—I'm ruined. Do you hear me? Ruined!"

"Listen, Sully." Lucas placed a hand on Sully's shoulder, turning his back to the party. "I need you to use your influence to push the wealthy citizens of this town toward buying into Whitetail. If they see you pulling out, that will squirrel the whole deal and I'll lose millions. I can't let you do that."

"Lucas, please…"

"I'll let you in on a little secret, my friend." Lucas glanced over his shoulder once more. "And I'm only telling you this because I need you out there pushing this resort—"

"Tell me what?"

"There is no resort being built on the mountain," Lucas revealed.

"What!" Sully gasped at Lucas's insidious revelation.

Lucas laughed boisterously to cover Sully's outburst. "Shhh, keep your voice down," Lucas sternly warned, looking deeply into Sully's fearful eyes, keeping his hand firmly resting on Sully's shoulder. "Now you know the truth."

"Why are you telling me this?"

"Well, because now that I have you by the short hairs, you will stay in the game and you will use your considerable influence to bring in those investors who are on the fence. You *will* be on one of the luxury buses I chartered for next week, and you *will* do your very best to convince all those potential investors to purchase. I'm expecting forty or fifty more to commit out of those two buses full of prospects and put their twenty-five percent down. If you do that, I'll refund your money at the end of the two weeks, just in time to save you from the auditors."

Sully looked like someone had punched him in the gut. His eyes were glassy, and he was sweating profusely now, as his breathing appeared labored. No words came.

"Now," he handed Sully a napkin from the table, "wipe the sweat and that stupid look off your face—we're going to return to the party and you are going to act like the happy brother of the bride." Lucas used a warm, even tone, as his hand continued to rest on Sully's shoulder, squeezing. "Agreed?"

Sully pulled away from Lucas's grip and he found his voice. "What about Maggie?"

"Maggie doesn't know anything. If you help me—which you will—she won't know anything until the day of the wedding when she finds that I've left town. I don't want to hurt her, she's a sweet gal and very easy on the eyes. She deserves someone far better than me. When she finds out what I've done, I'm sure she'll get over me fast enough."

With a stoic stare, Sully nodded his understanding.

"We should get back to the party before people start wondering about us." Lucas turned and walked back to the deck, wearing a satisfied grin, rather pleased with himself.

~*~

"Where's Sully?" Emily asked Lucas as he stepped up on the deck.

Lucas turned, looking. He cleared his throat. "I think he got a phone call. He must have had to take care of something."

He breezed past her, avoiding her gaze, and took his place next to Maggie.

Emily had observed their private pow-wow. She was suspicious. Why would Sully have left the party without saying good-bye to his sister? That wasn't like him.

Turning the music down, Camille's husband, Jonathan, vigorously jangled a cowbell to gain everyone's attention as his wife stepped through the French doors, holding a platter full of barbecued chicken.

"Well, now that everyone's here, let's get this barbecue started," Camille exclaimed from the top of the deck. "The food is ready. Grab a plate."

She placed the platter on the long table she had set up for all the barbecued meats and side dishes she'd prepared. Like a mother hen, she rounded everyone up and encouraged them to fix their plates and dig in. Once the guests served themselves, they sat to eat. A collection of square and round tables, covered with red-and-white-checkered tablecloths, were scattered around the deck and the lawn. The music started up again and so did the chatter.

Camille had done a fabulous job, her friends praised, putting on a spread of ribs and chicken, corn on the cob, potato salad and more.

Lucas sat and ate for a while with Maggie, Gloria, and Emily before excusing himself to spend time with the other guests. Emily watched as he moved from table to table, looking as though he was trying to make sure everyone was having a good time and thanking them for coming.

Emily's attention was drawn back to her table as Maggie described Emily's beautiful gazebo to Mrs. Wakefield. Maggie went on to describe the flowers and yards of cascading tulle she planned for the gazebo and the perimeter of the garden. The older woman seemed delighted by the picture of the setting Maggie had painted for her. She nodded and smiled in-between bites of her dinner.

When Camille brought the massive Texas Sheet Cake out, many groaned that they were already stuffed.

Josh had gone in to use the bathroom. As he was drying off his hands the doorknob jiggled and there was a light tap on the door. He called out, "Occupied," and straightened his shirt before opening the door.

Expecting someone to be right outside the door waiting, his attention turned to muffled conversation coming from the den just beyond the bathroom. The glass atrium door was shut and covered with closed blinds, and a woman was standing close with head leaned in, listening.

He couldn't make out all that was being said inside the den, but a few phrases came through clearly. "When you and I leave…we'll split the money between us…cut the boss out."

Suddenly, the woman spun around to leave, and in her haste to get away, she bumped into Josh who was standing behind her, also listening to the voices.

"Excuse me," the woman muttered as she scurried past him.

Josh moved closer to the covered glass door.

"I can't wait," Josh heard a female voice, followed by a small giggle. Then he recognized Lucas's voice as he replied something to her. Josh slowly pushed the door open, catching Fiona reaching up to wipe a smear of lipstick off Lucas's lip with her thumb and observing Lucas smiling down at her.

The pair's eyes grew wide in surprise as they realized the door was open and Josh stood staring at them, his face twisted into a snarl.

He charged Lucas like an angry bull. Fiona had stepped aside just in time or she would have been caught up in the skirmish, as well. She made herself scarce, leaving Lucas to fend for himself.

Standing toe to toe, Josh pinned Lucas to the wall with his powerful forearm pressing on the man's throat. After turning the air blue with a few choice expletives, he tore into him about what he just saw. "You're already cheating on my mother! I won't have it—you hear me? There's no way in hell I'm gonna let you marry my mom knowing you were just in here doin' God knows what with your assistant."

"You have it all wrong, Josh," Lucas faltered. "Fiona and I just had to straighten something out—about the promotional trip up the mountain next week."

"You're lying," Josh seethed.

"There's nothing between us." Lucas fought to get the words out, struggling to breathe. "I love Maggie."

"You think I'm stupid?" Josh's eyes widened as the stress in his voice rose. "I saw her wiping lipstick off your freakin' lip."

"That wasn't lipstick—it was barbecue sauce," Lucas squeaked under the forceful weight of Josh's muscular arm.

"I'm not buying it! You two are way too friendly to be all business. I swear, you break it off with my mother or I'm going to tell her what I saw tonight." Josh stepped back, releasing his pressure against Lucas's neck.

Lucas grabbed at his throat and coughed a few times. "I promise, Josh, it's not what you think," he sputtered. He bent over, putting his hands on his knees, trying to catch his breath. "I would never hurt your mom. I love her." He drew in a few more breaths. "Let's get through this party and then I'll let her down gently tomorrow."

"Tomorrow?"

"Just give me some time to do it in my own way."

"I'll probably regret it, but I will give you until tomorrow at six or I'll tell her myself."

Emily passed by the den as Josh stormed out. She noticed Lucas in the room, doubled over and breathing hard. "What on earth?"

"Not now, Emily," Josh growled as he stomped away.

"Lucas?" she asked from the doorway. "What's going on?"

"Nothing to worry about." Lucas pulled himself upright. "Just a difference of opinion." He squeezed past her, smoothing his hair with his hand, and he returned to the party.

Emily immediately went looking for Isabel to fill her in on what she'd seen and she hoped they could put a plan together to find out what was really going on. The Semanski trial be damned—they had put off the background check long enough.

After watching Lucas's interaction with Sully on the lawn, and now this conflict with Josh, Emily was convinced something was up. She had to find a way to get Sully and Josh to talk to her. If Maggie was set to marry this guy in two weeks, then time was running out to find out what was going on and save her friend from perhaps the biggest mistake of her life.

# THE HEART OF LIES

# CHAPTER 10
## Sully's Regrets

SULLY HAD LEFT HIS SISTER'S engagement party without even saying good-bye to her. He felt terrible about it. The rude departure was so unlike him, but there was no way he could appear happy in front of her when her husband-to-be was ruining his life—and hers too. And the worst part of it was that he couldn't even warn his sister what was happening without bringing his own crime out into the open.

His wife, Carolyn, would be surprised that he'd returned so early from the party. Sully had tried to encourage her to come for a little while, but nothing he said changed her mind. The pain was becoming unbearable for her and she was embarrassed by the slurred speech and jerky actions her MS brought on.

Carolyn had been a vivacious and active woman before she became ill. Now, even though Sully's love for her was unwavering, she became a constant source of financial and emotional stress for him. The difficult conversations, the mounting hospital bills that were not covered by their insurance and his loneliness for a companion at the many functions he had to attend. His love for her remained solid, but his character was cracking under the constant pressure, causing him to make a bad decision that could ruin everything.

He had picked her up out of her wheelchair and placed her in her recliner before he'd left for the party, sticking her favorite romantic movie in the DVD player—*An Affair to Remember*—to keep her company while he was gone. When he'd returned home, he noticed she had fallen asleep with the movie still playing.

He went to turn the television off when he saw the scene in the movie, near the end, when Cary Grant learns his love, Deborah Kerr, is paralyzed, sitting on the sofa with a blanket over her motionless legs. She didn't want to tell him she was paralyzed, to burden him, because she loved him so much. When Cary Grant realizes she is an invalid, he rushes to her, throws his arms around her and kisses her passionately because he doesn't care—he loves her.

Watching that scene, it dawned on Sully for the first time that this was why Carolyn loved this movie.

He turned the TV and DVD player off and turned back to his wife. There wasn't anything he wouldn't do for her. Thinking about the hundred thousand dollars and the possibility of jail, he paced the floor, mumbling under his breath.

"Sully?" Carolyn's soft voice called his name.

Sully rushed to her side. "I'm here, Carolyn. What do you need?"

"Is something wrong?"

"What makes you ask that?"

"You look so worried. You're wearing a path in the carpet and talking to yourself. What's wrong?" Poor Carolyn struggled to get the words out.

"Nothing I can't handle, sweetheart. Don't worry yourself." He looked into her tired eyes and smiled tenderly. The last thing he wanted was to worry his wife—that would be too cruel. She had enough to handle with her illness—she didn't need his problems as well. "Worries are part of the job when you're the mayor."

He hoped that would satisfy her, but if he didn't get the hundred thousand dollars back into the city's retirement fund soon, he would not be able to hide the truth from her much longer. What would happen to her if he was in jail? Who would take care of her? Who would pay for her medical bills? He had to find a way to get the money back in the account.

"It's late, sweetheart. Why don't I take you to bed now?"

The next morning Josh stopped by his uncle's house to discuss what he had seen and overheard at the engagement party. He told him how he had struggled with it all night, avoiding his mother for fear he would blurt out what he'd witnessed. And because he had promised to give Lucas twenty-four hours to tell her what happened, he felt duty-bound to hold to it.

"I should've just confronted him in front of my mom last night at the party, not given him time to come clean. What was I thinking? If I had dealt with it at the party, my gut wouldn't be twisting like someone's big fist had a hold of my insides." Josh sat on the edge of the sofa, his shoulders slumped, and his head hung down. He looked up at his uncle. "But I didn't want to embarrass her, ya know?"

"Maybe you misunderstood, Josh. Is that possible?" Sully asked, taking a seat next to him.

"No, Uncle Sully, I know what I saw *and* what I heard." Josh was adamant. He shot up from the sofa and turned to face his uncle. "He was definitely fooling around with that girl—his assistant," he said through clenched teeth. His jaw twitched with anger as he began to pace back and forth.

"I want you to calm down, son," Sully tried to reason.

"I just want to kill him!" Josh slammed his clenched fist into the open palm of his other hand.

"Hey, don't ever say that," Sully warned.

"I promise you, Uncle Sully, if that man hurts my momma—"

He felt like a caged beast, holding back his rage. "I'll tear him apart with my bare hands!" Josh threatened, displaying his fists as the lethal weapons they were. He was so enraged, his body was trembling.

Sully rose from his seat and put a hand on Josh's shoulder. "Boy, you need to calm down before you do something you'll regret. That quick temper of yours is going to get you into trouble someday."

"You're saying I can fight to defend my country, but I can't fight to defend my mother?"

"It's not the same. Think about it. What'll hurt your mom worse? A man breaking her heart or her son ending up in prison for the rest of his life?"

Josh jerked back like someone had slapped him hard. Visions of being hauled to prison in chains and an orange jumpsuit flashed before his eyes.

"Now, son, as her big brother, my first instinct is to protect your mother, too—always has been—but when I jump in without thinking things through, I usually make matters a whole lot worse. Let's give Lucas the day to tell her, like you said. Then, I'll go see him at the end of the day and have a man-to-man talk with him."

Though Josh wanted nothing more than to rip Lucas's head off with his bare hands and feed it to the wolves, he considered that his uncle might be right. The last thing he wanted was to hurt his mother. He took a breath, sucked in hard, and released a cry of exasperation.

He would wait, he told his uncle, but if Lucas hadn't broken it off with his mother by tonight, he was going to take matters into his own hands and it wouldn't be pretty. Sully had until six o'clock to deal with the scoundrel, Josh said.

Sully spent the day agonizing over how he was going to protect his little sister and still get the city's money back from Lucas Wakefield. He knew that if he pushed Lucas to break off the engagement with Maggie, rumors would spread all over the valley and people would start pulling their money out of the Whitetail Resort. He and Lucas needed the prospects on the bus trip next week to invest their money or Lucas would not be returning the hundred thousand dollars to Sully.

Was Josh right about Lucas fooling around with his assistant? Was she involved in the scam? Or was she just working for Lucas and fooling around with him, unaware of what was really going on?

Sully remembered Maggie introducing Fiona to him at the welcome party for Lucas, telling him she had been in the area for a while and she hadn't had much luck finding a job. He recalled Maggie introducing Fiona to Lucas, as well. So, she couldn't have initially been part of the plan—but was she now? Had she been sucked in by this powerful and charming man, just as Maggie had?

It was going to be a long day, Sully told himself, waiting to see if Lucas would do the right thing and tell Maggie. If the town thought Lucas was stepping out on Maggie, he had to know it would ruin him. So why was he willing to fool around with his assistant with so much at stake? Knowing firsthand of Lucas's devious and manipulative ways, he would likely be planning his own damage control strategy to keep Maggie under his spell, keeping her from believing that Josh was right in what he saw and heard, maybe even devising some way to get Josh out of the picture altogether.

Sully shuddered. Did he really even have any idea what Lucas was capable of?

~*~

Emily sat at her desk, in front of the computer in her office across the main hall from Lucas's office. She had been searching the internet all morning, trying to find something on Lucas Wakefield. She had attempted to call Isabel several times in the last few hours, but it always went to voicemail. Though it was frustrating, Emily knew that if Isabel was working hard on a case at the FBI, sometimes she could not be reached for non-FBI purposes.

Isabel had worked for months doing the financial analyses on the George Semanski murder and kidnapping case and it would be going to court soon. She'd had to go out of town a few weeks ago and lately had been putting in some fourteen to sixteen hour days. She had managed to get the evening off last night for Maggie and Lucas's engagement party, but Emily assumed she was back at her office working again.

All the intense work on the Semanski case, leading up to the trial, meant Isabel hadn't had the spare time to look into Lucas's background yet. Emily didn't have the federal contacts Isabel did, so she had to rely on her own investigative methods.

If Detective Colin Andrews had still been in town, she could have asked him for a few favors and he would have gladly complied. But his replacement, Detective Ernie Kaufman—good ol' Ernie—wasn't as cooperative. He was old school, by the book, and Emily wasn't romantically involved with him.

*Boy, I miss Colin.*

Emily had found several different Lucas Wakefield's on the internet, none of which seemed to match the description of her subject—a high school football player in the south, an insurance adjuster in the Midwest, a pharmacy owner in Texas, and a professor in England.

Something wasn't adding up. Maybe if she could get something with Lucas's fingerprints on it, she would have more success. She was hoping she could convince Isabel to squeeze the request for that analysis into the middle of her hectic schedule. DNA would be better, but that could take weeks to get the results. By then it would be too late.

Lucas and Maggie would be married.

Her cell phone began to ring and she dug it out of her pocket. "Hello."

"Hey, Em, this is Isabel. I see you tried me quite a few times this morning. What's up?"

"I wondered if you'd had a chance to do that background check on Lucas yet."

"Not yet. I've been buried with this case. But as soon as I get a breather, I'm on it."

"After what I saw at the party last night, I think we need to move quickly." Emily had discussed her observations briefly with Isabel after the party was over, but they hadn't had the chance to discuss it in depth and formulate a plan. "What if I can get you something with Lucas's fingerprints on it? Can you ask for a test to be run?"

"When would you have it?" Isabel asked.

"Tonight. I'm having dinner with Maggie to go over some of the wedding plans, so I'll have it after that, and I'll drop it at your house later."

"Sounds good. I'll take it in tomorrow."

"But tomorrow is Sunday."

"Ugh, don't remind me—I have to work—trying to tie up loose ends before trial. Tomorrow being Sunday, though, there won't be anyone to run the prints 'til Monday. But if I get it submitted, we can be first in line and I can push it on Monday."

"Thanks, Isabel. I'll let you get back to work."

# CHAPTER 11
## Josh's Confrontation

EMILY SHOWED UP AT MAGGIE'S little house around five, anxious to find something she could be sure had Lucas's fingerprints on it. Maggie lived in a cottage-style house just a few blocks from Emily in the charming, older section of Paradise Valley. It was pretty as a postcard with painted white clapboard and black shutters, set off by a deep red arched-top front door.

The front yard was profuse with flowers and blooming rosebushes, bordered with a white picket fence. It was the kind of home Maggie grew up dreaming of back in her dirt-floor shack in Texas.

"Come in, Em," Maggie squealed, giving her friend a warm hug. "I can't wait to show you the invitations I've picked out. I want you to tell me which one you think is prettiest."

"Okay."

Maggie took Emily's hand and dragged her to the cozy dining room. The table was covered with magazines and catalogs lying open with pads of colorful sticky notes strewn amongst them. Maggie excitedly pointed out which one was which, and how she had put bright yellow sticky notes on the items she liked.

"I don't think we can do all of this within the next two weeks, Maggs," Emily said.

"I know, but it's a nice idea, isn't it? My first weddin' was in front of a Justice of the Peace in Hollywood, so I was hopin' this one would be magical and romantic, with a big white weddin' dress—the whole shebang." Maggie's big blue eyes moistened and her lips thinned as she appeared to be fighting off the disappointment.

"We'll see what we can do," Emily assured her, patting her hand. "Let's make some plans. Guest list first so we can get the invitations out right away, then we'll set a time to go shopping this week for everything else."

"I knew I could count on you, Em." Maggie's expression brightened.

Emily took on a serious tone. "You know you can always count on me, Maggie, but I have to ask you…" She paused, trying to find the best way to say what was in her heart.

"What is it?" Maggie's countenance grew serious as well.

"Are you certain you're making the right decision? Marrying Lucas before you have a chance to truly get to know him?"

"What are you sayin'? You don't like him?"

"I'm saying Isabel and I—"

"Y'all have been discussin' me and Lucas?" Maggie spoke as if she felt betrayed.

"Listen to me, Maggie. Isabel and I are just concerned. We want nothing more than happiness for you, but we want to make sure you're doing the right thing." Emily could see she had upset Maggie, but this was too important to just drop it. "How much do you really know about him? About his background? Who he was before you met him?"

"We've talked for hours and hours over the past few months. He's never given me any reason to doubt what he's told me—or that he loves me."

"He may not be who you think he is."

"Like Evan?" Maggie asked pointedly. "Just because you're findin' out Evan wasn't who he said he was doesn't mean every man is like that."

"It has nothing to do with Evan," Emily snapped back, hoping she was right. Camille had also accused her of projecting her suspicions of Evan onto Lucas, and she had vehemently denied it. *Could they be right?*

"Are you sure?" Maggie questioned.

"Did you know Lucas had an argument with Sully at the party last night?" Emily asked, arching an eyebrow, trying to direct the discussion away from Evan.

"No. I did notice Sully left without sayin' good-bye, but Lucas told me there was some city emergency he had to deal with."

"Did you know he had a fight with your son, too?"

"With Josh? If that's true, why didn't Josh say anythin' to me about it?

"Where is Josh? Let's ask him," Emily posed.

"Uh, I don't know. We didn't really talk last night and he's been gone all day. I assume he's out with his buddies, doin' something with them while he's home.

"Why don't I give him a call?" Emily pulled her phone out of her purse.

"You don't need to do that," Maggie protested.

Emily raised a hand to shush Maggie.

"Josh, this is Emily. I'm at your mom's and we were wondering if you'd be home for supper?" Emily met Maggie's gaze as she talked.

"No, sorry. I should have let her know, I guess. Is she okay?" he asked.

"Fine. We're going over some final details for the wedding. Why do you ask?"

"So she's still going through with it." Josh spat.

*Why wouldn't she? What did he know?* Emily heard the tension in his voice and sensed he was not pleased with the prospect of this marriage either. Her eyes lowered as she tried to get a read on him.

"I'm headed over to Lucas's office. There's something we need to hash out."

"Josh, is there something you want to get off your chest?" Emily asked, hoping to snag a clue what this conflict between Josh and Lucas was about. She glanced over at Maggie, whose eyes were riveted on Emily's side of the conversation.

"I don't want to talk about it right now," he snarled.

"But, Josh—"

"Not now," he barked. "After I have it out with Lucas, I'll come home and tell my mom everything. I want you to be there, too, Em. She's going to need you." The line went dead.

"What did he say?" Maggie wrapped her arms around herself.

"He said he was going to have a talk with Lucas, then he'd be home."

"A talk? What does that mean?" Maggie pressed.

Emily shrugged her shoulders. "He said he'd be home afterward and explain. So let's give him the chance to do that, okay?" She tried to downplay it and not expose to Maggie the anger she'd heard in Josh's voice.

"Okay," Maggie reluctantly agreed.

"Didn't you say we'd be having dinner together, too? I'm getting kind of hungry," Emily said, changing the subject.

~*~

Josh pulled his car into the parking lot next to the historic Graystone Building and entered the main lobby. He meandered down the dimly-lit hallway and found the door to the suite of offices open. The reception area where Fiona would sit was dark, but light was streaming out of the partly open door to the next office. Male voices were coming from behind the door.

Josh crept nearer to see if he could overhear the conversation. He recognized Lucas's voice right away, then he realized who the other man was—his Uncle Sully.

"I need that hundred thousand dollars back, Lucas!" Sully demanded.

"I already told you that I would give it back to you in two weeks. You hold up your end of the bargain and I'll hold up mine."

*What bargain?* Josh couldn't believe his uncle was in cahoots with this scumbag. He leaned in a little closer.

"I need it now," he protested, "not in two weeks. That could be too late. I'll be ruined!"

"Don't be so dramatic, Mayor. You'll live."

Josh heard the coldness in Lucas's voice. His muscles clenched and his fists curled into a tight ball at what he'd heard.

"I can't let you do this to us," Sully cried out in a shaky voice. "When everyone finds out this Whitetail Resort is a scam, we'll all be arrested. Who'll take care of my wife if I'm in prison? And what about Maggie? She'll be ruined, too."

"Hey, put that gun away!" Lucas hollered.

*A gun?* Josh took a small step forward and clanked into a metal waste basket. Had they heard him? Footsteps were coming toward the door, so he crouched down behind a file cabinet in time to see his uncle fly out of the room and into the main hallway. The sound of a heavy door slamming in the distance echoed through the office and he knew his uncle was gone.

He stood and stretched to his full height of over six feet tall and faced the door to Lucas's office. Josh's athletic body was vibrating with pure adrenaline. He couldn't comprehend all of what was happening between Lucas and Sully, but he did understand that Lucas was planning to ruin his family, including his mother, and he wasn't going to let him get away with it. He stormed into Lucas's office to give him the beating of his life.

Lucas startled, likely expecting it was Sully returning. His eyes grew big when Josh reached out and grabbed him by the front of his shirt and dragged him to his feet. Lucas was a couple of inches taller than Josh, but he was not as young or physically toned.

Lucas threw the first punch, but Josh pummeled back until Lucas crumpled limp and bloodied on the floor. The man had gotten a few good punches in himself, but he was no match for the Navy-trained sailor.

"Get up!" Josh roared, standing over his nemesis, but Lucas did not move. Josh reached down and felt for Lucas's carotid artery, afraid he had beaten the man to death.

A female voice singing in the distance cut the silence of the empty building. Josh froze and turned an ear toward the sound. Each note brought the voice closer.

He slinked out of the darkened office and stuck his head into the hall. He could hear footsteps coming down the staircase. He gingerly sprinted down the dim hallway, ducked beneath the staircase, and waited for the woman to pass.

He watched as Fiona adjusted the earphones on her iPod as she walked into the almost dark office, then he made his escape out the front door.

## THE HEART OF LIES

# CHAPTER 12
## A Grizzly Discovery

EMILY WAS ABLE TO KEEP MAGGIE distracted during dinner, trying not to let her know how angry Josh had sounded. He said he'd be home after his meeting and he would explain what was going on, but he still wasn't home. Now that dinner was over and they had cleared the dishes, Emily wondered how she was going to keep Maggie's mind off her son.

"Em, I expected Josh home by now." Maggie looked at her watch.

Emily scrambled for something else to talk about. She glanced around the living room and her sight caught on a sparkling crystal paperweight on a book shelf. It was in the shape of a mountain with a sharp peak and spiky crags.

"Don't worry, I'm sure he'll be along soon." She rose from her chair and moved over to the shelf.

Maggie looked out the living room window, scanning the street in both directions.

"This is beautiful." Emily admired the artful piece.

"What's beautiful?" Maggie asked, turning around to see.

"This." Emily indicated the paperweight.

"Lucas bought that for me when we were in Sun Valley checkin' out the area." She turned back to the window.

"Lucas bought it?" Emily wondered if it might have his fingerprints on it.

"Yep, he surprised me with it." Maggie remained at the window, arms crossed, watching for her son. "I'd admired it at the gift shop and when we got home he gave it to me."

"That was thoughtful." Emily took advantage of Maggie's distraction at the window and slipped the paperweight into the plastic zippered baggie inside her purse.

"Lucas is wonderful that way. I can't imagine what he and Josh would have to disagree about." Maggie turned away from the window.

She went back to the dining table and put both hands out, leaning on the edge of the table, pouring over the open books and magazines. She flipped one closed.

Maggie stood upright, crossed her arms again, and looked at her friend. "I can't concentrate, Em. Where's my son? What's goin' on?"

"I thought he'd be back by now too, Maggie. Why don't we go down to Lucas's office and find out what's going on?" Emily suggested. She was getting a little concerned herself.

Maggie, with worry written all over her face, nodded in agreement.

~*~

At almost seven o'clock, Emily and Maggie entered the Graystone Building and headed directly to Lucas's office. The door to the suite was open, yet the front reception area was almost dark, lit only by the stream of light coming from where Lucas's door stood ajar.

They listened for voices before entering, but there were none. Emily half-expected to hear a shouting match the way Josh had described the encounter he was going to have with Lucas.

"Should we go in?" Maggie whispered, looking to Emily for confirmation.

Something didn't feel right. Maggie must have sensed it too. Emily pulled the gun out of her purse, and handed her bag to Maggie. She kept the gun pointed to the ground until she checked out the office.

"Stay behind me," Emily directed in a soft voice.

Emily slinked through the front office, peeking into Lucas's office through the six-inch crack in the door. Then she heard a woman's voice and she slowly pushed the door open.

Gloria Wakefield sat in a club chair next to Lucas's body. She had dialed nine-one-one and was asking for an ambulance and the police to help her son. Her breathing was hard and her face looked pasty and sweaty. She lifted her gaze to Emily.

"My son—someone's killed my son!" the elderly woman cried. "I tried to help him, but I think it's too late."

Emily stuffed her gun in the back of her waistband, not wanting Gloria to see it and become even more distraught. The woman's hands were covered in blood, as was the front of her dress. Emily crouched down beside her chair to see if she was all right, she appeared to be going into shock.

Maggie surveyed the brutal scene before her, then she ran in, throwing herself over Lucas. A flood of tears came spilling out and she sobbed uncontrollably.

"No!" She put her hand on his battered face, then laid her head down on the chest of his blood-soaked shirt. "Lucas! No!"

Emily was torn between tending to the murder victim's elderly mother and helping her friend who was hysterically embracing her fiancé's brutally murdered body. Then Emily had a sudden realization—could Josh have done this?

"Maggie." Emily reached for her friend's shoulders, pulling her gently back. "You can't be touching the body. You're compromising the evidence."

Maggie turned and glared at Emily. "He isn't evidence! He's my world."

"I know, I know, but the police are on their way and they can't find you like this. Come on, sweetie, why don't you sit down in this chair," Emily urged, motioning to the club chair beside Gloria.

With some coaxing, Maggie took Emily's hand to help her off the floor and into the chair. Lucas's blood was smeared on Maggie's pink blouse, and the side of her face and her hands were covered in it. Her mascara had run down her cheeks, but she didn't seem to care as the tears continued to flow.

"You doing okay there, Mrs. Wakefield?" Emily glanced over her shoulder at Gloria.

She quietly shook her head and stared down blankly at the handbag clutched in her lap.

The scream of sirens split the night air and soon there were police and paramedics swarming the parking lot and pouring into the building. Emily went to the office door and motioned them in from the main hallway.

Detective Ernie Kaufman stood in the doorway to Lucas's office. His eyes quickly assessed the crime scene. A bloody body on the floor and two women covered in blood sitting in chairs near it, he had to ask, "What on earth happened here?"

"Detective, this is the victim's mother, Mrs. Wakefield," Emily said, gesturing in the woman's direction. "You'd better get the paramedics to tend to her ASAP."

He took one look at the old woman's face and agreed. He stepped out of the office. "Hey, Willy," he called out to one of the EMTs, "we need you in here."

Two young men in uniforms brought a gurney into the office and one of them checked Mrs. Wakefield's vitals. Her heart was racing and her blood pressure was low, he said. He helped her out of the chair to assist her onto the gurney, but she went limp in his arms, grabbing at her chest.

"I think she's having a heart attack," the paramedic yelled. The other EMT took her legs and they lifted her onto the gurney. "Let's get her to the hospital."

Ernie picked up her handbag and laid it next to her as one of the paramedics put an oxygen mask over her face.

As the EMTs rolled Gloria out, the Detective assigned a policewoman to stay with her until he could sort out what took place. "Make sure you bag her clothes and get a swab of her hands," he reminded.

Ernie called for the coroner to retrieve Lucas's body, before turning to question Emily.

"What the heck happened here, Emily?" Ernie asked, staring into her face. "Dead guy on the floor, blood all over the old woman, blood all over Maggie—spill it."

Ernie had been on the Paradise Valley police force for over twenty years, but it wasn't until Colin had to take a leave of absence that Ernie took the promotion, against his better judgment, to be the town's only detective.

Emily took Ernie by the arm and led him into the other room while a couple of uniforms taped off the crime scene. "The dead man is Maggie's fiancé. I already said the older woman is his mother, or was."

Ernie's bushy eyebrows lifted in surprise, creating a cascade of wrinkles across his considerable forehead. "All right. Go on."

"Maggie and I came here together. When we walked in, Lucas was already dead on the floor and his mother was sitting in the chair calling nine-one-one. She said she found him like this, and that she'd tried to help him but she was too late. I'm assuming that's how she got the blood on her hands and her dress."

"So why does Maggie have blood all over her?" he asked.

"Because he's her fiancé, Ernie," she stressed, her eyes growing round with emphasis. "When she saw him on the floor, she didn't think about it being a crime scene, she just rushed to him and put her arms around him."

"I wish she hadn't done that," he mumbled.

"What would you do if you found your wife dead on the floor? You're telling me you wouldn't run to her and take her in your arms?" Emily asked, trying to put Ernie in Maggie's shoes.

"I guess I would," he replied, shifting his burly weight.

"Let me take Maggie home now. This is all such a shock to her. They were supposed to be married two weeks from today."

"I can't let you take her just yet. I have some questions for her," he said.

"Listen Ernie, Maggie was with me for the last few hours and we came here together just a little while ago. She saw what I saw, when I saw it. She's not going anywhere, so if you have any questions for her, call her in the morning. I'm sure she'll be willing to answer them."

"But I'll need her clothes."

"What? Why? I just told you she and I came in together and I saw her lay against Lucas, getting his blood on her. She did not have his blood on her prior to that."

"If I don't do it by the book, the DA will chew my butt."

"Please, Ernie, have a heart."

"All right, if you and she will sign a written statement to that effect and be willing to testify in court to that, if need be, then okay. If the DA has a problem with it, he can just demote me back to officer. I'd prefer that anyway."

"Thanks, Ernie." She patted him on the arm as she started to walk away.

"You know, Emily, I'm not cut out for this kind of work," he said, causing her to stop. "I wish Colin hadn't gone off and left me with this detective job. I liked just being a plain ol' cop in this town. We hadn't had a murder in more than twenty years, and now we've had three in the last twelve months. I can't wait 'til Colin gets himself back here. I sure miss that boy."

"Not more than me, Ernie. Not more than me." Emily smiled at him as she turned and went to collect Maggie.

As Emily helped Maggie out the front door of the building, the medical examiner and the equipment-laden crime scene investigators trudged in. She wished she could stay to observe, find out the truth of what happened, but she needed to get Maggie home before she had a complete meltdown.

~*~

Maggie didn't say a word the whole way home. Emily left her to her thoughts, having a few serious ones of her own. After having witnessed the clash between Josh and Lucas at the party, she couldn't help but wonder if he had been involved in Lucas's death in some way.

Emily helped her friend into her house and waited while she showered, storing Maggie's blood-stained clothes in an untouched plastic zippered bag, just as she had promised Ernie she would.

She asked Maggie if she wanted anything to eat, but Maggie said no, that what she wanted was to go to bed and wake up in the morning to find this was all just a bad dream.

Emily tucked her in and sat in the dark by her bed until she fell asleep.

Once she was certain Maggie was out, she tiptoed out of the room and gently closed the bedroom door. She grabbed her purse and started to reach for the front door handle when the door opened and Josh walked in.

He had a black eye and cut lip. Emily glared into his face, waiting for an explanation.

"Where's my mom?" He glanced around the house. "Mom!"

"Quiet," she admonished. "She went to bed."

"Before you left? What's up with that?"

"Where have you been, Josh?"

"Out."

She stared at him, evaluating. "Out where?"

"Just out."

"What's with the black eye and the cut lip?"

"You should see the other guy," he smirked, showing her his bloody knuckles.

"I have seen the other guy—he's dead."

# THE HEART OF LIES

## CHAPTER 13
## Colin's Return

"DEAD? I DIDN'T DO IT, EMILY—I swear." Josh proclaimed his innocence over and over again, as he paced the living room floor. "I beat the crap out of him, I'll admit that, but he was alive when I left."

"Why, Josh?" Emily was perched on the edge of the couch, keeping her voice down. "What could have possessed you to attack him?"

Josh looked her in the eye. "He was fooling around with his assistant, okay? I saw them."

"What do you mean you saw them?"

"At the engagement party. They were in the den giggling and probably making out. I walked in on them and they looked surprised."

"You said they were *probably* making out? You didn't see them actually doing anything?"

"Well, I think she was wiping lipstick off his lip. Besides, I stopped by his office yesterday afternoon. When I walked in on them, I thought they were a little too cozy then too. And now this. He tried to tell me they were talking business, but they looked pretty guilty."

"Why didn't you tell your mom last night?"

"I confronted Lucas right then and I told him I'd give him twenty-four hours to tell her, or I would. I warned him to break off the engagement, but I knew he hadn't done it yet when I talked to you on the phone. That's why I asked if the wedding was still on."

Emily remembered him asking that.

"So I went to see him, to make him pay for hurting my mom. Then I was going to tell her."

"Why didn't you come home after your fight with him?"

"I wanted to. That's what I had planned to do. It's just that I was having trouble working up the courage to break her heart."

He slumped into a chair and leaned forward, putting his elbows on his knees. "I thought a few beers would give me the courage," he said, hanging his head down, "but that didn't work."

Josh shook his head and raised his eyes to Emily. "Funny, I can find the courage to kill our enemies, but I couldn't find the courage to rip my mom's heart in two."

"Nothing funny about that," she assured him. "I hope this whole mess doesn't reflect badly in your military record."

He looked down at the floor and ran a hand over his face.

Emily braced herself for more bad news. "Something you want to tell me?"

"I got kicked out of the Navy—I'm so ashamed. I didn't want to tell my mom until after the wedding, but now it's going to come out and make her feel even worse."

"A dishonorable discharge? For what?"

"I did something really stupid, and let's just say they *strongly encouraged* me to take the early-out offer. I drank too much one night, and me and a couple of my buddies played a prank on an officer. Apparently he didn't think it was funny. We all got the same offer. I guess we're lucky they didn't throw us in the brig."

"Oh, Josh," was all she could manage to say.

"I know. It was stupid."

She didn't even want to ask what he did. She rose to her feet. "Let your mom sleep and have a good talk with her in the morning. She's going to need you more than she ever has. You can't imagine how hard it is to lose someone you love."

"You're talking about Evan, aren't you?"

She nodded, releasing a sigh. "I'm going to go now, but I'll check in with you tomorrow."

~*~

Daybreak came and the morning light began peeking through Emily's bedroom curtains. She was slowly waking from a romantic dream about Colin and she felt warm and tingly all over. Startled by a sharp knock at the door, she bolted upright and checked her digital clock, which read six forty-five.

"What the heck?" She swung her legs over the side of the bed and reached for her silky white robe. Irritated, she ran to the door, wondering who would be knocking at such an early hour. In the dim early morning light, through the row of small windows across the top of her front door, she saw the top of a man's head covered by a dark ball cap. After having been broken into recently, she stood still for a moment trying to decide what to do. Should she open it? Should she get her gun?

Another hard knock jolted her attention and she flinched. Only when she heard the man's voice did she relax.

"Emily? Open up! It's Colin."

With delight, she flung the door open wide. Wearing a big smile, he stepped inside, sweeping her up into his arms. "Good morning, sleepy head." He gazed into her eyes, then swept the door shut with his foot.

As he lowered his face to hers, she anticipated his long-awaited kiss. He brushed her lips with his, then smiled at her, as if he was waiting for an invitation. She pushed up on her tiptoes, pulled off his cap, and pressed her lips to his.

In response, Colin pulled her tighter into his arms and her body melted against his. He returned her kiss more deeply and passionately than she had expected, sending heat radiating through her body. She let his hat fall to the floor.

When he finally released her, she felt weak and dizzy under his power. "*Whew*, I think I need to sit down," she cooed.

He led her by the hand into the living room and sat beside her on the sofa, resting his arm on the back. She leaned against him, pulled her bare feet up under her, and nuzzled her face into the crook of his neck as she rested a hand on his chest. He lowered his arm around her shoulders and held her close.

"I'm thrilled to see you, Colin," she breathed in his masculine scent and savored the warmth of his body against hers, "but what are you doing here?"

"Ernie called me last night, said Maggie's fiancé was murdered. He thought you might need me." He brushed a stray curl back from her face with his finger. "Was he right?"

Yes, she needed him. She had ached for him since the day he left to help care for his dad. Being startled awake from that dream-like space between being asleep and fully awake, she had not yet given any thought to the events of the night before. His comments brought them rushing back at her—walking in on Lucas's bloody body, Maggie's avalanche of shock and grief, her probing conversation with Josh.

She sat up straight and stared wide-eyed at him. "Yes, Colin, I need you. You have no idea." She cupped his face in her hands and kissed him softly. "I'm thrilled you're here."

"I was hoping you'd say that. I drove through the night to get here."

"But what about your dad?"

"He's improving every day, so I'd already arranged for my aunt and uncle to come and help while I came up for Maggie's wedding. After I got the call from Ernie, I phoned them and asked them to come early. They're retired, so it was no problem. As soon as they got to the house, I hit the road."

"You must be starved," Emily said. "Why don't I make you something to eat? Then I can tell you all I know over breakfast."

He tapped his chin. "Hmm…As I recall, you're not the best cook." He offered a sly grin. "Why don't we go out to breakfast? My treat."

Emily had to agree with his assessment of her cooking skills, and she graciously accepted his invitation. "Just give me a few minutes and I'll be ready to go," she called out as she dashed down the hall to her bedroom.

~*~

"Can I get you anything else?" The young waitress smiled and refilled Colin's coffee cup.

"Just the bill, thanks," he replied, as they finished their breakfast at The Griddle.

"This was a great idea, Colin," Emily said, swirling her last bite of French toast in the remaining maple syrup on her plate.

"Lucas Wakefield sounds like a piece of work," Colin said. "For Maggie's sake, we need to get to the bottom of this thing fast."

"I agree. From the start, Isabel and I had a bad feeling about him—well, Isabel more than me, at least at first. She threatened to do a background check several times, but other things seemed to crowd her time and she put it off."

"I wish she'd done it early on. Maybe this whole mess could have been avoided." Colin sipped his hot black coffee and took his last forkful of omelet.

"I take part of that blame. I warned her Maggie wouldn't be happy if she found out we were checking him out behind her back. Now I wish I'd pushed more for it."

"And what about Josh?" Colin asked, sliding his empty plate aside. "You said he went to see Lucas last night and admitted he had a physical altercation with him?"

"Around here we call it a fight," she teased, "and yes, he admitted it, but he swears Lucas was alive when he left."

"And you believe him?"

"I want to," she said, dumping a packet of sweetener into her coffee. "But I wonder, if Lucas was alive when Josh left, but then died shortly after that from the beating. The medical examiner and CSI unit were coming in when I was leaving. I wish I knew what they found."

"The body's at the medical examiner's for an autopsy by now, I'm sure. They'll probably have a cause of death soon."

"Could you talk to Ernie and find out what's in the ME's report?" she asked.

"I can try," he offered. "Maybe he'll let me know what the CSI unit found, too."

Emily's phone began to ring and she dug it out of her purse. "It's Maggie," she whispered to Colin.

"Hello."

"Emily, I need you to come over right away," Maggie said, sounding frightened and breathless.

"What's wrong?" Emily looked at Colin and his eyes were riveted on her.

"The police are here. They've arrested Josh."

"Oh, Maggie, no," Emily exclaimed.

"I already called Isabel and Alex. Alex is headed down to the police station right now."

Emily could hear Maggie sniffling, and she felt a heavy weight in her chest, knowing what her friend was going through. "We'll be right over."

"What do you mean *we*?" Maggie questioned.

"Colin is here with me. He drove through the night when he heard what happened."

"That sweet man. Maybe he can get some information from the police—I couldn't."

"Don't worry, Maggs. We'll be there before you know it."

When Emily rang the doorbell, Maggie let them in, finding Camille and Jonathan had arrived minutes before them. Following a round of hugs, Maggie described what had happened that morning, the police showing up with an arrest warrant, taking Josh away in handcuffs, giving little information in response to Maggie's tearful stream of questions.

Emily did her best to try to console her friend, as did the others, but Maggie was beyond that. Maggie's fiancé had been murdered, and her son—her only child—had been accused of killing him. What could she say to make it better?

Dressed in jean shorts and a white t-shirt, Maggie had barely combed her hair and she had no makeup on. Emily wasn't used to seeing Maggie like this, but she remembered having days like that right after Evan was killed, hardly having the energy to get out of bed. It was Maggie, Isabel, and Camille that had gotten her through it.

"Did anyone call Sully?" Emily asked, wondering if Maggie's brother was aware of what had happened.

"I called him," Maggie replied, working to stifle her sobs, "but it just went to voicemail. I didn't want to leave that kind of message on his phone."

"I'll try him again for you," Jonathan offered.

"Thanks, hon," Camille said, lightly patting her husband's back. "Maggie, dear, have you had anything to eat this morning?"

"No," Maggie replied softly, her tears subsiding.

"Why don't you let me make something for you? You're going to need your strength today." Camille went to the kitchen and Jonathan stepped outside to make the call to Sully.

"Is Isabel on her way?" Emily asked.

"No, Alex said she had to go into work today, you know, that big FBI case she's workin' on." Maggie walked to the sofa and dropped onto it. She leaned into the cushions and put the back of her hand against her forehead, closing her eyes. "The trial starts next week and she has to tie up some final details. He said he'd let her know what was happenin' and have her stop by as soon as she could."

Emily remembered Isabel mentioning the trial. She also recalled having told Isabel she'd drop something off to her last night that would have Lucas's fingerprints on it so she could have the FBI run the prints first thing Monday morning. That's when she realized the crystal paperweight was still in her purse. With the murder last night, she had forgotten all about it. Keeping it now seemed unnecessary, but how could she return it without being noticed? She decided to keep it awhile longer.

Jonathan stepped inside from the porch. Before he went to help Camille in the kitchen, he told everyone about the call to Sully. He said Sully was going to head straight down to the police station to find out what was happening with Josh, and he'd let Maggie know as soon as he knew anything.

Emily watched Colin from across the room as he took a seat next to Maggie, promising they were all going to do their best to help her through this nightmare. Emily knew he understood Maggie's heartache as much as she did. All three of them had violently lost someone they loved.

Colin took Maggie's hand and spoke softly to her. Emily couldn't hear all of what he was saying, but his tenderness and compassion fanned the flame of her affection for him. She would have to thank Ernie later, for calling him last night.

He patted Maggie's hand and caught Emily's gaze as he stood and walked over to her. "I'm going to go call on Ernie and see what I can learn from him."

Emily pushed up on her tiptoes and gave him a quick kiss. "Thank you, Colin."

"For what?" He seemed puzzled.

"For being you. I saw how gentle you were with Maggie just now."

"You and I both know what she's going through. I simply wanted to help. But what I need to do now is go and talk to Ernie."

"I want to be there," Emily said, "hear what he has to say."

"I think it's best if I go alone, talk to him man to man."

"You mean detective to detective?"

"Something like that."

"I'm a detective. A *private* detective." She poked a finger at his chest, feeling like maybe he didn't think she was on par with them. She tried not to react the way she had in the beginning of their relationship when she used to prickle at what she considered to be his condescending attitude toward her lack of experience. They'd gotten past that. She had experience now—heck, she carried a gun and taught self-defense classes.

"I remember," he said with a grin. "Who do you think nicknamed you the smokin' hot lady PI?"

"So why are you shutting me out?" Emily asked.

"I think Ernie will be more forthcoming if it's just him and me. That's all. Don't get your panties in a twist."

"You know I hate it when you say that." Emily frowned.

"I know," he chuckled. He glanced over at Maggie, sitting with her eyes closed and her head leaned back on the sofa. "Stay here with Maggie and Camille and I'll let you know what I learn from Ernie."

Before she could protest again, he was out the door.

## THE HEART OF LIES

# CHAPTER 14
## The Arrest

COLIN WALKED INTO THE PARADISE Valley police station and surprised the receptionist working the front desk. "Hey, Stella!" he shouted, echoing the classic Tennessee Williams line from *A Streetcar Named Desire.*

She jumped to her feet. "Oh, Colin! It's great to see you again!"

"Thanks, Stella."

"Are you back for good?"

"Just a visit. Say, is Ernie in? I need to talk to him."

"Yes, go on back. You know the way." She smiled and pushed a release button to buzz him through.

He wandered down the hall and stuck his head in Ernie's doorway. "Hey, buddy."

Ernie glanced up with a look of surprise that quickly melted into a broad smile. "Hey, yourself. Was Emily happy to see you?"

"Of course, but that's not what I'm here to see you about. What can you tell me about the murder?" Colin asked.

"Why don't you come in and have a seat?" he said, gesturing toward the chair across from his desk. "And be sure to close the door behind you."

Colin shut the door and took a seat, his gaze roving across Ernie's desk. He watched with interest as Ernie pulled a thin file off the top of a short stack of folders and laid it open. Then he clasped his large hands on top of it. "What do you want to know?"

"Why did you arrest Josh Sullivan?" Colin asked.

"Well, ol' Pete Peterson owns the Graystone Building where Lucas Wakefield had his office. Pete is such a cheapskate, he pinches pennies 'til Lincoln bleeds," Ernie chuckled.

"Is this story going somewhere, big guy?"

"Of course. After Evan Parker was murdered in his office there last year, the other tenants pushed Pete to put security cameras on the building for their safety. So, he did, rather than lose some of his renters."

"If he'd done it sooner, maybe we'd know who killed Emily's late husband," Colin said.

"That's right."

"But what does that have to do with Josh?" Colin asked.

"Well, after getting the video, we found that Josh was the last one to leave the Graystone Building last night—that is, before Gloria Wakefield and Maggie and Emily came there. When one of my officers and I went to talk to Josh this morning, we found that someone had done a number on his face, and his knuckles were bloody and busted up. I asked him about it. He started to say he had gotten into an argument with Lucas until Maggie told him not to say another word until he got a lawyer. I had no choice but to bring him in. My officer waited with him while I called for an arrest warrant. While we waited, Maggie called an attorney, that guy who defended Delia McCall a few months ago."

"Alex Martínez?"

"That's the one. Say, isn't that the case Emily worked on?"

"Yes. You might say that's how our romance began."

"Now she's got you involved in this case," Ernie said, shaking his head.

"You're the one who called me, Ernie, not her."

"I called you to give her moral support, not to poke your nose in my investigation," Ernie scowled.

"I'm not poking my nose in your investigation," he said, defending himself. "I'm here to help."

Ernie's scowl turned into a wide grin. "Gotcha!" he shouted with a fist pump and let out a thunderous laugh.

"You old coot."

"Hey, watch it young man."

"What else do you have?" Colin looked down at the open file.

As a seasoned detective in San Francisco, he had worked nearly a hundred murders. This was only Ernie's second murder case. The first one he worked was as an officer aiding Colin, who at the time was Paradise Valley's only detective. Since Colin's departure, Ernie now held that esteemed position—the entire case rested on Ernie's big shoulders.

"Well, since Lucas Wakefield appears to have been beaten to death, and Josh all but admitted having been in a fist fight with him, what else do I need?" Ernie asked smugly.

"Was there anyone else on the security video?" Colin questioned.

"Yes, but no one else that would have done it."

"Tell me who was on the video around the time of the murder," Colin pressed. "You do have a time of death don't you?"

"Yes." Ernie looked at the notes in the file. "Doc Walters says time of death was between six and seven last night. Around that time, the video showed Mayor Sullivan entering the building, then Josh Sullivan. Shortly after that, it shows Josh leaving, then Mrs. Wakefield, Lucas's mother, entering, then Maggie and Emily going inside."

"Have you questioned all of them?" Colin asked.

"Not yet, but I will. I'm working through the list, but it's a little tricky. The mayor, the victim's mother, the fiancée—you know what I mean?

"It's gotta be done, Ernie."

"Step by step, I'm working through it. Hey, did you hear Mrs. Wakefield is in the hospital? She had a heart attack last night, right after she found her son dead. They had to rush her to the emergency room." He pulled out a small notepad and began to write. "I'll have to check on her status."

"I hadn't heard that. Poor woman, losing her son and having to be the one to find him."

"Just a crying shame all around," Ernie said. "You know Josh is military, like you were."

"That's what Emily said. I hope you're wrong about him, Ernie."

"Me, too."

~*~

Alex phoned Maggie from the jail. Emily sat next to her on the couch, watching Maggie's expression for any sign whether the news from Alex was good or bad.

Maggie nodded her head at what Alex was saying. Her eyes were red and swollen and the remnant of her mascara bled below her eyes. Her mess of blonde hair was pulled haphazardly into a ponytail. She clicked her phone off and tossed it on the wooden coffee table, leaning back on the sofa, closing her eyes.

"What did he say?" Emily asked.

"He said Josh won't be arraigned 'til Monday," she replied, her eyes still closed, "but he'll try to get me in to see him today. He didn't know when, though." She stifled a cry that almost broke through.

Camille ambled into the living room, wearing her face of motherly concern. "The kitchen's all clean, everything from breakfast is put away. What else can I do, Maggie?"

Maggie sat up and looked at her through watery eyes. "Can you explain to me how this happened?"

"I don't understand, Maggie." Camille rushed to the sofa and sank down on it. "What do you mean?" Camille had a look of confusion in her eyes and she glanced at Emily for some help.

"Yesterday, I was engaged to a wonderful man and we had our whole lives ahead of us. I was so thrilled to have my boy home, and happy he could be here for the weddin'."

Maggie thrust her elbows on her knees and buried her face in her hands. Her shoulders began to shake as she wept. "Now everythin' has gone to hell! My Lucas is dead and my son is in jail, accused of killin' him!" she bawled.

Emily patted Maggie's back softly as she wailed, and Camille put her arm around Maggie's waist.

After a few torturous minutes of sobbing, Maggie sat up and Emily handed her a box of tissues.

"What a big blubber baby I am," she said, wiping her nose with a tissue.

"Don't say that, Maggs." Emily remembered having been a crying mess, too, after Evan's death.

"We would expect no less, hon," Camille said, lightly running her hand up and down Maggie's back. "Whatever you need, we're here."

"Em, do you think my son could have killed Lucas?" Maggie dabbed at her eyes, the sobs subsiding.

"I would hate to think so, but I guess it's possible," Emily replied. She didn't want to tell her friend that, but she had to be honest. The evidence so far certainly did point to him. She could feel Camille's stare heating her skin. "I'm sorry, Camille, but I have to be honest with her."

"We're here to support Maggie, and by extension, Josh," Camille snapped at Emily.

"I am being supportive, but Maggie asked me a question and I'm not going to lie to her," Emily defended. "It doesn't look good, but that doesn't mean he did it. Colin went to find out what the cops have. Let's wait until we hear back from him before we start jumping to any conclusions."

"Until I have absolute proof, I'm choosing to believe Josh is innocent," Camille declared.

"I agree, Cam," Emily said, "but I'm not going to stick my head in the sand and hope it all goes away."

"Enough!" Maggie shouted and shot up off the sofa.

Both Camille and Emily sat back, stunned.

Maggie walked to the windows and looked out, before turning back to face them.

"Emily, can I hire you to investigate this murder, clear my son. I have some money saved."

"No, Maggs—"

"Why not?" Maggie interrupted.

"Let me finish. No, I won't take your money, but I promise you that Colin and I will do all we can to find out who murdered Lucas, and why."

"If my son killed Lucas," Maggie dropped her gaze to the floor and crossed her arms, "then I'll have to deal with it, although I'm not sure how. But if he didn't do it," she raised her head and looked Emily in the eye, "then the real killer needs to be rooted out and caught."

Maggie turned back to the window and wiped a stray tear from her cheek. "I just can't imagine why anyone would want to kill my sweet Lucas."

~*~

When Maggie went to lie down again, Camille agreed to stay with her, leaving Emily free to meet up with Colin and find out what he'd learned from Ernie. She phoned him and he swung by Maggie's place and picked her up.

Colin filled her in on the security tape the police had, showing Josh was the last to leave the office before Lucas's mother showed up, which he said lined up with the time of death the medical examiner determined. That evidence, together with Josh's admission that he and Lucas had had a fist fight before he left the office was all the evidence Ernie needed to hold him.

"I want to sit down and interview Josh," Emily told Colin, "get his side of the story."

"I thought you talked to him last night when he came home."

"Yeah, but I have other questions for him. Something's just not adding up," she said. "Why was Sully there? Who else was on the security tape? What about—"

"Whoa, slow down, Emily. You're going to blow a fuse," he warned. "I'm sure Ernie can get us in to see Josh, but we'll probably have to have Alex with us. I'd like to talk to the medical examiner, too—see if we can get the cause of death dialed in a little clearer."

# CHAPTER 15
## A Conversation with Josh

ERNIE AGREED TO ESCORT THEM to the medical examiner's office on Monday, but he would make arrangements with the county jail to let them in to see Josh that Sunday afternoon if his attorney was with them.

Emily phoned Alex and informed him she was setting up a meeting with Josh. Maggie had already told him she wanted Emily on the case. Alex agreed to meet them down there.

Colin and Emily drove to Boise, the county seat about fifteen minutes from Paradise Valley where they found Alex already waiting for them. They were escorted into the sparse interrogation room and seated, and then an officer brought Josh in, wearing the standard orange jumpsuit and handcuffs.

"Are the handcuffs really necessary, Officer?" Emily asked, pursing her lips for emphasis.

"He's a murder suspect, ma'am. The handcuffs are for your protection and mine," the man said as he turned and walked to the door. "Just holler when you're done here," he instructed before he left.

"We haven't met yet, Josh." Out of habit, Colin stood to shake Josh's hand. When Josh flashed the handcuffs in response, Colin smiled apologetically and sat back down. "I'm Colin Andrews, a friend of Emily's."

"And your mom's," Emily added, digging around in her oversized leather bag. "You know Colin was military too—he was a Marine a number of years back."

"Nice to meet you, sir," Josh said, taking a seat at the table next to Alex.

"I've filled him in on your current military status and he's here to help me find the truth about Lucas Wakefield." Emily placed a voice recorder on the table. "I'm only taping what you say in case I need to go back and remember something, Josh. No need to worry."

Josh looked at Alex, who nodded his approval. "Okay," Josh consented.

"The first thing we need to know is, did you kill Lucas Wakefield?" Colin asked.

"No. I don't think I did." Josh looked Colin square in the eye. "He was alive when I left—I checked his pulse to make sure—then I got out of there when I heard someone coming."

"Who?" Emily asked.

"It was his assistant, Fiona."

"You know her?" Emily questioned.

"Met her at the engagement party," Josh nodded, "and, you know, I saw her and Lucas *together*."

"Did she see you at the office that night?" Colin asked.

"No, I hunched under the stairs. After she passed by, I beat it out the door."

"I don't think the detective knows she was there." Colin glanced at Emily, then at Alex. "She never showed up on the security tape. Ernie listed all the people coming and going, and she wasn't one of them."

"Maybe she went out the back door," Emily suggested. Since her office was in the same building, she knew there was another way out. "I don't think there is a security camera out there."

"Terrific," Colin said sarcastically. "That makes our job more difficult."

"Sorry, Josh. Keep going," Emily said.

"I went to the office to confront Lucas because I had caught him messing around with his assistant at the engagement party. Remember, I told you about that the night he died?" Josh reminded Emily.

She nodded her acknowledgement.

"I gave him twenty-four hours to come clean with my mom and call off the wedding. I warned him what would happen if he didn't."

"Did anyone else hear you threaten him?" Emily crossed her arms on the table and leaned forward.

"Fiona, maybe."

"Then what happened," Colin pressed.

"I went into Lucas's office. He was sitting behind his desk. We argued. I dragged Lucas out of his chair and we argued some more. The more we argued, the hotter we got until he threw the first punch. Of course, I hit him back."

Josh still wore the black eye and busted lip Lucas had given him, proving it wasn't just a one-sided beating.

"Is there anything else you can remember, Josh?"

"I went to a bar to have a few beers, hoping to work up the courage to tell my mother the truth about Lucas."

"I remember you telling me that the night he died," Emily confirmed. "And you told the police about that?"

"Yeah, but it didn't seem to make any difference."

"Anything else?" she asked.

Josh stared back at her, and Emily could almost see the wheels turning in his mind. He opened his mouth as if he was going to speak, something was right there on the tip of his tongue, then he closed his lips and shook his head no.

"Josh?"

Alex put his hand on his client's shoulder for a moment.

"What is it?" Emily was certain he had something more to say. She glanced at Colin. She could tell he wasn't buying Josh's story either.

"Nothing."

"You seem irritated—we're here trying to help you." Emily crossed her arms and leaned back in her chair.

"I just don't get it. I already told the cops all of this, and Alex too. Why do I have to keep going over it and over it?"

"Hearing the course of events straight from your mouth might help us discover something the others missed. That's all," Colin assured him.

"There's nothing more to tell." Josh remained stone-faced.

There was something, though, something he wasn't telling them. His face and his body language were betraying him.

"What are you not telling us?" Emily challenged him, casting a sideways glance at Colin. "If you want us to help you beat this thing, you've got to be completely honest with us. What are you hiding?"

"If you have something to say, just say it," Alex insisted.

Josh sat silent.

Colin's eyebrows furrowed into a frown as he shot out of his chair, which went flying backwards against the wall. He slammed both hands on the table and stared down hard at Josh. "You want to go to prison for the rest of your life?"

Josh hung his head and shook it.

"Because that's exactly where you're headed if you're not straight with us."

Alex flashed him a look and Colin stood up straight, then dragged his chair back to the table. "You think this is some sort of a game?"

"Don't scare him, Colin, he's just a kid," Emily insisted.

"He's not a kid, Emily," Colin snapped. "He's almost twenty-one, and he had better wise up and tell us everything he knows if he's going to have any chance in hell of beating this murder rap."

"I'll give you one last chance to tell us or we're out of here. What are you holding back?" Emily's eyes narrowed as she focused her attention on Josh's response.

Josh raised his head and set his clasped hands on the table. Tension hung in the air as he looked at Emily with sad eyes. He licked his lips and swallowed hard before he spoke.

"Don't be afraid, Josh. Just tell us," Emily pleaded.

"When I got to the office that night," Josh began slowly, "Uncle Sully was already there talking to Lucas. They were arguing about money. I've never heard him so angry." Josh shook his head as he looked down at his folded hands. "He even pulled a gun on Lucas."

Emily gasped at the thought of Sully pulling a gun on anyone. "Did you believe Sully was going to shoot him?"

"I thought he might, 'cause he was real mad. I was in the dark outer office and I stepped closer to the open door, trying to hear better, but I bumped into something, a trash can I think. The noise must have startled Uncle Sully, because he came running out of the office and took off."

"Did he see you?" Colin questioned.

"No, I hid behind a file cabinet as he raced by. That's when I went in and had it out with Lucas myself. You know the rest."

"Is there anything else you haven't told us?" Emily pushed, studying his expression and body language for any tells.

"No, that's it. I just didn't want to drag my uncle into this. He's always looked out for me, like a dad. I don't want you trying to pin this on him to save me."

~*~

"Let's get some lunch, Emily," Colin suggested, driving out of the county jail parking lot. "I'm famished. Why don't we head over to Goodwood?"

"You and your barbecue." She grinned at him. "I'd like to call Sully first, see if I can meet with him to get his side of the story, you know?"

Emily dialed Sully's personal cell phone number as they drove. It rang a few times. "It's just going to voicemail," she told Colin. Then, Emily left a brief, vague message asking Sully to call her back.

"Maybe I should call Camille and see how Maggie's doing," she suggested, "or head over there after we have lunch."

As they drove down Main Street toward the rib joint, they passed the Paradise Valley police station and noticed a crowd gathering around the main entrance. It looked like maybe thirty or forty people.

"I wonder what's going on over there." She pointed toward the station.

"I can't imagine. Why don't we check it out?" Colin made a U-turn in the middle of the street.

"Hey, you can't do that! U-turns are illegal here," Emily scolded. "Only police with flashing lights and sirens can do that."

"Sorry, I'm used to the big city. Let's just say it was an emergency. Looks like Ernie could use our help," he chuckled.

Colin pulled the car into the police station parking lot and then he and Emily wormed their way through the crowd. He tried to open the front door, but it was locked. They turned and faced the men and women milling around.

"What's going on, Mr. Peterson?" Emily asked. The gray-haired man standing in front of her was her office landlord and the scowl on his face told her he was not happy. "Why are all these folks here?"

"We all heard what happened to Lucas Wakefield on the TV news last night and we've been calling each other, trying to figure out what's happening with our money," he explained, with crossed arms and a deep frown. "We all invested quite a bit of dough in his resort. What's going to happen now that he's dead?"

"I don't know. That's an excellent question, Pete, but you can't believe the police chief would have the answer, do you?" she asked.

It sounded like it would be more of a question for the bank Lucas put the money into, or an escrow company who may be holding the funds, neither of which would be open on a Sunday.

"We tried to call the mayor, find out what he knows about this, but no one can seem to reach him. I left a message, so did Ralph and Kaye and John and Travis—heck, most of the people here probably left him a message. The city offices are closed today—it is Sunday, you know—so of course no one is answering the phones. So a bunch of us thought we'd ask the police chief or Ernie—I mean, Detective Kaufman, see what they know."

"So why are the front doors locked and all you guys standing out here?" Colin asked.

Mr. Peterson's face flashed with recognition. "Hey, I know you. Aren't you that California guy who was the police detective here before Ernie? You didn't last long."

"Yeah, that's me," Colin replied with a sheepish look, "but I hope to be back before long."

"Yes, Pete, Colin will be back in Paradise Valley before you know it." Emily winked at Colin, then turned her attention back to the elderly man. "You didn't answer the question, though. Why are the front doors locked?"

"A bunch of us went in and I guess we filled up the reception area. Stella said there were too many of us and we were making too much racket, so she shooed us out and locked the doors. She said the police chief would come out and talk to us as soon as she located him and got him to come down here. It is Sunday, you know."

"Yes, you said that." Emily turned to Colin and whispered in his ear. "I'd be interested to know what's happening with that money, too."

Colin nodded, then figuring there wasn't anything they could do, they continued on to the barbecue place down the street for lunch.

Colin got his finger-lickin' fix, while Emily, having only a salad, took pleasure in watching him devour the ribs.

"Did I mention how good it is to have you back? Even if it's only for a little while." Emily had her eyes fixed on him—the crop of dark hair, his smoky hazel eyes, his strong angular jaw. She would enjoy what little time they had together, hoping that in the midst of the murder investigation and comforting Maggie, she and Colin would have a little time for themselves before he dashed back to San Francisco.

"I think you may have mentioned it." He grinned and licked his fingers. "Once or twice."

"I was very surprised to see you this morning. It made me so happy when you took me in your arms. I miss that—you holding me."

She reached across the small round table to wipe a little drop of barbecue sauce from his lower lip and he caught her hand in his. He provocatively licked the sauce off her finger and kissed the top of her hand, bringing it in close to his chest.

"Do you feel that?" he asked.

"Feel what?"

"My heart. When I'm not here, that's where I hold you."

# CHAPTER 16
## The Crystal Paperweight

AFTER LUNCH, COLIN RECEIVED a phone call from Ernie, asking him to meet down at the county coroner's office. The medical examiner had some news and Ernie said he figured Colin might want to hear it. Colin didn't ask if Emily could come, but he knew she'd be miffed if he failed to take her with him.

Ernie seemed a little surprised to see Emily when they showed up, but he put on a smile, hiked up his pants by the belt, and offered his hand. "It's good to see you again, Emily. I wish it was under happier circumstances."

"Good to see you, too, Ernie."

"Doc's expecting us, so let's not keep him waiting." Ernie ushered them into the autopsy room.

"Dr. Walters, you know Colin Andrews," Ernie introduced.

The doctor was an older man with a thick head of snow-white hair and wire-rimmed glasses. His hunched back was evident under his standard white medical coat that he wore over his street clothes.

Colin politely extended his hand, but the doctor had latex gloves on and raised his hands to show him.

"And this is Emily Parker. She's a private investigator working on this case for the suspect who's been arrested, Josh Sullivan."

"Ms. Parker," the doctor said as he nodded in her direction.

"What do you have for us, Doc?" Ernie asked.

The medical examiner walked over to the sheet-covered body lying on the examination table. "As you know, my initial observation stated that the victim had been beaten to death—" Dr. Walters pulled the sheet back to expose Lucas Wakefield's head.

"But he wasn't?" Emily interrupted, averting her eyes.

"Now hold on, ma'am, let's not get ahead of ourselves," the old doctor warned. "He was beaten pretty badly, but when I examined him more fully, I found that he had actually been hit in the upper rear quadrant of his head with some sort of sharp jagged object."

"A jagged object?" Ernie questioned, scratching his head. "Like what?"

"I can't say for sure. We'll have to figure that one out." He took a couple of steps over to the computer on his desk. "I made a digital mold of the wound. Here, let me bring it up on the screen." Dr. Walters hit a few keys on the keyboard and turned his computer screen toward the others. "Have you any idea what would make a deep gaping wound like that?"

The screen showed a digital outline in 3-D of an object approximately four inches wide with several rough, pointy areas about three inches high.

"Maybe a big rock or something hard that broke and left a jagged edge?" Colin suggested.

"Perhaps," Doc Walters replied with a nod.

"Could he have hit his head on the corner of his desk when he fell?" Ernie asked.

"Not likely. It would need to be more uneven, more jagged," the doctor answered. "It could be the size of what's on the screen, or that mold may be the tip of a larger implement."

"Emily? What do you think?" Colin glanced at her, but she remained silent. "What's wrong? You look like you've seen a ghost or something."

Without a word, she reached into her large leather handbag and held out the mountain-shaped crystal paperweight, still in the plastic zip-lock bag.

The three men stood silent, gazing with quizzical looks at the sharply-peaked paperweight.

"Could this be it?" she asked.

Their collective gazes moved from her hand to her eyes.

"Let's see," Dr. Walters said, taking the mountain of crystal from her. He held it up to the screen at an inverted angle to match the wound, then he took some measurements. "I think this could be our murder weapon, fellas," he announced.

They all looked relieved at finding what made the unusually-shaped gash that ripped through Lucas

Wakefield's skull—for a few moments, that is. Then all eyes turned to Emily as if they simultaneously realized the same thing. Why did she have the murder weapon?

"Emily? Care to explain? Why do you have the murder weapon and why is it in a baggie?" Colin questioned.

She shook her head. "This couldn't be the murder weapon." There was no way. She'd had it with her the entire time. "Doc, you said the time of death was approximately six thirty to seven o'clock. Well, I was with Maggie at her place, from five-thirty up until we walked into Lucas's office, *after* he'd been killed."

"Where did you get this thing, Emily?" Ernie asked with an inquiring tilt of his head.

"Off Maggie's bookshelf at her house," she explained. "I slipped it into a new plastic bag and put it in my purse when Maggie wasn't looking. I had hoped to get Lucas's fingerprints from it."

"You stole it?" Ernie's eyebrows rose in surprise.

"No, just borrowed it. Look, I had every intention of returning it. I just didn't want her to know we were investigating Lucas."

"We?" Ernie questioned.

"My friend, Isabel, and I. She works for the FBI and she was going to have their lab try to get his prints off of it."

"That's too bad. I guess we didn't find the murder weapon after all," the medical examiner said, disappointment lining his voice.

"It must be something similar though."

"Agreed," the doctor concurred.

"Now that Dr. Walters has the body here," Emily flashed a coy smile at Ernie, "can you take his fingerprints and run them through the system? Find out if he was hiding something?"

"Why do you want me investigating the victim?" Ernie scratched at the stubble sprouting on his chin. "Seems to me we already know Maggie's boy killed him. He had opportunity and motive, and from the video tape, their brawl fits the timeline."

"Ernie, with all due respect, I think there's a lot more to this than what we're seeing on the surface," Emily asserted. "Won't you please just run his prints?"

"What could it hurt, Ernie?" Colin put a hand on the detective's shoulder. "Do the lady a favor."

"All right, I'll run 'em," Ernie agreed. "I always was a soft touch for a pretty girl."

"Ain't that the truth," Doc interjected with a chuckle.

"Then I can slip this paperweight back on Maggie's bookshelf before she notices it's gone," Emily said.

"Not so fast, Emily," Ernie said.

"What do you mean?"

"Well, I'm going to need to take that into evidence—at least have Crime Scene spray it with Luminol to check for blood. If it's clean, I can give it back to you."

Emily now wished she hadn't brought it out. She should have known better. There was no way it could be the weapon and now she couldn't sneak it back onto Maggie's shelf. She handed it over to Ernie. "Try to be quick, Ernie, please. I don't want Maggie asking about it."

Colin put his hand on her arm. "We better get out of here while we're ahead, Emily." He placed a guiding hand at her waist, prompting her toward the door.

"Oh, and can I please get a copy of those prints, too?" Emily requested, throwing a glance at Ernie over her shoulder. "I'd still like to have the FBI do their thing."

~*~

Emily tried Sully's cell phone again as Colin drove back to her house. Still no answer, just voicemail.

"Sully, this is Emily Parker again. Please call me back as soon as you get this message. It's critical that we talk. Josh is in trouble and he needs your help. Call me."

"No luck?" Colin glanced at her as she clicked her phone off and tossed it in her purse.

"Not yet." She crossed her arms. "I have to find out how Sully is involved in this and why he pulled a gun on Lucas."

"There must be more to it. You said it was unlike Sully to do such a thing and Josh said they had been arguing about money—that Sully sounded really angry. That does make his uncle look bad." Colin reached across the seat and took her hand. "We'll get to the bottom of this. That's why I'm here, Emily, to help you."

She squeezed his hand and nodded. "I appreciate it." Then she turned and stared out the window.

"What are you thinking?" he asked.

"Poor Maggie. Do you remember those first few days after Miranda died?" she asked, still looking at the buildings blurring by the window as they drove. "I sure remember the first days after Evan died." She reached up and wiped a stray tear from her cheek.

"Hardest days of my life," he said. "Maggie's lucky to have her friends."

"I need to return the favor, be there for Maggie, but seeing her like that brings it all back to me."

"Maybe the best way you can help Maggie is finding out what really happened, hopefully clearing her son—if he didn't do it."

"Do you think he's guilty?"

"He might be." Colin shrugged and turned the car into her driveway, cutting the engine. "He certainly had motive and opportunity. There's no denying he beat the crap out of the man right before he died. If it's true what Josh said, that Lucas threw the first punch—no, even that is a stretch. Self-defense only goes so far. We need to follow the evidence, Emily, find the facts, you know?"

She nodded.

"Since I'm not as emotionally connected to Maggie and Josh as you are, I'll try to be the voice of reason and help you work through this investigation."

"Are you saying I'm an emotional female?" she snapped. He certainly knew how to push her buttons, whether he was trying to or not.

"No, but they're close friends of yours," he replied. "If the evidence points to Josh, or Sully, or one of your other friends, please don't shoot the messenger."

"No promises," she responded.

"What?" he asked with a grin. "I tell you, woman, if you weren't so, so—"

"So, *what*?" she asked with a smirk, leaning her body toward him, her face not far from his.

"So pig-headed, so irritating, so funny and adorable, yet so frustrating and stubborn, so sexy, so—"

"I get it," she interrupted. "You just couldn't stay away."

"No, I couldn't."

"I love...*um*, having you here." She caught herself just in time. Emily needed him to be the first to say those three little words—but, by God if he didn't do it soon, she was going to explode. "I wish you didn't have to leave again."

"Me, too," he agreed, "but it won't be for long. Let's not talk about it, though, let's just enjoy the time we have." He leaned in and kissed her softly.

She pushed back and giggled. "Yes, let's, but we should go enjoy it inside, before the neighbors start gawking at us making out in the car like a couple of teenagers.

## CHAPTER 17
### Sully's Admission

WHILE COLIN MARINATED THE STEAKS and fired up the grill, Emily slid up on a barstool and phoned Maggie to see how she was doing. Camille answered the phone and reported that Maggie was sleeping, that she'd given her some of her Xanax to help her relax. She said Isabel had stopped by in the afternoon and that she and Alex were bringing dinner back for them. Jonathan would be back later in the evening, too.

Then Camille asked Emily when she was coming back over—Maggie had asked for her.

"Colin and I have been working on the case, Cam, trying to figure out what happened to Lucas."

She held back from telling Camille how she was afraid the deep despair she'd experienced when Evan was murdered would come flooding back to her if she was there, comforting Maggie.

"We were able to speak with Josh at the jail, too, and we're trying to piece it all together," she told Camille.

"I don't understand, Em. Josh got in a fight with Lucas and accidentally killed him, didn't he?"

"Oh, Cam, is that what Maggie thinks?"

"I believe so. No one has told her anything since the police came and arrested Josh. What else are we supposed to think?"

"Colin and I learned some things today and we're trying to fit the pieces together. It's a lot more complicated than we thought."

"How so?"

"I'm not at liberty to say at this point," Emily hedged, "but we'll figure it out and let you all know as soon as we can."

Feeling somewhat disloyal, it was hard for Emily not to blurt out all she knew to her friends. They had shared everything with each other for the last five years. But this was different from when she had lost Evan. When she was in Maggie's shoes, her friends were constantly by her side, supporting her, comforting her, encouraging her—but they couldn't help her figure out who killed her husband—or why—not even Isabel.

Out of their tight circle of friends, only Emily had the skills to give that kind of help to Maggie. Sure, Isabel could give an assist, she had the FBI connections, but as an overworked financial analyst, she couldn't take the lead.

"I'll try to make it over there tonight," Emily promised before hanging up.

"How's Maggie?" Colin asked, picking up the tray of marinating meat.

"Sleeping for now, but I should go see her tonight. Everyone's going to be there with her for dinner—everyone except me." Even she could hear the sadness in her voice, knowing she should be with her friend, but that she chose to stay away a little while longer.

"We could go, you know. This meat will keep." Colin set the tray down on the counter and moved to stand closer.

"Maybe later," Emily said, slipping off the stool. She slid her arms around his torso and he wrapped his arms around her, pulling her snuggly into an embrace. She laid her head against his strong chest and listened to beat of his heart.

"I don't understand. Why are you holding back, Em?" He gently kissed the top of her head. "That isn't like you."

"Self-preservation, I guess. The situation hits a little too close to home."

"For me, too," he whispered.

She had been so consumed with her own feelings, for a moment she forgot about his. Guilt pricked her and she forced her eyes to meet his. She noticed they glistened with emotion—turning the guilt from a prick to a sharp stab.

"I'm sorry, I was so self-absorbed, I wasn't thinking about your loss." She laid her head back down against his chest.

He did not reply, but his arms tightened around her and she felt safe, hearing the soft thumping rhythm of his heart. They stood clinging to each other and the world seemed to fade away.

"I would be a wreck without you," she muttered.

"Not you, babe. You're a rock."

Emily felt his hold loosen. She pulled back a little and looked up into his face. "Maybe on the outside, but total mush on the inside."

"Just the way I like you," he quipped, a slow smile spreading across his face. His head dipped close and he covered her lips with his. He kissed her tenderly and she felt a gentle sensation radiate down to her toes.

Emily had missed his kisses and his warm hands gently caressing her body. These last few months apart had been agony. As much as she would prefer to spend their brief time alone in each other's arms, she knew it would mostly be spent working the case. Priorities dictated it.

Maggie needed Emily. Emily needed Colin.

Disrupting their private moment, the ringtone on her cell phone began to jingle.

"Phone," she murmured.

"Let it ring." Colin moved in for another kiss.

"Can't," she chirped. "Could be important."

He groaned and released her.

She grabbed her phone off the counter. "Hello."

"Em, this is Isabel. Do you have a minute?"

Emily glanced up at Colin with a grin. "Can it wait? I'm kind of in the middle of something."

"It's about Jethro."

"Jethro," Emily repeated. She shot Colin a serious look as she settled onto a stool.

"I don't want to talk about it over the phone. Are you coming to Maggie's later?"

"Yes, Colin and I."

"We can talk then."

Emily clicked her phone off and set it on the counter.

"Who's Jethro?" Colin asked.

"A retired FBI agent. He's the one I showed the old photo to, the one of Evan and the woman."

"He has news for you?"

"I don't know. Isabel didn't want to talk about it over the phone. I guess we're going to Maggie's this evening, after all," Emily said, scrunching up one corner of her mouth.

"Then we better get back to business. Now where were we?" Colin leaned in, as she sat perched on the stool. His lips met hers, warm and moist. Just when she was relaxing into the kiss a sharp knock came at the front door.

"Expecting anyone?" he questioned, looking in the direction of the noise.

"No." She slid off the stool and padded to the front door. Colin trailed closely behind her. Emily could see sandy blonde hair skimming the bottom of the little windows spread across the top of her front door.

"I think it's Sully," she whispered over her shoulder.

She opened the door and found the mayor standing on her porch, dressed in casual jeans and an un-tucked button-down shirt.

"Hello, Sully," she greeted politely.

"If I could have a few minutes of your time, I really need to talk to you, Emily." The dark shadows under his eyes were evidence he hadn't been sleeping, and she detected a slight quiver in his voice.

"Certainly, come in." Emily stood aside.

"Colin Andrews, Mr. Mayor." Colin took a step forward and offered his hand, which Sully grabbed and shook firmly. "I had worked for the city of Paradise Valley for a while."

"The police detective, right?"

"Yes, sir, Mr. Mayor," Colin replied.

"Please, call me Sully." He offered a weak smile.

Emily noticed a nervousness about Sully that she'd never seen before—shifting eyes, a jittery resonance to his voice, the dark circles. It wasn't that they were ever close friends, but because he was Maggie's brother, they were well acquainted.

"Would it be possible to speak to Emily alone?" Sully asked, eyeing Colin.

Emily glanced at Colin and quirked an eyebrow.

"Sure, I'll just go check on the grill." Colin made himself scarce.

"Let's go in the living room and sit down." Emily gestured toward the sofa. What could Sully want with her?

Sully took a seat at the end of the couch and Emily sank down on the chair perpendicular to it.

"Can I get you something to drink, Sully? I could get you a glass of wine or something."

"No, thank you. You left me several messages, so I thought it best to come and talk to you in person. I don't have much time, so let me get right to the point." His voice was quiet, his gaze darting around. "I don't want Colin overhearing this conversation. I know he's not working as a cop right now, but he will be again. And if he knows I did something illegal, he'll be duty-bound to arrest me."

"Oh, Sully, what have you done?"

"Lucas came to me last week and offered to let me buy a couple of condos at his new resort, for a deeply-discounted price. He convinced me that if I bought them, with a quick turn around, I could make a lot of money. With Carolyn so sick," his voice began to crack, "the doctor and hospital bills are piling up." He worried his hands in his lap. His eyes moistened and he appeared as if he was fighting back tears. Sully took a deep breath.

Emily had questions, but she held her tongue and let him continue.

"He knew I was desperate enough to jump at the opportunity. I told him I didn't have the money, that I'd have to pass, but he convinced me to borrow it from the city retirement fund."

"Oh, Sully, no."

"I thought I'd have time to sell the condos and get the money back in the account before anyone noticed it was missing. I knew it was wrong, but I…I…aw damn, I don't know what I was thinking," he exclaimed under his breath.

He went on to explain how he'd received the notice from the auditor and had asked Lucas for the money back at the engagement party.

*The private pow-wow—I knew something was wrong.*

Sully described how Lucas had told him no and that, in fact, the whole resort project was a scam.

"I don't understand. Why would he come right out and tell you that?" Emily questioned. "I wouldn't think he'd want anyone to know."

"He said he was telling me so he could hold it over my head. He wanted me to use my influence to get others to invest in the project, knowing that if I didn't, he would expose me. If I did what he asked, he said he'd return the hundred thousand dollars to me before the audit."

"So, basically, he was blackmailing you."

"That's right. The night he died, I paid him a visit. I went to his office and begged for the money back. I threatened him with a gun, but it didn't seem to make any difference. He said he wouldn't give me the money back yet."

"You pulled a gun on him?"

"He knew I wasn't going to kill him, because if I did I'd never get the money back. He warned me that if I breathed a word of this to anyone he would ruin me, and he would ruin Maggie."

"Oh, Maggie…poor Maggie. She was going to marry that shyster."

"No," Sully said, shaking his head, "that was never part of the plan."

"What? What do you mean?"

"He was never going to marry her. He said he was going to disappear with all the money before the wedding, that Maggie was just a front, a beard, a way to involve me to help him suck in more investors."

"Maybe knowing what a slime-ball he was will help her get over him," Emily hoped.

"He was more than a slime-ball, he was a—" Sully's face flushed red with anger and the whites of his eyes seemed to grow as his eyes widened. Pulling in a deep breath and releasing a low guttural sound, he appeared to get control of his anger. His rage deflated and he flattened his voice. "Well, we'll leave it at that."

"You do realize Josh overheard you that night."

"No, I didn't know that. He never said anything."

"Colin and I interviewed him this morning and I could tell he was hiding something. He didn't want to tell me, but when I pressed him hard, he told us he'd gone to the office that night to have it out with Lucas, but you were already there. He overheard part of your conversation and knew you'd pulled a gun on him."

"I didn't know." Sully hung his head as he propped his forearms on his knees. "I'm so ashamed, Emily."

"I don't understand why you'd steal the city funds and invest in this scheme. That isn't the Sully Sullivan I know."

"When you're desperate for money, you do things you never thought you'd do. It changes you. Between the crappy economy and Carolyn's illness, everything I had has been wiped out. I didn't look at it as stealing—Lucas had me convinced I was only borrowing the money." Sully sat up and ran a hand over his face. "I can see now he was never going to give me the money back. He was just hanging a carrot out to get me to do what he wanted."

"But it was stealing—grand theft is what you'll be charged with."

"I know." Sully's voice sounded weak and shaky. "I don't know what to do."

"As much as I'd like to help you, Sully, my main concern is Maggie. She needs me to find out who killed Lucas and I hope to God it wasn't Josh."

"Me, too," he agreed.

"I hate to say this, but you had motive and opportunity, too. You're on my short list."

"Emily, you can't think I would do this." He raked a hand through his hair. "Like I said, if I killed him I'd never get the money back."

"In a fit of rage, knowing he was never going to let you have it, I could see you killing him."

"He wasn't shot to death, was he?"

"No, someone hit him hard in the head with something, shattered his skull. That someone could have been you."

"I'm not a murderer!" Sully's sunken eyes bulged with anger. "I could never kill someone."

"Anyone could kill under the right circumstances," she shot back.

"So now you think I'm a murderer *and* a thief?" He jumped to his feet at the accusation.

She rose to face him. "Like you said, Sully, a desperate man will do things he never thought he would do. Those were your words."

"You've got to believe me, Emily," he begged, grabbing her by the arm. "I did not kill Lucas. When I ran out of the office, someone else was there. I heard a noise—that's why I left. From the sound of things, that someone was Josh. I bolted out of there and went home to Carolyn. She'll verify it."

She yanked her arm loose from his hold and glared at him.

"Everything okay in here?" Colin asked, his hands planted protectively on his hips, filling out the doorway.

"Fine. The mayor was just leaving." Emily's hand motioned toward the door.

Sully stepped close to Emily and whispered in her ear. "You'll keep the other thing just between us, won't you?"

"For now," she replied softly.

"Sorry to bother you," Sully muttered to Colin as he breezed past him and out the door.

"What was that all about?" Colin approached Emily.

"I guess the Mayor didn't like me accusing him of killing Lucas." She slipped her arms around Colin's torso and he returned the gesture. She didn't want to lie to him, but she agreed with Sully—if Colin knew what Sully had done, he'd have to do something about it. For Maggie's sake, she'd keep her brother's secret for as long as she could.

"You accused him? To his face?" Colin sounded stunned. "You're getting pretty gutsy."

"I didn't actually accuse him straight out. I simply told him he was on my short list."

Colin laughed. "Almost as bad."

"Yeah, I guess." She giggled. "Steaks ready yet? All this gutsiness has made me hungry."

# THE HEART OF LIES

# CHAPTER 18
## Taking Care of Maggie

"WE SHOULD GET GOING pretty soon." Emily rolled her wrist to check her watch. "I'll do the dishes later."

Colin brought their plates from the table and set them in the sink. "It'll only take a minute to rinse them off and stick them in the dishwasher." Because of his military training, Colin always liked things squared away when he left them.

"I'm anxious to talk to Isabel. She was so mysterious on the phone." Emily cleared the glasses and silverware off the table and set them on the counter next to the sink.

"Get your shoes on, and your purse, and we can go," he said, sticking the glasses in the dishwasher and closing the door.

She put a hand gently around the back of his neck and drew his face down to hers, giving him a quick kiss. "Thanks for making dinner and cleaning up."

"My pleasure." He slid his arms around her waist and pulled her tight.

She made an exaggerated fanning motion with her hand. "Why, whatever will I do when you're gone, Mr. Andrews?" Emily teased with a heavy Southern drawl, purposely sounding like a helpless female.

"Miss me like crazy?" he replied with a grin.

"Absolutely." She threw her arms around his neck and planted a wet, passionate kiss on him.

"I thought you were in a hurry to leave."

"I am." She released him and stepped away. "Just wanted to make sure you were going to miss me like crazy, too." She sauntered down the hall after her shoes, swaying her hips, assuming he was watching her go. She slanted a quick look behind her—she was right.

~*~

By the time Emily and Colin arrived at Maggie's, the small gathering of friends had already eaten, and Camille and Isabel were cleaning up the kitchen. Emily could hear the girls chattering in the kitchen and noticed through the rear kitchen window that Jonathan and Alex had retreated to the back deck. The guys were sitting on canvas director chairs, when Colin stepped outside and joined them.

"Hey, Em, so glad to see you made it." Isabel looked up from the suds-filled sink as Emily stepped into the small, cozy kitchen.

Maybe the 1920's cottage lacked a dishwasher, but it definitely oozed with charm. A fair trade-off, Emily always thought.

"Yes, we were starting to wonder about you." Camille was drying a platter with a well-worn, checkered dish towel.

Before she could respond, Maggie came rushing into the kitchen with her arms outstretched to Emily. She looked exhausted and frail in her sweatshirt and jeans, nothing like her usual vibrant self. Her face was bare of makeup and her hair was pulled up into a messy ponytail.

"Emily!" Maggie cried out, squeezing her firmly.

Emily returned the hug. "How are you holding up?" Emily asked once Maggie released her grip.

"I slept most of the day, but I'm doin' better now. Havin' everyone here helps so much." She smiled at Camille and Isabel, still doing the dishes.

"I'm assuming your brother came by to see you too," Emily said.

"Yes, Sully was here this afternoon for a bit. He was so worried about me and Josh—and about the project with so many people in town puttin' their money into it."

"How's Josh doing?" Camille asked, drying the last of the dishes.

"Alex saw him today." Isabel wiped her hands on a towel. "He said Josh was nervous about being able to get out on bail tomorrow. I hope my husband can convince the judge he's a low flight risk."

"I don't understand how they can think my son would kill Lucas." Maggie had tears welling up in her eyes. "What possible motive would he have?"

Since walking into Lucas's office the night before and finding Gloria seated beside his bloody and battered body, Maggie had been pretty much in the dark—literally—mostly sleeping and sedated.

Maggie was not aware of the facts that had unfolded during the day, and Emily wasn't sure how much to share with her at this point. Taking a moment to consider her best move, Emily decided that if Maggie knew what a scumbag Lucas was, it would help her get over him faster.

"Why don't we all go into the living room? I'll explain what I learned today," Emily suggested.

"That would be great, Em. I feel like I don't know what's goin' on," Maggie replied.

Camille shot a questioning glance at Isabel, as if to ask if they should go, and Isabel nodded her agreement. Emily turned and led the way back to the quiet living room.

Emily took a seat next to Maggie on the floral-print sofa, rearranging the jumble of pillows behind them, while Camille and Isabel settled into the sage-green overstuffed chairs that flanked the stone fireplace, facing them.

"Listen Maggs, I know getting through this is probably the hardest thing you've ever had to do—you know it was for me, when Evan died—but there are some things I need to tell you."

"That doesn't sound good." Maggie pulled her legs up cross-legged on the sofa, grabbing a tissue from the box on the white painted end table.

"It won't be easy to hear, but you need to know the truth." Emily searched for the right words while every eye in the room was fixed on her. "There's no easy way to say this—"

"So spit it out, already," Camille directed, shifting in her seat.

"Calm down, Camille." Isabel reached out and put her hand on Camille's forearm. "Let Emily find her own words."

"Sorry, I'm just a bundle of nerves," Camille apologized, running her fingers through her short fiery locks.

"Emily?" Maggie muttered, her eyes growing large with alarm.

"Okay, here it goes." Emily sucked in a deep breath. "You wanted to know what possible motive your son could have, well, Josh caught Lucas fooling around with Fiona at the engagement party."

"Fiona?" Maggie gasped. "No! That couldn't be. He loved me. He was going to marry me. That doesn't make any sense at all." She pulled an accent pillow in front of her and wrapped her arms around it, clinging tightly.

"I'm so sorry, Maggie. Josh said he ordered Lucas to come clean with you about Fiona, to break off the engagement within twenty-four hours, or he would tell you himself."

"I thought she was my friend." The tears began to flow once more. "I introduced her to Lucas."

Emily scooted closer to Maggie and put an arm around her, as Maggie leaned into Emily and began to sob.

"I never liked that woman," Isabel said, her eyes narrowing. "There always seemed to be something *evil* about her. Even at the presentation the other night, she seemed resentful that Lucas had proposed. Remember that, Em?"

"How come y'all never said anythin' about that to me?" Maggie looked from Isabel to Emily, dabbing her eyes.

"She seemed a little jealous of the two of you at the welcome party, too," Isabel added. "And didn't you say, Em, you saw them together in the lounge at the Hilton Hotel a week or so ago?"

"Why am I the last to know?" Maggie bawled, throwing her hands in the air.

"If it makes you feel any better, I didn't know either," Camille said to Maggie while scowling at their other two friends.

"We're not saying they had sex, Maggie," Emily tried to explain.

"You think they were havin' sex?" Maggie queried. "We weren't havin' sex, but do y'all think they were?"

"We don't know what they were doing, Maggs." Emily rubbed her hand over Maggie's shoulder. "Josh is the one who said he saw them fooling around, those were his words."

"Foolin' around, huh?" Maggie murmured, patting the tissue under her eyes. "I still don't understand why y'all didn't say one word about it to me."

"They were just observations we made, we didn't know anything for sure. And we certainly didn't know they were playing around," Emily tried to justify.

"You could have at least told me," Camille pouted.

Isabel twisted in her chair to face Camille. "We didn't tell you because we didn't want Maggie to know until we were sure. Let's face it, Cam, you're not the best at keeping secrets."

Camille frowned at the characterization.

"We just thought Fiona was attracted to Lucas, maybe had a little crush on him," Isabel said.

"He was handsome and charming." Emily had to give him that much. "If we had known something for certain, we would have come to you with it," she assured Maggie, patting her hand. "Let's get back to Josh, hmm?"

"Okay," Maggie mumbled.

"When Josh found out Lucas hadn't told you about Fiona, he went to Lucas's office to confront him."

"Oh, Emily, no," Maggie whimpered.

"Josh confessed to me that he beat Lucas for what he did to you, but he swears Lucas was alive when he left," Emily explained. "The cops have a security video showing Josh coming and going from the office building, and Josh admitted to them about the fist fight."

"Why did he let the cops question him without his attorney?" Camille asked.

"Just looking at him, anyone could see he'd been in a fight," Emily said.

Maggie took a long cleansing breath, gaining control over her sobs. She dried her eyes with the tissue and blew her nose. "Yesterday mornin' when I got up, I saw Josh looked like he got in a fight, but the police showed up and arrested him before he got a chance to tell me what happened. Right away I called Alex and he headed down to the jail."

"Doesn't Josh get military representation?" Camille asked.

"Oh, I never even thought of that," Maggie said.

"Well," Emily looked at Isabel, who through Alex, also knew about Josh's current status. "He's kind of not in the Navy anymore."

"What?" Maggie cried. "Does anybody tell me anythin' anymore?"

"I'm sure he'll fill you in later, Maggie. He didn't want to burden you with it before your wedding." Emily rubbed Maggie's shoulder.

"Do you think Josh did it?" Isabel asked Emily.

"Isabel!" Camille's eyes darted to Maggie. "How can you ask that? Especially in front of poor Maggie."

Maggie's eyes widened, looking at Emily in anticipation.

Emily bit her lip, wondering how to best respond without inciting another round of wailing from Maggie.

"I'm so sorry, Maggie. I don't mean to be insensitive." Isabel sat forward in her chair. "I was just wondering what Emily thought Josh's odds were."

"Isabel," Camille reprimanded again. "Why don't you talk about this in private with Emily—later."

"All right," Isabel relented, plopping back in her chair and crossing her arms like a child who had just been scolded.

"Emily?" Maggie asked. "Do you think my son killed Lucas?"

"I don't *want* to believe it, Maggs—and if he did do it, I don't think he meant to kill him—but I have to be honest, the evidence is pretty compelling." Emily squeezed Maggie's hand. "Just know Colin and I will do everything we can to find the truth." Emily hoped that meant proving Josh innocent.

"I appreciate that." Maggie's voice was small and trembling.

"But you do have to consider the possibility that he did it," Emily warned. "He was furious, he admitted to beating the snot out of him, and he was there very close to the time Lucas died."

"I'm gonna support my son, no matter what, Em. He's my family."

"I understand," Emily replied.

"Whatever I can do," Isabel offered, "if there's anything Emily needs from the FBI resources, I'll do my best to get it done."

"There is one thing on Josh's side," Emily remarked. "The murder weapon hasn't been found."

"I thought he was beaten to death," Camille said.

"Well, according to the medical examiner, the cause of death was being hit in the head from something sharp and jagged," Emily explained.

"What on earth?" Maggie exclaimed.

"Something like that paperweight you said you got in Sun Valley, the one in the shape of mountain peaks," Emily told her.

"How do you know that?" Maggie asked.

"Um, well, you're not going to like this, but—"

"But what?" Maggie interrupted, her blue eyes turning gray with worry.

"I *borrowed* your paperweight when I was here Saturday."

"Borrowed? What for?"

"Well, that's the part you're not going to like." Emily glanced at Isabel, then back to Maggie.

Maggie frowned at her as a perplexed expression washed over her face.

"I wanted to give Isabel something that might have Lucas's fingerprints on it. Isabel and I had an uncomfortable feeling about that man and we wanted to find out more about him." Emily braced herself for Maggie's reaction.

"You did what?" Maggie's face turned from confusion to anger. "Behind my back? How could you, Emily? Isabel?"

"It appears we were right to do it, Maggie," Isabel said in their defense. "I wish we had done it sooner, maybe he would still be alive, and Josh wouldn't be in jail."

"Why are you sayin' that?" Maggie cried.

"Isabel's right, Maggie. I haven't told her this yet, or Alex for that matter, but I just learned the whole Whitetail Resort was a scam," Emily admitted. "But that information doesn't leave this room. Understood?"

Maggie and Isabel nodded in agreement.

"I knew it," Isabel muttered angrily. "A hundred grand gone."

"Camille, not a single word to anyone about this—not even to your husband," Emily warned.

"I understand," Camille agreed.

"A scam? Oh, Em, are you sure?" Maggie buried her head in her hands.

Emily gently stroked her back. "Yes, I'm sure, but we'll help you through this, Maggs. Whatever you need."

"Wait a minute," Maggie gasped, shooting up straight in her seat. "You said the murder weapon was like the mountain paperweight?"

"Yes," Emily replied. "Dr. Walters said the peaks are a perfect match to the wound."

"Was it my paperweight?" Maggie asked. "Or did they find the paperweight in Lucas's office?"

"In Lucas's office? No, I had it with me the whole time," Emily said.

"No, Em, you don't understand." Maggie shook her head, causing her blonde ponytail to flop from side to side. "There were two."

"Two?" Isabel's expression changed from surprise to comprehension.

"You know what that means," Emily deduced.

"The other one could have been the murder weapon," Isabel answered.

"Where is the other one?" Emily asked.

"Lucas gave me one and he put the other on his desk," Maggie said. "He said it would keep us both close to our dream."

"Maggie, you may have solved the mystery," Camille congratulated her.

"Not so fast, Cam," Emily cautioned. "That still doesn't clear Josh. There was no paperweight on the desk. I was in there for a while, I never saw one, and I would have noticed it. The police will say Josh used it, took it when he left, and then disposed of it."

Maggie's face had held the briefest of smiles for the first time since the murder, but it quickly faded to a frown.

"We have to find the second paperweight," Emily stared directly at Isabel.

"But where?" Isabel asked.

"First thing we have to do is let Detective Kaufman know, get his people to go over Lucas's office again with a fine-tooth comb. This time they'll know what to look for. Let's pray it doesn't have Josh's fingerprints on it," Emily said, hoping it didn't have Sully's prints on it either. She wondered if it might have Fiona's.

"Shouldn't you call him tonight?" Maggie asked.

"It's late, Maggs. They won't do anything about it until tomorrow. I'll fill Alex in and we can get a hold of Ernie first thing in the morning."

"Fill Alex in on what?" Alex asked as the men sauntered into the room.

"Somebody's ears were burning," Camille joked.

"On what we've discovered in Josh's case. Why don't we step out to the deck and talk?" Emily suggested. She assumed Colin would have refrained from sharing information in front of Jonathan the way Emily just did in front of the girls.

"We'll start dishing up dessert while you talk," Camille offered. "Peach cobbler a la mode."

"You tryin' to make me fat?" Maggie laughed weakly.

The girls got up to head for the kitchen, and Isabel leaned over and whispered to Emily. "Don't forget we need to talk. Jethro?"

"I haven't forgotten. After I brief Alex."

## CHAPTER 19
### Evan's Identity

COLIN DROVE EMILY HOME from Maggie's after Emily and Isabel had a chance to talk about Jethro on the front porch. She was quiet on the drive home, lost in thought about what Isabel had disclosed to her.

Colin walked her to the front door, the interior lights giving the porch of her bungalow an inviting warm glow.

"Would you like to come in for a few minutes?" she asked as she unlocked the door.

"I'd better get going. It's getting late and I still have to pick up my gear from Ernie's house. I don't want to wake them.

"I thought you drove directly to see me."

"I stopped at Ernie's first, I had brought something for him. It was in my bag and I accidentally left it at his place."

"I wanted to go over what Isabel told me tonight." She moved in close to Colin, placing her hands on his muscular chest.

He responded by sliding his hands around her waist.

"Aren't you even a little curious?" she asked.

"I'm very curious, but—"

"You have a funny way of showing it," she cut him off, her lips forming a pout. "Besides, I thought you'd want to stay and enjoy a little private time with me." She did—he would be gone back to California soon. "But, I guess you don't." She let go of him and started to turn away.

"Hey, don't be like that," he said, catching her by the hand. "If I can finish up with Ernie quickly, I'll come back. Otherwise, I'll just head to my apartment and see you tomorrow, then you can fill me in on all of it. Okay?" His lips curled into a sexy smile, and before she could answer, he pulled her into a tight embrace.

She felt the warmth of his body as she pressed against him. He kissed her thoroughly and removed any doubt that he truly wanted to stay. She would have to settle for this one satisfying kiss to keep her until tomorrow.

He stepped off the porch and waved good-bye as he got in his car and drove away, only waiting long enough to make sure she had gone safely inside.

Kicking off her shoes, she headed to the bedroom to slip into her pajamas, then to the kitchen for a cup of chamomile tea. As she waited for the tea kettle to whistle, she thought about what Isabel had told her. Jethro had put out feelers, he said, asked around and showed the photo to a few colleagues. One man thought that maybe he recognized Evan, but not the girl.

He did say, Isabel recalled, that when he had another friend run Evan's photo through facial recognition, there seemed to be a match, for a different name, but access to any information was denied. As for the woman, his friend did not find a match, however, he thought he remembered the girl, the daughter of an FBI agent he knew, who had been tragically killed in France years ago.

The kettle whistled and Emily turned the burner off and poured the boiling water into a mug, bobbing the tea bag in it. She was disappointed he couldn't tell her more, but his promise to keep searching encouraged her.

Isabel also said Jethro had asked about seeing the gun again, but she reminded him it was just a hypothetical question Emily had asked. Emily wasn't ready to show anyone and she was almost sorry she had mentioned it. She was quite sure he didn't believe the questions were hypothetical.

She ripped open a yellow packet of Splenda and stirred it into her cup, again thinking of the photo that was now missing.

*Why didn't I make another copy?* Emily questioned herself as if she could have known she would need it. *Why didn't I email it to Isabel as I'd planned?* Then she remembered she had scanned the photo, to email it to Isabel the day they met with Jethro, just in case, but she had gotten distracted and not actually sent it.

She ran to her laptop which lay open on the breakfast bar and she searched through her downloaded files. *Yes!* There it was, not lost after all. Relieved, she attached it to an email and sent it off to Isabel. Now they'd both have it.

~*~

The alarm clock sounded its rhythmic screech and Emily slapped at the snooze button. Bleary-eyed, she rolled over, hoping for a few more minutes of sleep. Tossing and turning most of the night, she had replayed Lucas's murder scene in her mind and her conversations with Josh and Sully, along with some eerily-realistic sensual dreams about Colin, who would morph into Evan, and then back to Colin again.

Not bothering to check the time on the clock, the sun streaming in her windows told her it was time to get up. Her cell phone chimed on the night table, alerting her to a new text. She rubbed her eyes, pushed back a few strands of hair, and picked up the phone, trying to focus on the tiny words.

The text was from Colin and read, *Sorry I didn't come back. It was late. Didn't want to wake you. Bringing breakfast. Be there in 15.*

"Shoot!" She flew out of bed and straight into the shower as her nightgown flew over her head and onto the floor.

Dabbing a little mousse into her tousled curls, brushing her teeth and throwing on her favorite jeans and T-shirt, as well as a little lip gloss and mascara, she dashed to the front door just as he rang her bell.

"*Whew*," she exhaled before opening the door to him, greeting him with a bright welcoming smile.

"Good morning, beautiful." Colin stepped inside with a box from her favorite coffee shop, Moxie Java, full of Chai latté for her and black coffee for him, along with fresh slices of lemon poppy seed bread. He swept her up in his free arm and kissed her soundly.

When he let go of her, she was breathless. She grabbed hold of his arm to steady herself. "You sure know how to greet a girl," she laughed, giving him a playful push for not showing up the night before.

"Let's have our coffee while it's hot and you can tell me all about your talk with Isabel last night."

He followed her into the kitchen and took a seat at the table while she grabbed a couple of small plates. "Sorry I couldn't come back last night—I know you wanted to talk." Pulling the bounty out of the box, he waited for her to sit. "I'm all ears."

She laid the plates on the table and sank down into her chair. "Isabel didn't have much for me, but little by little, maybe I can piece this thing together."

"What did she say?"

"She said Jethro told her he'd asked around, emailed the photo to a few of his connections in the FBI and the CIA, hoping someone could identify either of them. He said one of his contacts thought he recognized Evan, thought he had been in the CIA years ago, but that wasn't his name, which I kind of figured at this point."

"What was his real name?"

"The man was hesitant to divulge the name, but I guess Jethro convinced him that it would be all right since he was dead, that his widow had a right to know. The other man said he thought it was David Gerard. Isabel asked that I keep it confidential, though."

"I won't tell anyone, Emily—cross my heart." He made a crossing motion on his chest with two fingers. "Was that one of the names on the passports you found?" Colin took a sip of his coffee and waited for her answer.

"No, but it makes sense he wouldn't have used his real name," she replied, picking at her lemon poppy seed bread.

"What about the woman?"

"Isabel said he found out that the woman was the daughter of an FBI agent and she had been killed in a shootout between Evan, or David Gerard, and someone else—a terrorist or enemy spy, or something."

"The daughter of an FBI agent? Did he know who?"

"Jethro said he couldn't reveal the father's name, but maybe the man wanted payback against Evan for his daughter's death. It was just a theory Jethro had."

"Are you okay, hearing about all this?" Colin stroked her arm gently.

"It's upsetting, of course, knowing the man I married was not at all who he said he was, but I've been dealing with that fact for months now and Isabel's been preparing me for something like this. She warned me he was probably running from a previous life."

"A previous life? Like what?"

"She said I might find out he was an NSA agent, or a CIA assassin, or maybe he was in witness protection because he'd been a criminal who testified against someone high up in a criminal organization, like the Irish mob, or something like that. I kind of laughed it off at the time, but it stuck in the back of my mind and I wondered about it now and then."

"You seriously thought he might be a CIA assassin? Or a member of the mob? You never said anything to me about it."

"It was just a possibility. I didn't want it to be true, so every time the thought popped up, I beat it back down."

"I wish you'd told me."

"I might have, eventually, but then you took off back to California."

"I had to, I didn't have a choice. You make it sound like I ran off and left you," he defended.

"No, I know you had to go. Your mom and dad needed your help. Sorry, I'm just being a little selfish, throwing myself a pity party."

"You know what they say about pity parties," he grinned, lightening the mood.

"No, what?"

"Few people want to come and they don't bring presents," he replied with a smirk, making her laugh.

"Touché." She stuck the last bit of lemon poppy seed bread in her mouth.

"So what's on the agenda for today?"

"First up, we need to get a hold of Ernie and get him and the forensic team back to Lucas's office to search for the murder weapon."

"Why is that?" Colin cocked his head with a perplexed look.

"Oh, I forgot to tell you. When you and the boys were out on the deck last night, I was talking to Maggie and the girls about the mountain-shaped paperweight. Remember how the medical examiner said it was a perfect fit for the wound?"

"Yeah," he nodded.

"But the one I had couldn't have been it?"

"Right."

"Well, get this. Maggie told me Lucas had one, too, just like it, sitting on his desk." She sat back in her chair and crossed her arms, letting that bit of news sink in. "If we can find it, I'm sure it'll have his blood all over it. Whoever's prints are on it will be our murderer."

"Assuming it hasn't been bleached, this could break the case wide open."

"It could."

"We need to concentrate on finding that paperweight. If it's not at the office, Ernie's going to have to search some homes," Colin stated.

"He'll want to search Maggie's place first. Josh had better be telling us the truth. If they find a paperweight at Maggie's and they already know they have the one I took—if it has his prints on it—he's hung." She grimaced. Ernie would most certainly want to search Sully's as well as Fiona's homes, too.

"Since you're the one with the relationship with good ol' Ernie, could you give him a call? Tell him about the other paperweight and get him back out to search the office again."

"Be glad to," Colin agreed, flipping out his phone and punching in the numbers.

While he was busy on the phone, Emily climbed up on a stool at the breakfast bar and went on her computer to Google the name David Gerard. She found a magician, a cartoonist, a musician, and a few others with the name David Gerard. When she had more time, she'd have to dig a little deeper.

"Ernie's rounding up a team right now to search the office." Colin stuck his phone in his pocket and joined Emily.

She was finished searching for now and she closed the program, leaving the photo of Evan and the woman on the screen.

"Isn't that the picture someone broke into your house for?" he asked.

"Yes, I thought it was lost, but I remembered last night that I had scanned and saved it."

"That was lucky," Colin remarked.

"It was, just don't mention it to anyone. I don't want someone breaking in and stealing my computer next."

She'd said it half joking, but someone didn't want her to have the picture and it wasn't that far-fetched to think they would take her computer, too.

"Okay, boss, what's next?" Colin asked.

Emily's phone sounded its tone alerting her to a new text. Alex had texted, *Josh's arraignment is 10 a.m. today.*

"I'd better call Maggie and see if she's up to going," Emily said. "She may need me to be there for support."

Emily dialed Maggie's phone and Camille picked up. Alex had already called and given them the time and Maggie was set on going, she said. Emily assured her they would be there too, and told them not to worry—Alex was the best trial lawyer in town and Josh was in good hands.

When she hung up, she noticed Colin studying the photo on the computer screen.

"You're going to think this is funny," he said, "but she looks a little like Delia, only younger."

"Delia McCall?" Emily questioned. "Yeah, a little. It's probably just the dark hair."

"Yeah, you're right. Besides, Delia would have been older than this woman, even back then, don't you think?"

"Maybe." She slid off the bar stool, brushing against Colin's chest with hers. "I should go change for court," she said with a little smile spreading on her lips. She hadn't intended to brush against him like that, but he had just been standing so close to her, looking over her shoulder at the screen. His nearness made her heart skip and a tingle feathered up her spine. Peering up into his smiling eyes, she could tell he enjoyed the sensation too. "I'll be right back."

She felt his gaze on her as she padded off to the bedroom.

# CHAPTER 20
## The Hospital Visit

WHEN EMILY AND COLIN ENTERED, Maggie was seated in the courtroom, first row on the left, flanked by Camille and Isabel. Alex had waited on the aisle seat for Josh's case to be called.

Isabel saw them and waved them over. Alex stood and stepped into the aisle to let them in, shaking Colin's hand as he passed by.

They scooted past their seated friends, and Emily stopped long enough to bend down and give Maggie a quick hug and squeeze Camille's hand before taking a seat on the bench next to Isabel.

"How's she holding up?" Emily whispered to Isabel.

"As well as can be expected, I guess," Isabel quietly replied.

Another attorney stood at the front of the courtroom at the defendant's table—a young man in a cheap, blue suit that Emily thought looked like someone fresh out of law school, likely a public defender. The female defendant stood next to him, her bleached blonde hair a wild mess, looking none too pleased to be wearing orange.

The judge barked out the bail amount and slammed his gavel down. "Next!" he hollered.

A deputy escorted Josh into the courtroom, and Alex rose and strode to the defense table.

"Joshua Sullivan?" the judge asked.

"Yes, sir, Your Honor," Josh replied respectfully, standing at attention.

Alex bowed his head and stood with his hands clasped behind his back. "Alex Martínez, attorney for the defense, Your Honor."

Across the aisle was the Assistant District Attorney. She stood and introduced herself, as well. "Alison Laraway, for the State, Your Honor."

Emily recognized her even before she'd introduced herself. She was the same formidable, blonde ADA that had worked to prove Delia McCall guilty of murder, and she was the same attractive woman who'd had hopes of a relationship with Colin when he had first come to Paradise Valley.

Emily had won out on both counts and she was sure Alison would not forget it. Emily slinked down in her seat, trying not to be seen by the ADA.

"How do you plead?" the judge asked, after the charges were read.

"Not guilty, Your Honor." Josh peeked over his shoulder at his mother.

"Your Honor, the defendant is charged with the brutal murder of his mother's lover and the State asks that no bail be allowed," Laraway stated.

It was Alex's turn. "Your Honor, the defendant was a proud member of the US Navy and he fought for this country. He is a man of honor with deep roots in this community and he does not have the financial wherewithal to be a flight risk. The victim, Lucas Wakefield, was not his mother's lover, as Ms. Laraway is salaciously trying to suggest, he was engaged to the defendant's mother, to be married shortly. Also, we have recently learned that the victim had duped quite a number of local people out of millions of dollars. The murderer could have been any number of people. The State has a very flimsy—"

The judge raised his hand. "Save it for the trial, Mr. Martínez." He folded his hands in front of him, and looked directly at Josh. "Young man, I appreciate your brave service for our country. That being said," he paused, "this is a serious crime and the State seems to believe they have enough evidence to charge you with Lucas Wakefield's murder."

The judge momentarily glanced over at ADA Laraway before proceeding. "Bail is set at two hundred and fifty thousand dollars, in cash or bond."

The banging gavel echoed throughout the courtroom. Emily and her friends watched as Alex leaned over and said something to Josh before the deputy escorted him from the courtroom. Words of encouragement perhaps.

The row full of friends sat with their eyes riveted on Alex, waiting for news of the next step, like hungry baby birds waiting to be fed by their mother. He picked up his briefcase and walked through the low, swinging door to speak with them.

"Maggie, I'll need to take you to arrange for the bail."

"I can put my house up for collateral," she offered. "I don't owe much on it."

"What about Josh?" Camille asked. "What's going to happen to him?"

"I'll do all I can to get Josh out today," he assured them all, looking from face to face. "Why don't we step out into the hallway?" he suggested, motioning toward the door with an outstretched arm. "There's another arraignment coming up."

They all filed out of the row and congregated in the wide hallway.

"I was half expectin' Lucas's momma to be here," Maggie said.

"She's probably still in the hospital," Emily suspected. "Maybe Colin and I could stop by and check on her."

"I can't even imagine walking in and finding my son lying bloody and dead on the floor. No wonder she had a heart attack," Camille said.

Isabel elbowed her and shot her a harsh glance.

"What?" Camille snapped at Isabel.

Then as suddenly as she spoke, she seemed to realize her inappropriate comment with Maggie staring at her, tears filling her tired, bloodshot eyes. "I am so sorry, honey," she gushed, putting her arms around Maggie. "Me and my big mouth."

"Seems like a good time to get to the bail bond office, Maggie. Shall we?" Alex held out his hand to her.

Camille released her embrace. Maggie took Alex's hand, and then he brushed a light kiss on Isabel's cheek as he led their distraught friend away.

"See you for dinner?" Isabel called after her husband as he and Maggie rushed down the hallway.

"I'll call you," Alex yelled back over his shoulder.

~*~

Emily and Colin arrived at St. Luke's Hospital and checked in with the gray-haired woman at the circular information kiosk in the lobby. She happily looked up Gloria's room number on the computer and wrote the room number on a slip of note paper.

"Thank you, Mrs. Grimaldi." Emily took the note from the woman and turned to walk away.

"You're welcome, dear. Bye, now."

They boarded the elevator and glided up to the third floor.

"You know that woman?" Colin asked while in the elevator.

"No," Emily answered, watching the numbers change above the door.

"You called her by name."

"It was on her name tag," Emily replied, threading her hand through the crook in Colin's arm.

"I thought maybe you knew everyone in town," Colin laughed.

"Actually, I do know her," she admitted, "or at least I did. I listed and sold her home in my first year in real estate. She was quite a talker. Nice lady, but lonely. She moved into senior housing after the house sold and I never saw her again. She probably forgot who I was."

"Why didn't you mention it to her?"

"Did you want to be stuck there, talking for the next hour?"

"Not really." He patted her hand that was still clinging to his arm.

The elevator doors opened and they stepped out. The nurse's station was directly in front of them and a young Hispanic nurse dressed in blue scrubs sat behind the counter. Emily recognized her too—she had helped the nurse and her husband buy a home a few years before. After a few words of pleasantries and greetings, they inquired about Mrs. Wakefield's condition and asked if they could visit her.

"She's doing better, she should be checking out before too long. Her daughter is with her right now."

"Her daughter?" Emily peered up at Colin with a curious look. There had never been any mention of Lucas having a sister.

"Yes, but I'm sure she won't mind you visiting. She's been here every day since Mrs. Wakefield checked in," the nurse said. "She might welcome a break."

The nurse directed them to the room number, and they thanked her as they strolled down the wide sterile hallway toward her room.

"I'll ask the nurses again when I come back, Mom. Try to get some sleep," Emily and Colin overheard the female voice say as they opened the door to the room, almost bumping into the young woman coming out.

"Fiona?" Emily questioned with surprise.

*Wait. What? Did I just hear her call Gloria, Mom?*

"Uh, Emily, hi. What are you doing here?" Fiona looked surprised, as well. "Let's talk out here," she said in a low voice, pulling the door shut. "Mrs. Wakefield is trying to sleep."

"We came to see how Gloria was doing. We didn't think anyone else would be here," Emily said.

Fiona looked up at Colin. "Hello, I'm Fiona. I don't think we've met." She extended her hand.

"I'm Colin, a friend of Emily's." He gave her hand a quick shake.

"I'm Lucas's assistant, that is, I *was* his assistant..." her voice crackled and trailed off as she began to tear up.

"Oh, I see," Colin said.

"That must have been quite a shock to hear he died, Fiona." Emily exhibited sympathy but she wondered how much of a shock it really had been. "I guess you'll be looking for another job now."

"Yes, but not 'til Mrs. Wakefield is out of the hospital. Lucas would want someone looking after his mother, don't you think? It's the least I can do. He was always good to me. He was a wonderful boss." Fiona looked past Colin and Emily. She wiped a tear with her hand as it trickled down her cheek.

Fiona's tears definitely exposed her real feelings for Lucas, confirming what Emily had already suspected— that they shared more than just a working relationship. But was she really his sister?

Should she bring it up? Emily decided against parading what she knew, hoping to learn more first.

"I'm sure he was good to you, Fiona." Emily nodded, placating her. "By the way, did I just hear you call Mrs. Wakefield, *Mom*?"

"Yes," Fiona giggled nervously. "But only so the nurses would let me see her," she replied softly, peering around as if to make sure no nurses were within earshot. "She has no one else. After I heard what happened to Lucas on the news, and that his mother had a heart attack from the shock of it, I rushed right over here. I'm glad I did—the poor woman is all alone in the world now."

"Did she know who you were?" Colin asked.

"Yes, she did. I had met her at the engagement party, so she recognized me as her son's assistant. She seemed glad for the company. After the doctors and nurses started letting me see her without questioning me, she asked me if I'd keep calling her Mom. She said it would make her feel better, since her only child was gone now. So, I'm just doing it to humor her." Fiona turned and glanced back at the door. "I feel sorry for the old woman."

"Well, if she's trying to sleep, we'd better not bother her," Emily remarked. "Let her know we were by, all right?"

"Sure, I'll tell her," Fiona promised.

Emily and Colin left Fiona standing in the hallway and made their way back to the elevator. As they passed the nurse's station, the young dark-haired nurse looked up from a file on her desk. "That was a short visit," she commented.

"Mrs. Wakefield was trying to sleep, so we'll come back another time," Colin explained.

"That's probably just as well. She hasn't gotten much sleep, she must have had a bad experience in the hospital before."

"What do you mean?" Emily asked.

"Oh, you know women—we like to keep our personal items and valuables close by. It seems she and her purse got separated when she was checked in downstairs in Emergency and we haven't located it yet."

"Valuables?" Colin questioned.

"We women keep our entire lives in our handbags," Emily said, thinking about all the things she had stashed in her own.

"Yes," the nurse agreed. "She said it had her cash and credit cards, the keys to her Mercedes—family photos."

"We'll be back to see her another time," Emily told the nurse as she and Colin walked to the elevator.

The doors opened and they stepped inside.

"What now?" he asked, taking her hand as he watched the numbers descend. "Check in with Ernie? See if they've searched the office again?"

"That's exactly what I was thinking."

# THE HEART OF LIES

# CHAPTER 21
## The Short List

"HEY, ERNIE." COLIN GAVE A FRIENDLY clap on the older detective's back, catching Ernie standing in the office building's main hall, staring into the taped-off crime scene. "We hoped we'd catch you here."

Ernie turned and noticed Emily coming up behind Colin. "Hello, Emily. You've been with this clown all day?" Ernie asked with a smirk, hiking up his pants.

"We were wondering if you found anything new," she said, staring up into the face of the tall, burly detective.

"Like a bloody paperweight?" Ernie asked. "Sorry, no. I had the CSI team comb this place from top to bottom."

"What about the dumpster out back?" she asked.

"Yep."

"Under the stairs?" Colin asked.

"Got it covered."

"You went through Fiona's desk, too?" Emily questioned.

"They did."

"That could only mean one thing," she said.

"What's that?" Ernie asked, rubbing his chin.

"The killer took it," she answered.

"No, really?" Ernie asked sarcastically, raising his eyebrows and dipping his chin. "Nothing like the obvious."

"So who are you going to search next, Detective?" she asked.

"I don't want to say just yet, but I have a search warrant in the works. It should be ready within the hour. If nothing turns up at the first place, then we'll go down the list."

"And what list would that be?" Emily arched an eyebrow at him.

Colin seemed amused by the banter between the two of them.

"Well, little lady, who do *you* think should be on that list?"

"As much as I hate to say it, I think you'll have the mayor at the top of that list."

"Well, yes. He is Maggie's brother and he might have been defending her honor," Ernie agreed. "Then again, he was the first to invest in the new resort, and we know he was here about the time Josh was."

"How do you know that?" Emily asked.

"Turns out, he was on the security tape coming in, but not leaving."

"Did you interview him?"

"Not yet. I've left messages at his office and his home, but no response. I even stopped by his house, but no one answered the door. I won't need his permission to search his house, though, once I get the search warrant.

"Okay, then there's Fiona," Emily added to the list.

"Fiona? The assistant?" Ernie's voice rose with surprise. "Why would she be on the list?"

"When Colin and I interviewed Josh he said he heard her coming down the stairs as he left. He hid under the stairs over there," Emily motioned down the hall toward the alcove under the central staircase, "and watched her pass by and go into the office. Josh said he made sure Lucas was still breathing before he left, so she would have been the last one to see Lucas alive."

"That's assuming he was telling the truth," Ernie shot back.

"Did he tell you about Fiona when you questioned him?" Colin asked.

"He did, but I figured he was just trying to cover his six, you know."

"His butt, Emily. It's a military term," Colin explained.

"Yes, I know. You use it all the time." She grinned at him. "Are you already forgetting all the time we spent together?"

She turned back to Ernie. "Well, Ernie, did you know Lucas and Fiona were having an affair?"

"I might have heard something about that. Doesn't mean she killed him. Besides, she never showed up on the security video," Ernie said.

"You do know there's a back door to this building, right? And there's no camera out there?" she asked.

"Anyone who knew that could have come and gone without being caught on tape."

"Yeah, but I can only work with what I have. Josh Sullivan is who I have admitting he was in a knock-down, drag-out fight with the victim *and* he's on tape coming and going around the time of the murder."

"Doesn't mean he killed him." Emily used Ernie's words against him and he winced. "Fiona could have been jealous of Maggie, that Lucas was choosing Maggie over her." Emily planted her hands on her hips. "Josh might be the easiest suspect, Ernie, but he can't be the only one."

"All right, who else is on your list?" Ernie asked, crossing his arms over his girth.

"Just about anyone who invested in the Whitetail Resort."

"Yeah, I had a whole passel of folks storming the police station yesterday morning, wondering where their money was," Ernie said. "How was I supposed to know where their money was? That job's far above my pay grade."

"I'd say start with the short list first, Ernie," Colin recommended. "Then, if the murder weapon doesn't turn up at any of those places, I'll help you narrow down the investor pool to possible suspects."

"The police chief isn't going to like me burning through city funds chasing after all these potential suspects," Ernie waved his arms as he spoke, "when we already have our prime suspect under arrest—especially ones like the mayor and some of our wealthiest citizens."

"Just tell him Doc Walters has identified the murder weapon and you'll leave no stone unturned in this town to find it. Besides, you're on the payroll whether there's a case or not, so you might as well be working for your pay. He'll understand that," Colin encouraged him.

Ernie nodded in agreement.

"You don't think anyone's gotten into this office since the murder, do you?" Emily asked, stepping past Ernie, peeking into the office from the barrier of the yellow crime scene tape.

"I can't imagine how. I used Lucas's key to lock it up. It's here in my pocket," Ernie replied, digging the key out.

"What about Fiona? Wouldn't she have a key?" Emily scanned the room.

"She swore to me she didn't have one, claimed Lucas was very private about the project, and didn't want anyone in the office when he wasn't here." Ernie shoved the key back in his pocket.

"And you believed her?" Emily asked pointedly, as she turned her attention back to him.

"Why shouldn't I?" Ernie asked, cocking his head and knitting his eyebrows together.

"Think about it, Ernie. If she does have a key, she could easily have gotten in and taken whatever she wanted since the murder. She probably has access to the files on Lucas's computer, too."

"I guess I could post an officer here, night and day, but I doubt the police chief would approve that," the detective suggested, pushing his hands into his pants pockets.

"My guess is that if she wanted something out of this office, Ernie, she's already been here and taken it." Emily scrunched her lips sideways in exasperation.

"She's right, Ernie." Colin crossed his arms, shifting his weight to one hip. "Are you having a techie go through his computer? There may be clues there—emails, banking information, documents—who knows."

"Well, I can tell you the CSI team took both Lucas's and Fiona's computers with them this morning. They said they'd let me know if they found anything." Ernie hiked his pants up by the waist again. "I hope there's a clue to where all that money went."

At the word *money*, Emily's thoughts immediately darted to Sully Sullivan and the hundred thousand dollars he desperately needed back. She wondered if Lucas had kept any incriminating notes in the computer about the mayor's indiscretion.

"If there isn't a clue," Ernie predicted with a slight shake of his head, "there'll be hell to pay."

~*~

"Why don't we stop at Moxie Java, Emily? I could use some coffee," Colin suggested as he drove down Main Street on his way to drop her off at home.

"Mmm, that sounds good. I could use a pick-me-up right now. I didn't get much sleep last night."

"Why not?" His voice showed concern, as he glanced in the rearview mirror, then took a quick look at the side mirrors.

"Just a lot on my mind," she watched him, "with the murder, and Maggie and Josh, and Jethro, and you—" she noticed him checking the mirrors again, "—is something wrong?"

"Don't look, but I think we're being followed."

She spun around and looked out the rear window.

"Hey, didn't I say don't look? Why do people always do that?" he grumbled.

She whipped back forward, eyes staring straight ahead. "Is this better?"

"I'm serious. Why is someone following us?" He looked in the mirror again as he pulled into a parking space in front of the coffee shop. This time the car was gone.

"Maybe it was nothing," she said.

"I guess when you turned around and looked, he saw he was made and turned off."

"What kind of car was it?" she asked.

"Black, mid-size sedan, late model, not sure which make—he was several cars back, and they're all starting to look the same these days."

"What makes you think he was following us?"

"I saw the car behind us at the courthouse, then again when we left the hospital."

"Did you get a look at the driver?"

"No, he was too far away."

"Then how do you know it was a man?" she asked.

"I don't, just assumed."

"It could be a woman then, right?"

"Could be," he conceded.

"Well, they're gone now. Let's go inside." She gave his hand a light press.

He caught her before she could draw her hand back, and he held it firmly in his, turning his head to catch her gaze. "You were talking about not being able sleep last night? You rattled off a laundry list of things on your mind, and you probably thought I wasn't listening, but I was. You tacked me on the end. What did you mean?"

Emily lowered her eyes, a little embarrassed as the memory of her dreams flashed back to her, feeling a warm sensation rush over her core. She wasn't sure how much to tell him. The dream, as much as she could remember, was romantic and sensual.

The unsettling thing about the dream was that she was with Colin, sitting on her sofa, talking, then kissing passionately—she could clearly see his face, like watching a movie—but suddenly the scene changed and he became Evan, and they were in bed.

She remembered being thrilled Evan had come back to her. He'd made glorious love to her in the dream—as if he was still alive, still her husband—and she'd felt the full pleasure of it.

In the afterglow, he lay next to her in their bed and held her in his arms, pressing his warm lips to her temple. She'd felt loved and protected, the way she had always felt with him.

Then he morphed back into Colin, who was now the one holding her and kissing her forehead, assuring her everything would be okay, sitting on the sofa. Even though her feelings for Colin were strong, she had to admit, part of her longed to have Evan back.

She had awakened from the vivid dream in a sweat, feeling confused and wrung out. How could she possibly explain that to Colin? She decided to keep it short.

"Only that you were one of the many things on my mind last night." Her lips curved with mischief, as she gazed into his sexy hazel eyes. "I've missed you and I'm glad to have you back, if only for a little while."

Emily was never one to read much into the interpreting of dreams, but she wondered if this dream meant something. Maybe it was just that she hadn't totally let go of Evan yet, as she thought she had.

She hoped learning who Evan really was would help her move on, and finally shut the door on that chapter of her life. How could she ever be happy with anyone else if Evan kept sticking his size eleven shoe in the closing door and reeling her back in?

"Just so you know, you're often in my dreams too." He lifted his hand tenderly to her cheek as he leaned over and kissed her. "Often."

# THE HEART OF LIES

# CHAPTER 22
## Searching Maggie's House

"DO YOU THINK THEY'VE SEARCHED Maggie's place yet?" Emily asked Colin as she finished her mocha cappuccino and dug in her purse to refresh her lipstick.

He checked his watch. "Maybe."

"You'd think if they found the murder weapon," she wagged the tube of lip color at him, "or anything else incriminating, Ernie would have called us." She pressed her freshly-coated lips together.

"He will. Be patient." He pitched his empty disposable coffee cup in the nearby trash can, then hers, as if he was making free-throws with a basketball.

As Emily stuck her lipstick back in her purse, her phone began to ring and she saw it was Maggie.

"The cops are here!" Maggie burst the words out without even giving Emily the chance to say hello. "They're tearin' my place apart," she cried.

While Maggie went on ranting, Emily had visions of Maggie's neat little cottage in total disarray with drawers overturned and the contents of her closets and cupboards strewn all over the place. She hoped Ernie and his people had more decency than that. Emily shot an expressive look at Colin as she scooped up her purse and stood to leave.

"Don't worry, Maggs, we'll be right over," she assured her before hanging up. "We need to get to Maggie's. I guess Ernie and his people are searching her place and she's all in a lather."

"Is Josh there?" he asked, following Emily out the door.

"She said Alex just brought Josh home, so they're both there—Isabel too."

"With all those people there, why does she need you there too?" Colin opened the car door for her.

She paused and stared at him, resting her forearm on the top of the door. "You're joking, right?"

"No, but from your tone I'm guessing I should be." He skirted around the car and slipped in behind the wheel.

"Friends are there for you, Colin, when you're going through the tough stuff," she said, climbing into her seat and closing the door. "That's what makes them friends." She shifted in her seat to face him. "You *know* how I feel about that. And what she's going through is more awful than what I had to. I can't imagine anything worse than having your child accused of killing the man you loved."

He looked at her for a moment without speaking, as if he was thinking through what she just said. Then he turned to check for traffic and pulled away from the curb.

"Weren't your friends there for you when Miranda died?" Emily recalled him telling her what he'd gone through, trying to get past the pain and move on, but she didn't remember him mentioning any friends at the time. His parents, yes, but not any friends.

"Guys aren't like girls, Emily. We don't get all emotional and touchy-feeling with each other—especially Marines. We're told to buck up, don't cry, be a man."

He checked the rearview mirror, then straight ahead. He had both hands gripping hard on the steering wheel, and Emily noticed his knuckles clenching.

She reached out and put her hand gently on his forearm, sorry she had brought up the painful memories.

"Can you imagine my Marine buddies giving me a hug?" he asked, letting out a hollow laugh. "Or my fellow officers crying with me? Or wanting me to talk with them about my feelings?"

He checked the rearview again before taking a right turn onto Maggie's street. "My family was there for me, but that was it."

"Oh, Colin." Emily sighed. She couldn't imagine not having the support of close friends.

"I don't have the kind of friendships you have, babe." His expression softened as he glanced over at her briefly, eyes glistening. "Not that my buddies don't care…"

Her chest tightened and she felt a small lump growing in her throat as she realized the pain this conversation was dredging up for him, so she decided to change the subject. She reached a hand up and lightly stroked the back of his neck. "Listen, why don't I let you take me out to dinner tonight? A little food, a little wine, a little dancing—what do you say?"

Colin pulled the car over to the curb in front of Maggie's charming little house and turned the engine off.

He gently cupped her face in his hands and studied her eyes. "I think I'd like that." He kissed her, softly at first, then more urgently, moving his hands to her back, pulling her toward himself.

When they came up for air, Emily drew in a breath and released a long sigh. "*Whew*," she exclaimed as she fanned herself with her hand.

"Emily, I—"

Colin was interrupted by a rap on the car window.

Emily whipped her head around, startled. Isabel was standing outside the car. With her cheeks flushing dark pink, Emily pushed the button to lower the window.

"Sorry to have to break up the party, kids, but you're wanted inside." Isabel put a few fingers to her lips in exaggerated pretense to cover her giggles.

Blushing, Emily climbed out, knowing her friends had seen them from the house.

Colin came around the car, as well, and they all meandered into the cottage.

"Emily!" Maggie cried out as soon as Emily came through the door with Isabel and Colin trailing behind her. Maggie ran and threw her arms around her, and Emily returned the hug, patting her friend sympathetically on the back.

"It'll be okay," Emily said, trying to soothe her friend's frazzle over having her house torn apart. She could hear voices and movement, like drawers and cabinets slamming, coming from the rear of the house, out of one of the bedrooms. "Where's Josh?"

Maggie released her embrace. "He's out back on the deck with Alex and Sully. The detective said it was best if they stayed out of the way."

"Let me go see what I can find out for you," Colin offered, skirting around the women and stalking down the hallway.

"Camille's in the kitchen. You want somethin' to eat? She's made a big pitcher of sweet tea and some kind o' sandwiches. I think she's workin' on a pie of some sort."

"No, I just had a cappuccino, but thanks."

"I'll have some," Isabel piped up as she headed to the kitchen. "I'm starved."

Colin and Ernie came down the hall, toward Emily and Maggie, with a couple of other officers behind them, speaking in low voices.

Emily wasn't able to make out what they were saying, but the tenor of their voices seemed to be friendly.

"Maggie," Ernie called out as he approached, "we're finished. Sorry for the inconvenience, ma'am."

"Did you find what you were lookin' for?" She crossed her arms tightly over her chest and glared at him.

"No, but I had to do my job and take a look. Tell Josh he can come back inside." Ernie marched out the front door with his entourage.

"I'll go tell him," Colin offered, traipsing off to join the men.

"Look at this mess," Maggie moaned.

Emily skimmed the living and dining rooms. There were things out of place, but it certainly wasn't the disaster she was expecting. "Don't worry, we'll help you put everything back the way it was."

"I'm gonna go see how badly they tore up my bedrooms," Maggie declared, stomping off.

Sully poked his head out of the kitchen and whispered to Emily. "Is my sister with you?"

"Hello, Sully. No, she went to check on her bedroom. If you like, I can—"

"No, it was you I wanted to talk to," he said in a low voice, glancing around. "Can we step out front?"

"Okay."

What was this about? She walked outside first and he pulled the door shut behind them.

"Em, you haven't mentioned our little discussion the other night to anyone, have you?" Sully gestured to Emily to move down the walkway a bit.

"No, no one."

"I'm going crazy, Em. I have no idea what to do."

"I don't know what you want me to say, Sully."

Emily believed Sully was basically a good man who had been sucked into this scheme because he was desperate for money. She always thought Lucas was a smooth operator and he obviously took advantage of the man's weak point, but what did Sully want from her? How was she supposed to help him?

"Is there any way you can find out where Lucas hid the money he stole from the investors?" His eyes were glassy and the dark circles below them told her he still wasn't sleeping much.

"The police have impounded the computers and their techs are going through them, trying to put the pieces together."

"I'm ruined, Emily. I'm just plain ruined." He hung his head and rubbed a hand across his forehead. His normally straight and confident shoulders now slumped in worry.

"Sully," she said, putting her hand on his arm, hoping to calm him down, but he drew it back sharply.

"I'm not worried for myself, you understand." He seemed to struggle to look her in the eyes. "I'll take what's coming to me. I screwed up and I'm willing to take my lumps, but this will—" His voice broke and he coughed to clear his throat, staring down at the ground. "This will destroy my wife, not to mention Maggie."

"I'll do what I can to find out where the money is, Sully, but I can't guarantee you that finding it will get you the hundred thousand back." She didn't want to believe he was capable of murder, but she couldn't deny the possibility his desperation may have driven him over the edge the night Lucas was killed.

His phone shrilled in the holster on his belt and he pulled it out and looked at it. "It's Carolyn. I have to take it." He stepped away and cleared his throat again before answering.

Emily looked toward the house and noticed Colin standing in the living room window watching them. She wondered what he had seen and if he could have overheard any part of their conversation. Certainly if he had seen her reach out for Sully's arm and him whipping it back, he would have questions.

The front door opened and Isabel came bounding down the few steps. "Hey, Em, do you have a minute?"

Emily glanced over to Sully who was walking toward her, sticking his phone back in its holster.

"I have to go. That was my wife and she's extremely upset. Apparently our house was next on Ernie's list of searches and she doesn't understand why. I guess I have some explaining to do." Sully backed away. "Tell Maggie I had to go," he said as he turned and hurried down the walkway.

"What was that about?" Isabel questioned.

"Sully's wife just called. Ernie is searching his house next for the murder weapon."

"Why are they searching Sully's house? Ernie suspects Sully might have it?"

"Not as much as he suspected Josh, but since he didn't find it here, I think he wants to rule out Sully."

"If he doesn't find it there, then who's next?"

"Fiona is my guess," Emily speculated.

"Why Fiona?"

"Why not Fiona? Remember the daggers she was throwing Maggie's way at the sales presentation where Lucas proposed?"

"Daggers?"

"Well, not real daggers, but if looks could kill…" Emily raised her eyebrows as she crossed her arms.

"A woman's scorn and all that?" Isabel said in a hushed voice, laying her hand on Emily's forearm for a moment.

"That and the money." Emily rubbed the tips of her fingers together with her palm facing up. She glanced at the living room window again, but Colin had moved away.

"Oh, yeah, the money," Isabel agreed, nodding her head.

"No one seems to know where it is, but I have a sneaking suspicion that Fiona might know. Another good motive for murder."

"Maybe we should wring her scrawny little neck until she tells us where it is." Isabel made realistic gestures with her hands and Emily could picture Fiona's neck being twisted. "Alex and I want our hundred thousand dollars back."

"You and half the town."

"Half the town?"

"Well maybe not half the town, but certainly a lot of people."

Isabel nodded her agreement.

"Anyway, what did you want to talk to me about?"

Isabel glanced around and stepped closer to Emily, speaking in a soft voice. "I heard from Jethro today. He asked again if he could see the gun, have it run through ballistics to see if it was involved in any open cases."

"What did you tell him?" Emily asked, feeling her heart beat quicken its pace. She wasn't ready to hand it over to anyone. She wanted to know more before she let it out of her control.

"I still told him you were simply talking hypothetically, but I don't think he bought it."

"I have a bad feeling about that, Isabel. I don't want to give him the gun just yet. I don't even want him to know for certain that I have it."

"Knowing him, he probably won't let up now that he knows about it," Isabel warned.

Goosebumps rippled across Emily's arms and she suddenly felt exposed standing out in the open in front of Maggie's home. "I don't know why, but something doesn't feel right. We should go inside, now."

"Why?" Isabel asked as Emily grabbed her by the arm and pulled her toward the house.

As they climbed the few steps to the front door, Emily shuddered and turned to look toward the street, then she shoved Isabel inside, hurrying in after her.

"What are you doing, Em?" Isabel moaned, catching Colin's attention.

He had been sitting in the living room, talking to Alex, enjoying a glass of Camille's sweet tea, but he shot out of his seat and rushed to Emily.

"I got an eerie feeling outside. The sense someone was watching me," she whispered to Colin.

"What's going on?" Isabel pressed.

"We think someone has been following us," Colin answered. "Black sedan, late model, not sure of the year and make and I haven't seen a license plate yet."

"Black is a very common car color in this town, Emily" Isabel pointed out.

"Maybe, but it's giving me the creeps." Emily felt a slight shiver run up her back.

Colin put his arm around her and patted her shoulder. "I won't let anything happen to you."

"I appreciate that," she told him, shrugging away from his arm, "but it's not like I'm some weak little woman." Looking back at him, she instantly realized she had probably embarrassed him a little in front of Alex and Isabel.

Fumbling with how to lighten the mood, she thought of something that might do the trick. "You're the one who nicknamed me the pistol-packin', smokin' hot lady PI, remember? You wouldn't want me doing anything to tarnish that title, now would you?" she teased, flashing him a toothy grin.

He burst out in laughter, as did Isabel and Alex.

~*~

Colin dropped Emily off at home to get ready for their dinner date and he headed to his apartment to shower and change. But first, at his insistence, he briefly went inside to help her search the house to make sure no one was there hiding, waiting to pounce.

After that, she promised she'd call him if she felt in danger, assuring him that she had him on speed dial.

He hadn't wanted to leave her alone, not after being so certain they were being followed, but she didn't want to be coddled. He thought back to when he had first met Emily. She had recently decided to leave her career as a real estate agent and had taken on her first case as a PI.

Emily was so new to private investigation that Colin had given her a bad time about her lack of experience—or so she told him. They were at a barbecue at Alex and Isabel's house, a set up by the girls. Seated next to her at the dining table, he'd felt the physical attraction was mutual. He had casually asked her what she did for a living.

"Well, I was a real estate agent, but I am currently transitioning into being a private investigator," she'd said.

He nearly choked, coughing and sputtering. He grabbed his glass of iced tea and took a couple of gulps.

"Did something go down the wrong way?" she'd asked.

"You could say that," Colin replied, coughing a few more times. "You said you're transitioning into being a private investigator?"

"Yes...why?"

"Well, you can't just be a real estate agent one day and decide to be an investigator the next."

The pleasant smile that had graced her face then twisted into a grimace, as she'd seemed to bristle at his comments. She'd picked up her plate and stomped to the kitchen. She told him later, after they'd begun dating, that on that first night he had offended her so deeply that she didn't care how handsome he was—his words were so condescending she'd had to get away from him before she'd told him what she really thought of him.

Thinking back now, Colin wondered how he'd ever convinced her to give him a chance.

Since those early days, Emily had developed into a skilled investigator and had learned to adeptly handle a gun. She was a bulldog for details and confident in her abilities. He hoped that confidence wouldn't be her undoing.

She was lovely and kind-hearted and she looked for the best in people. Yet at times she was stubborn to a fault. Altogether, these were the qualities that made her so endearing and attractive to him—in her line of work those qualities could also get her killed.

He had already been down that road once, losing a woman he loved, and he had been reluctant to go down it again, but he was so in love with Emily he couldn't help himself. He had almost told her several times that he loved her, but each time something stopped him, something got in the way. He wondered if maybe he wasn't supposed to say it, wasn't supposed to lay his heart out bare to her.

She had been the only woman in the last two years to break through the wall he had built around his heart after Miranda's death. He'd had no intention of falling for her like that, but Emily had systematically dismantled that wall with her sweetness and her charm, her vulnerability and her strength. But now that his heart was exposed and ready to love again, he was beginning to feel the need to start rebuilding the wall again.

The other night when Sully came over to her house, Emily had glossed over the truth when Colin had asked her what they were quarreling about. And earlier at Maggie's, he had seen Emily talking to Sully out front, it looked like they were arguing about something, but she wouldn't tell him what. She was hiding something from him—he knew it—but what?

How could he trust her if she was holding something back from him?

He looked in the rearview mirror as he drove. The pair of headlights in the mirror could have been anyone's, but now he was keenly aware of impending danger and was taking no chances. He abruptly pulled the car to the curb and watched as the next few cars passed him. No black sedans.

Collin rejoined the flow of traffic and headed to his apartment, just a few more blocks ahead.

Was he the object of the pursuer, or was she? Did it have to do with the murder case Emily was working, or something else?

He knew she was still following leads in her late husband's murder, even talking to a former FBI agent to see if he could be any help in uncovering Evan's true past. The agent had friends in the CIA as well as the FBI, Emily had told him, and the man had assured her he would try to find out something. Did the mysterious tail have anything to do with that?

# THE HEART OF LIES

# CHAPTER 23
## Date at DaVinci's

COLIN RETURNED TO EMILY'S bungalow, showing up with a big bouquet of daisies and freesia.

"Right on time," Emily greeted, still wearing her white silk robe and bare feet. Her hair was twisted into a pile of loose curls on her head.

"These are for you." Colin held the flowers out to her.

"They're lovely. I love daisies!" she squealed, taking them from him.

"I know."

She pushed up on her tiptoes and kissed him. "Thank you. Just let me put them in a vase and I'll be ready in a second. I just need to slip into my dress. Why don't you have a seat in the living room and I'll be right out."

He wandered over to the sofa as she hurried back to the kitchen for the vase. In a few minutes she emerged from her bedroom in a little black dress, sticking diamond studs into her ears.

He rose when she entered the room, an old habit his mother had drilled into him as a boy, he'd told her.

She glided over to him and spun around. "Will you zip me up?"

He bent his head down and kissed the nape of her neck which sent heat radiating down her spine. He slowly pulled her zipper up and kissed her neck again, just below her ear, sending a shudder of pleasure through her.

She turned to face him and met his lips with hers. "I've missed you," she whispered, looking into his sultry eyes.

"We should go," he said. "We have reservations."

There was coolness in his voice and his expression that puzzled her. She wondered what he was thinking. He was the one who kissed her first, but then it felt like he pulled back.

Once they got to the restaurant, he relaxed a bit and she seemed to have the old Colin back, warm and funny. After dinner, he led her onto the dance floor and held her close as the small jazz band played a slow song.

Emily laid her head against his cheek, closing her eyes to shut out the whole world around her. She remembered their first date at DaVinci's, when their bodies had swayed in unison, as they did now, and their attraction to each other had moved to another level.

In her thoughts, as they danced, she imagined their hands and arms curling around each other, embracing, as if they couldn't get close enough. She had forgotten how deeply and thoroughly kissed Colin could make her feel, sending her senses to places she had only gone with her husband. She willed her mind to other thoughts before she groaned out loud.

As she thought of Colin's return to Paradise Valley for good, she desired to find that soul-felt intimacy with him again. By the time he was back, she hoped to have Evan's murder solved and that disturbing chapter of her life closed. As long as suspicions and questions went unanswered, she wondered how she could ever be free to give herself fully to another man.

"A penny for your thoughts," he murmured in her ear.

"Thinking of you, enjoying the music," she responded truthfully, her eyes still shut. "I was thinking how wonderful it'll be when you come back here for good. What about you?"

"I'm remembering how good you feel in my arms, and thinking how sad it is that people wait for a tragedy to visit the ones they care about." He kissed her temple gently and held her hand close to his heart as they continued to slow dance.

The song ended but she didn't want to open her eyes and be sucked back into reality. She didn't want to let go of him. She relished the warmth of his body against hers and she felt safe in his strong, protective arms. Fighting reality was a useless endeavor, she conceded, and she forced her eyes open.

"Do you want to get out of here?" Colin asked, still holding her hand.

"What did you have in mind?" she asked eagerly.

"Let's get our dessert to go and head back to your house," he suggested. "I think we need to talk."

"About what?" Her head tilted slightly.

"Not here. I just think there's some things we need to talk about." He brought her hand up to his lips and kissed the top of it lightly, gazing deeply into her eyes. "Nothing to worry about," he promised.

"Forget the dessert, let's just go home," she replied flatly, letting him lead her out. Even though he assured her there was nothing to worry about, clearly it wasn't the romantic evening she had hoped for.

~*~

Emily walked into the living room carrying a bottle of white wine and a couple of crystal goblets. Colin was seated on the sofa, waiting for her return, leaning back and resting an arm across the top of it. After Emily poured the wine and they each had a glass in their hands, she snuggled into the curve of his arm.

"Thank you for dinner, Colin. I especially enjoyed the dancing."

"It was nice."

"How's the wine?" she asked.

"Good."

She wasn't sure what else to say, as she waited for him to bring up whatever he had on his mind. She set her glass down and laid her head on his chest, running her hand across his abdomen.

His arm slid down off the back of the sofa and hugged her gently. "I love being with you, Emily. I love everything about you—even the annoying things," he said.

*Here it comes! He's going to tell me he loves me.*

"I hope you feel the same way."

"I do," she agreed.

"But I think you're hiding something from me."

*What?*

She pulled away and sat up with start.

"What's going on with you and Sully?" he asked.

"What do you mean?" she asked innocently, looking away, knowing full well what he meant.

"There's something going on between the two of you, and I don't mean romantically. Something you're hiding from me and I want to know what it is. How can I trust you if you keep things from me?"

She wasn't sure how to reply. She had promised Sully to keep his secret as long as she could, but if she shared his secret with Colin, he would feel obligated to turn him in. The ruination of the Sullivan family would not be on her head, she decided. What could she say to appease Colin?

"You're not going to answer me?"

She shifted her body to face him. "Sully told me something in confidence and made me swear not to tell anyone."

"Not even me?"

*Especially not you.* "No one."

"You'd never agree to that if he'd confessed to murdering Lucas, so I know it can't be that."

"You're right. He is still a suspect, though, at least in my book. He had motive and maybe opportunity. Ernie headed over to his house to search for the murder weapon after he left Maggie's. I wonder what he found."

"Don't change the subject. What is the secret then?" he insisted, his eyes narrowing and his brows knitting together.

"I told you, I can't say." She stood and collected the wine and the glasses. "Don't be mad," she said as she walked out of the room.

Colin followed close behind her to the kitchen. "Does it have anything to do with the person that's following us?"

"No," she replied flatly.

"What am I supposed to think?"

"If someone told you something in confidence," she set the wine and goblets on the counter, "I wouldn't expect you to tell me, unless it directly affected me."

He planted his hands at his waist and stared at her. "You're saying it's none of my business and I should stay out of it?"

She rested her hips against the cabinet and crossed her arms over her chest. "I'm saying Sully told me something in confidence and it doesn't concern you. I agreed to keep his secret for Maggie's sake, nothing more."

She pushed away from the cabinet and stood in front of Colin, looking up into his eyes as she ran her hands up his chest. "Please, just trust me on this."

"For Maggie's sake, huh?"

She nodded.

He raked a hand through his hair and peered down at her. He appeared to be studying her lips, then her eyes. He pushed a wayward strand of loosely curled hair back from her face and slowly traced her cheek with his finger.

"Emily, you have me under your spell," he uttered, as he wove his fingers into her tousled curls. He brought her mouth to his and kissed her as she'd envisioned when they were dancing—deeply and thoroughly.

Her arms slid around his waist and up his back, and she held on as she melted at his touch.

*I guess this is turning into a romantic evening after all.*

~*~

The next morning, Emily awoke to rain slapping against her bedroom window. She ran a finger over her lips, tracing their outline, remembering the sensation of Colin's passionate kisses and she felt a wave of gentle heat ripple over her body.

Relieved to have staved off Colin's curiosity about Sully's secret, she reclined in bed wondering what else Sully was hiding. Had he been the one to kill Lucas? He certainly had motive—between Lucas stealing the money and using Maggie the way he did. And he may have had the opportunity to double back to the office after Josh left, before Mrs. Wakefield showed up. Except that Josh had said Fiona was there after him. The only thing completely clearing Sully of Lucas's murder, in her mind, would be finding the crystal paperweight in some else's possession.

As for Josh, she'd had her doubts, but it appeared more and more that he was telling the truth. If Lucas was alive after Josh left, and if Josh didn't know anything about the paperweight, then, with Fiona coming in after him, he could be innocent.

She flipped the covers back and slid out of bed. Heading for the shower, she wondered if there was any news from Ernie on his searches of Sully's and Fiona's homes. She hoped Sully was in the clear, but as for Fiona, her suspicions of that conniving woman were growing.

She didn't show up on the security camera, so she must have gone out the back way.

She could have killed him and thrown the heavy paperweight in the river that runs behind the office building. If that was the case, they may never find the murder weapon.

As she stood under the warm cascading water, she ran through the facts in her mind, searching for something she was missing.

When she turned off the water, she heard a noise, like a door closing in the distance. She threw a bath towel around her body and ran to her nightstand for her gun.

With her firearm ready, she crept through the house, searching for anyone who may have gotten in. She made her way to the back door, from where the sound seemed to emanate, and found it unlocked. She stepped onto the deck and peered over the crest of the back fence, noticing a sliver of the top of a black sedan speeding away down the alley.

*What are they looking for? They already took the photo.* Then the thought hit her. *The gun. Someone wants Evan's hidden gun. Could it be Jethro? Or someone he told?*

"Good morning, Emily." Her elderly neighbor greeted her over the fence from his covered deck, raising his coffee mug in Emily's direction.

Startled, she realized she was standing on her raised deck in only a towel with dripping wet hair—holding a gun.

"Good morning. Beautiful day," she replied, spinning around and darting back into her house. *Beautiful day?* She shook her head. *It had been raining outside.*

After making sure her doors were securely locked, Emily headed back to her bathroom to finish getting ready. As she grabbed a black, button-front blouse and gray slacks out of her closet, she noticed her everyday leather handbag sitting on the floor. Retrieving her wallet, she checked the coin purse for the bronze key she had been trying to match.

She held the puzzling key in her open palm and wondered what part it played in Evan's mystery. What other secrets would this key unlock?

Emily finished getting dressed, poured herself a bowl of cereal and climbed on a stool at the breakfast bar. She dialed Colin's number on her cell phone.

"Hello," he answered.

"Morning, babe. I wasn't sure you'd be up yet."

Hearing his voice calmed her nerves, but she wasn't sure she should tell him about someone being in her house again. He would worry, want to rush over—probably try to convince her to stay with Isabel for awhile.

"I'm awake, but still in bed, just dreaming about you," he said in a deeply seductive tenor. "Did you call just to hear the sound of my voice?"

"No. I mean, I do enjoy the sound of your voice, but I had another reason. I wondered if you'd heard from Ernie yet about his search of Sully's and Fiona's places. I'd call him myself, but I think he'd be more forthcoming with you."

"That's true. I'll throw some clothes on and go talk to him. You want me to swing by and pick you up?"

"No, he'll probably tell you more if I'm not there." She had other plans for the morning that she was not ready to share with him. "I'd love to hear what you find out, though."

"Will do."

"Colin?"

"Yes."

"I had an amazing time last night," she said.

"Me too. Makes it hard for a guy to leave."

"That's nice to hear." She wasn't sure if he meant leaving last night or leaving to return to San Francisco. Either way, she was glad to hear the words.

~*~

She decided to drive down to the bank again and revisit the safe deposit box. With someone lurking around her, she wanted to make sure the gun was safely hidden away.

Standing before the metal box the bank manager had set in the middle of the table, she waited for the man to leave before opening it. Then, lifting the lid, the fluorescent light glinted off the steel of the gun and her stomach lurched. Could Evan have used this gun to murder someone?

Emily rifled through the rest of the contents—the three passports, the Euros, the wads of cash—trying to get a handle on what any of it could mean. Picking up the rolls of bills, secured by fat rubber bands, she speculated about how much money might actually be there.

She glanced toward the door to make certain no one was approaching. Pulling the band off the first bundle of money, she began counting the bills, mostly hundreds. Soon she grabbed the second bundle and then the third, becoming more excited with each. Unrolling the fourth one, she found a note, folded several times into a square small enough to hide in the middle of the bundle.

She unfolded the note carefully and started to read the handwritten message—it was definitely Evan's erratic scrawl. Her heart pounded so hard in her chest she thought she might pass out, so she pulled out a chair and sank down onto it to finish reading.

*Dearest Emily,*

*If you've found this note, it means I'm dead. I hope you'll forgive me for keeping things from you. You may have figured out Evan Parker was not my real name. My name is David Gerard. Again, I'm sorry.*

*The gun belongs to someone who tried to kill me once, after moving to Paradise Valley. I wrestled it away from him before he got away, but I don't know who it was. He must have succeeded on a second attempt or you wouldn't be reading this note. I hid the gun because I had hoped to track him by it. (Sorry I never told you, I didn't want to worry you.)*

*The woman in the photo was a girlfriend when I worked for the Agency. Her name was Natalia Banderas. She was a natural history student at the Sorbonne that I met at a café in Paris. She was killed in France when a case I was working on went south and she was caught in the crossfire.*

*I blame myself for her death. I should have known better than to get involved with a civilian. That's why I left the Agency when I fell for you, Emily.*

*I figure the gun could belong to someone seeking revenge for her death or it could be related to another*

*case—it's hard to say. I don't know how they found me, but if you're reading this note, it means they did.*
*Keep these things hidden.*
*Trust no one.*
*I love you, Emily.*
    *Evan (aka David Gerard)*

She dropped the letter on the table and covered her face with her hands. Tears trickled through her fingers and spilled onto the paper, as the enormity of Evan's words sunk in. *David's words.*

He said he was responsible for the death of the woman in the photo. Someone killed him, likely in retaliation. Trust no one. He loved her. David Gerard.

Time came back into focus and she realized she had been there too long. Piles of cash were spread out on the table and she hadn't finished counting it. She hurriedly wiped the tears from her cheeks. Her hands flew over the table as she scrambled to gather the bills together and haphazardly rubber-band them once more, shoving them back in the metal box. She hastily refolded the note a few times and tucked it in her purse, sniffed a few quick breaths and shut the lid on the box.

"Are you almost finished in here, Mrs. Parker?" The bank manager stuck his head just inside the doorway. "I have another customer waiting."

"Yes. Thank you." She shoved the safe deposit box in its place in the wall of steel, closing the door securely. "All done."

## CHAPTER 24
### Trust No One

ON THE DRIVE HOME, EVAN'S words continued to replay in Emily's mind—trust no one.

*Trust no one?*

What about the girls? Especially Isabel. Was he saying they shouldn't be trusted? Had Isabel only been pretending to be Emily's friend all these years to gain her confidence, or to gather information? Was she working with Jethro to try to get Emily to give up the gun? Isabel's family was back east—or so she said. Emily had never met any of them. Did Isabel marry Alex when she moved here to maintain her cover?

Emily shook her head. "Now I'm just sounding paranoid."

But she couldn't stop. Emily was on a roll.

Had Colin's new job as Paradise Valley's police detective been arranged? Normally a police department would promote from within, but in Colin's case they put him at the head of the line and hired an outsider. Did he come to Paradise Valley to insinuate himself into her life—with Isabel's help—as part of the plan? After all, Isabel was the one who introduced them. Was he just trying to get close to her to get information on her late husband? Or did he truly care for her?

How much did she really know about Colin, anyway? She'd never met his parents. Had he actually gone back to San Francisco to help his mother care for his ailing father? Or was that all a lie? Was he ever even *from* San Francisco? He could be from Timbuktu for all she knew.

Emily was relatively certain she could trust Camille and Maggie. Camille had grown up in the area, as did her husband, and their now-teenage children were born in Paradise Valley. Maggie had brought Josh to Paradise Valley when he was four because her brother, Sully, and his family already lived here.

Camille and Maggie were long-time residents with deep roots in this community, but how would she know for sure if she could trust Isabel or Colin, after what Evan said in his letter. *Trust no one.*

A sick feeling curled in her stomach as she drove, and she suspected she might have to pull over and give up her breakfast.

~*~

"So what is your timeline, Ernie?" Colin asked, sitting on the edge of the detective's desk, his eyes fixed on the enormous whiteboard that took up most of one wall of Ernie's office. "Walk me through it."

Colin had gone to see Ernie to find out if he'd turned up anything of significance when he and his officers conducted their search of Sully's and Fiona's homes. They hadn't found anything worth mentioning, Ernie told him. The mayor was livid that they had upset his sick wife, not giving him notice so he could be there to prepare her.

"I got an earful about that," Ernie said.

"What about Fiona's apartment?"

"We didn't find anything out of the ordinary. She walked in on us during the search, and she was pretty steamed, too. She said she's been at the hospital with Mrs. Wakefield for most of the last few days."

"Yeah, Emily and I ran into her there. Seemed a little odd to us."

"The old woman doesn't have anyone else, Fiona said. I think it's kinda nice of her."

"Back to the timeline." Colin gestured toward the whiteboard.

Ernie rose from his squeaky, leather desk chair and sauntered to the board. "Tuesday night was the Whitetail Resort presentation where Lucas asked Maggie to marry him." He pointed to the notation of the event with his large hand. "Then Friday was the engagement party, here," tapping the board with his index finger. "Now it gets interesting."

"Give it to me," Colin encouraged.

"The security tape shows Mayor Sullivan entering the building at six fifteen, then Josh Sullivan entering at six twenty-eight. After that, Josh is seen leaving at six thirty-seven."

"When did the mayor leave?" Colin asked.

"I don't really know. He doesn't show up on the tape leaving. He claims he left through the back door and he never saw Josh. So, if he's telling the truth, I figure it had to be before six twenty-eight."

"Or he could have hidden out somewhere in the building and come back to Lucas's office after Josh left. He could have gone out the back any time," Colin proposed.

"You're right," Ernie had to agree.

"What about Fiona?" Colin questioned.

"I don't really know about her either." Ernie turned to face Colin. "She never shows up on the video tape. That darn cheapskate Pete Peterson! If he wasn't such a penny pincher we would have a camera outside the back door and one covering the parking lot, as well."

"What does she say? I mean, you did interview her, right?"

"Of course I interviewed her. I didn't just fall off a turnip truck." Ernie scowled.

"Well?"

Ernie walked to his desk and grabbed a file folder from a short stack. He flipped open to Fiona's interview report and began reading what he'd written. "She said she'd been at work all day. Late in the afternoon she went upstairs to the shared copy room, making copies of marketing materials for an upcoming presentation. She didn't know how long she was up there, but it must have been a few hours because she had quite a bit of contracts and brochures to print and collate. When she returned, she said, her outer office was dark and a light was on in Lucas's office, but the door was almost closed. So, she grabbed her purse and called out that she was leaving, assuming he heard her. She said she figured he was working on something and didn't want to be disturbed, having his door nearly shut. She said she went out the back door because her car was parked closest to that entrance."

"So there actually was no way to know what time any of this took place or if she's telling the truth, is there?" Colin asked.

"Not really, except that Josh says he heard her coming down and he hid under the stairs. He said he waited for her to pass by and go into her office before he came out the front door, and we know he left at six thirty-seven, so that would have been about the time she came down from the copy room. But that doesn't prove when she left."

"And it doesn't confirm she didn't talk to Lucas or prove she didn't see him lying on the floor," Colin pointed out.

"No, you're right," Ernie said, nodding his agreement.

"Lucas actually could have come to, then they argued about something, and she could have killed him," Colin supposed. "She could have smashed him on the head with the paperweight and took it with her, disposing of it somewhere we'll probably never find."

"Anything's possible, but why would she stick around? You'd think if she murdered the guy she would have packed up and left town by now."

"Hmmm." Colin scratched his head. "You have a point. Maybe there's something she's waiting for. Maybe she can't get at the money yet or something like that."

"Back to the timeline," Ernie said, moving again to the board. "Gloria Wakefield is shown entering at six forty-six, then Emily and Maggie at six fifty-five," he muttered, following the notations with his thick pointer finger.

"What time did the nine-one-one call come in?"

Ernie searched through the file and pressed a sturdy finger on the page. "Six fifty-five."

"Exactly when Emily and Maggie entered?" Colin asked.

"Looks that way, which makes sense because Emily said Mrs. Wakefield was on the phone calling the police when they walked in."

"I wonder what she was doing there for nine minutes." Colin pushed off the corner of the desk and stepped up to the whiteboard.

"I tried to question her that night, but she'd had a heart attack, probably from the strain of finding her son murdered. You should have seen her, she was pasty white and sweaty with blood on the front of her clothes. Emily said Mrs. Wakefield told her she'd tried to revive her son, but when she realized he was gone, she just held him for a while. She was sitting in a chair calling the police when Emily and Maggie walked in. It's a good thing the ambulance was already there when she went into cardiac arrest."

"Did you ever question her?" Colin asked.

"Yeah, I went to the hospital the next day, but the doctor wouldn't let me talk to her for long. She told me pretty much what Emily told me."

"Hmmm." Colin pressed his lips together as he rubbed his chin, his eyes studying the whiteboard. "That back door is killing us, Ernie."

"Anyone could have come in and out of it unseen. It could be someone who isn't even on this timeline," Ernie commented. "Maybe someone who invested in the resort found out they'd been duped out of a ton of money."

"My guess is this wasn't Lucas's first rodeo. It might even have been some mark from a previous scheme that found out where he was and came to make him pay."

"You really think so?" Ernie asked, arching his eyebrows.

"Anything's possible, Ern," Colin surmised, clapping his friend on the back. "Anything's possible." Colin collected his jacket off one of the chairs and headed to the door. "I promised Emily I'd fill her in, so I better get going."

"Thanks for helping me talk this thing through," Ernie said, turning away from the whiteboard.

"You're welcome." Colin paused in the doorway and turned back to face his friend. "I only wish it got us somewhere. Seems like it only brought up more questions."

"I don't know that I'm up to this job, Andrews. It should be you in this office, solving this case. This is your area of expertise, not mine. When are you coming back?"

"Soon, I hope. I hate being away from Emily and this place."

"Have you told her yet?" Ernie shot his friend a mischievous grin.

"Told her what?" Colin asked, as if he didn't know what Ernie was talking about.

"That you love her, knucklehead."

"I'm working on it."

"Work a little faster. You can't expect a great girl like Emily to wait around forever."

"I don't."

"You're not the only buck in town sniffing around that doe."

"What does that mean?"

"Just means there are other eligible bachelors in town that would love a chance with Emily."

"Like who?"

"No names," he replied with raised hands and a cock of his head, "I'm just sayin'."

~*~

Emily returned home and cautiously entered her house, the uneasy feeling of knowing a stranger had been there that morning settled on her again. She didn't want to feel this way every time she came into her house. She had to find out who the person was and put an end to this madness.

She kicked off her flats and pulled her gun from her purse, slinging her handbag over one shoulder. Moving slowly through the house, she listened carefully for any sound of movement, a creak of the old floor or a bump against a wall. She ended up in the kitchen, confident she was alone and set her gun and purse down on the breakfast bar.

Emily stood before her open refrigerator, and considered making something for lunch. As she pondered her choices, her phone shrilled in her pocket. She jumped. Her nerves were frazzled and raw. Not only was she trying to find Lucas's killer, and dealing with someone stalking her—but now she wondered if she could trust her boyfriend and her best friend.

*Trust no one.*

"Hello," Emily answered.

"Hey, Em. This is Isabel. Everything okay, you don't sound like yourself."

"Sorry, just distracted. What's up?"

"I got the results back on Lucas's fingerprints. Turns out his name wasn't Lucas Wakefield after all. It was James Belden."

"James Belden." Emily pulled a carton of yogurt out of the refrigerator and shut the door. "What else?" She grabbed a spoon from the drawer and nudged it closed with her hip.

"I thought I'd get more reaction out of you than that. Are you sure you're okay?"

"Someone broke into my house again this morning, so I'm a bit spooked by it," Emily shared. She considered filling Isabel in on the note she'd found at the bank, but thought she'd better keep things to herself for now. *Trust no one.*

"Did they take anything?" Isabel asked.

Emily thought she heard sincere concern in Isabel's voice, but what if it was just part of the act? She couldn't be sure. Should she tell her about seeing the black sedan speeding off down the alley? She hesitated to divulge too much until she was certain that Isabel could be trusted.

"No, not that I can tell," Emily replied. "Enough about me, what else did you learn about Lucas, besides his real name?" Cradling the phone between her shoulder and her jaw, she ripped off the cover to the yogurt and pushed the spoon down into it.

"He has a record, spent some time in prison for petty theft. He was arrested for fraud a few years back, but he disappeared while out on bail and he never went to trial."

"Fraud, huh? That's no big surprise. Seems like a lot of people are not who they say they are." She sank down onto a chair at the kitchen table.

"Are you sure you okay?" Isabel asked. "Like I said before, you don't sound like yourself."

"You know…if he isn't actually Lucas Wakefield, then his mother couldn't really be Gloria Wakefield, could she?"

"I had that same thought. She's probably still his mother, but if she knew he was going by a different name and she went along with the name change, then she's probably part of the scheme. Or at least she agreed to go along with it so he could pull it off. Imagine using your mother like that."

"We'll need to find out for sure, won't we?" Emily said. "I think I'll drop by the hospital and pay that woman a visit."

"I'd come with you, but I'm stuck at work."

Another call was beeping through Emily's phone and she saw it was Maggie. "Sorry, Maggie's calling. I need to take this call. We'll talk later?"

"Sure."

"Hello, Maggie?" Emily answered, feeling confident this was one person she could trust.

"Emily, I'm so glad I caught you. I wondered if you'd go to the hospital with me. Carolyn is runnin' a fever and had a major episode. Sully rushed her to emergency."

"Absolutely—but where's Josh?"

"Colin came by and took him to lunch. He said he wanted to talk to him, maybe about the case or somethin'. I tried callin' him, but he must have his phone off in the restaurant."

"I'm at home right now, so I can be there in just a few minutes. Don't worry, Maggs, I'm sure she'll be fine." Emily knew Maggie had had enough stress in her life—she didn't need to add more.

# THE HEART OF LIES

# CHAPTER 25
## A Surprising Discovery

SULLY HAD PHONED MAGGIE to let her know Carolyn had been examined by an ER doctor and moved to the third floor. So, Emily and Maggie took the elevator up and an attendant at the nurse's station directed them to her room.

The women rushed to the assigned room and found Sully sitting by his wife's bed, holding her hand. Her eyes were closed and she looked peaceful as she rested.

Sully turned toward the door, looking like he'd slept in his clothes. He dragged himself to his feet and put a finger to his lips, signaling them to be quiet.

"She's sleeping," Sully whispered, stepping close to his sister. "The doctor got her temp down and he thinks she'll be fine with some rest. We can't upset her or get her excited."

"How are y'all holdin' up?" Maggie asked him.

"Let's step out in the hallway," he suggested, looking over his shoulder at his sleeping wife.

The women nodded in agreement and went out into the hallway.

"This whole Lucas thing has taken a toll on all of us," he snarled. His face softened when he looked at Maggie. "Sorry, Sis, I shouldn't have said that. It's been hardest on you, most of all."

She shook her head and waved off his apology. "No, this is all my fault," she asserted in a weak and shaky voice. "I'm the one who brought Lucas to Paradise Valley. If I hadn't met him on that dang datin' site, none of this would've happened."

"No, Maggie," Emily assured her, putting an arm around her shoulder. "This is not your fault. Tell her," she said, looking at Sully.

His eyes grew big and his face flushed, as she forced him onto the hot seat.

"Tell me what?" Maggie asked.

"No, Em, it'll just hurt her more," Sully pleaded, shaking his head.

"If she knows the truth, I think it'll help her see him for who he was," she insisted, "then she can stop blaming herself."

Maggie waited with wide, expectant eyes and a straight face, as though she was bracing for the worst.

"Maggie," he said, gazing at the floor and then off to the right, pausing as if he was struggling to find the right words to tell her what she needed to know, without divulging the entire truth of his indiscretion.

"I'm waitin'," she said coolly, crossing her arms as she tapped her foot.

He slowly brought his eyes to meet hers. "I hate to tell you this, Sis, but Lucas told me he only responded to your dating site profile to get to me."

"What?" she screamed.

"Keep your voice down," Sully ordered, glancing up and down the hallway.

"What on earth does that mean?" Maggie demanded.

"Not that he wasn't attracted to you, but he had this resort scam planned out for months and he needed an in with someone who could influence people in this town to invest in his project. He said he saw the advantages of your being the mayor's sister, so he chose you. I'm sorry, Maggie. It kills me to have to tell you that."

"Y'all knew about this scam and didn't tell me?" she sputtered.

"I only knew because that SOB made it a point to tell me so he could blackmail me. It was after he asked you to marry him and after I had already invested in the project that he told me. He said I had to help him or he would ruin you and me both."

Maggie seethed as she stepped close to her brother and poked a finger in his chest. "And y'all think this whole mess turned out better than if you'd been honest with me?"

Sully looked past Maggie to Emily, with a pained look on his face, as if pleading for her help. She shook her head, unwilling to rescue him.

Emily knew the whole story and she watched him squirm as he attempted to skirt around the truth of his embezzlement. Maybe he didn't want his sister to know out of shame or maybe it was out of self-preservation. Either way, it was clear he was dancing around the issue, looking for a way out.

"Emily!" The familiar young Latina nurse approached, holding a large, beige leather purse.

Sully's hunched shoulders relaxed, as he had been given a temporary reprieve.

"We finally found Mrs. Wakefield's purse," the nurse said, "but she checked out this morning. We tried calling her, but the phone rings in her purse. So I wondered, since you're a friend of hers, could you make sure she gets it?"

"A friend?" Emily mumbled to herself, a bit taken aback by being called the old woman's friend. "Sure," Emily agreed. She was happy to jump at the opportunity to go through that woman's things and find out who she really was. "I'll track her down and make sure she gets it."

"A woman's whole life really is in our handbags." The nurse laughed as she handed it over. "That one feels like it has everything in it but the kitchen sink."

Emily grabbed it by the handle and her wrist strained under the surprising weight.

"Thanks, Emily," the nurse sang as she hurried back to her station.

Emily tried to control the smile that threatened to break across her lips as she anticipated the opportunity to dig through the woman's private things. "I need to go," she announced. "You want to stay here with Sully," she asked Maggie, "or do you want me to drop you off at home?"

"Uh, I'm going to be here for quite a while sitting with Carolyn, so you probably want to go with Emily," Sully quickly suggested.

Emily understood his desire to end the painful conversation with his sister. He was probably worn out, she assumed, from all the fancy footwork.

"I'll go with Em," Maggie said, stepping toward her brother, standing toe to toe, "but don't think for one single minute this discussion about Lucas is over, mister."

"No, I know you better than that." Sully sighed and backed toward the door, rolling his eyes as he pushed it open with his back and disappeared into his wife's room.

The girls strolled to the elevator and boarded, watching the doors glide shut.

"What does that woman have in this purse? My gosh, it must weigh fifty pounds," Emily complained, unzipping the top of it as the elevator floated down.

"Emily, it's not nice to be goin' through her purse. Isn't that against the law or somethin'?" Maggie frowned, watching Emily open it.

"I hate to tell you this, Maggs, because you think the best of everyone, but Gloria Wakefield isn't who you think she is."

"What are y'all talkin' about?"

Emily did not reply, but a wide grin spread across her face as she pulled out a white handkerchief wrapped around a hard object. The cloth was stuck to the crystal with dried blood. She held the thing out in her palm and peeled back the corners of the hanky.

Maggie gasped.

Emily had found the bloody mountain-shaped paperweight. She had found the murder weapon.

"Oh, my. There's a gun in here, too," Emily exclaimed.

~*~

Emily and Maggie drove directly from the hospital to the police station, phoning Colin on the way.

"I knew you'd figure this case out, Emily," he commended her. "I'll call Ernie and let him know you're on your way to see him. Do you have any idea where Gloria is?"

"Not yet, but I think I know a way to find her. Just be aware, though, she may not have been the one who put the paperweight in her purse."

"What do you mean?" he asked.

"The purse was out of her possession for days. Any one of our suspects could have taken the purse, tucked the paperweight inside, and hid it in an out-of-the-way place in the hospital."

"You could be right. Ernie said Mrs. Wakefield was pretty out of it when the paramedics took her away."

"And if the ER was busy that night, someone could have snatched the purse and not been noticed."

"One of those people might have been Fiona," he suggested.

"My thoughts exactly. I wondered why she was hanging around the hospital so much with a woman she barely knew. Maybe she hid the purse somewhere in the hospital and it got moved before she could retrieve it, so she had to stay at the hospital and search for it."

"Besides, why would Gloria want to kill her own son?" Colin asked.

"I don't know for certain that he was her son."

"What are you talking about?"

"I'll explain when I see you. You need to get off the phone and call Ernie. I'll call you back in a bit with my plan."

"Ay, ay, Captain," he joked as he hung up.

"Maggie, I need to drop you at home."

"No, I want to come. This sounds like it's just gettin' good," Maggie exclaimed, rubbing her hands together. "Please let me stay, Em...please. I deserve to know."

"That would save some time. All right, but you'll need to stay out of the way, okay?"

"Yes, ma'am."

"Do you have Fiona's cell phone number?" Emily asked.

"I do, right here in my phone. Just a second and I'll have it for ya. See, I can be helpful to y'all." Maggie smiled as she searched her phone, probably the first time she'd smiled in days.

"All right, Maggie, don't get full of yourself now."

Maggie turned her phone screen to Emily and Emily punched the numbers into her own phone.

"Hello?" Fiona answered and Emily swore she heard a hint of suspicion in her voice.

"Fiona, this is Emily." Emily worked to keep her own tone casual and upbeat.

"Hello, Emily. I'm surprised to hear from you."

"I was at the hospital earlier and one of the nurses found Gloria's purse. Isn't that great?"

"Yes, Mrs. Wakefield will be thrilled."

"The nurse said Gloria had already checked out and you were taking her home."

"That's right. I'll let her know you have it."

"I can drop it by your place, if you like, but it won't be for a while, I have to go somewhere first. But then I can come by," Emily offered.

"Hold on, let me ask Mrs. Wakefield what she wants to do. I'm sure she'll want to get it back."

There was a silent pause for a couple of minutes. Emily put her hand over the phone and whispered to Maggie that she was on hold. Fiona returned to the phone.

"We're leaving for the airport shortly. Mrs. Wakefield wants to go home to recuperate in her own bed."

"I don't blame her. After what she's been through, she probably wants to get out of here as soon as she can." Emily tried to act natural and sympathetic, avoiding any sense that either woman was under suspicion.

Emily wondered how the woman could get a plane ticket and get on the flight without her driver's license and credit cards that were still in the purse she'd lost. Then she realized Gloria and Lucas must have had someone who provided their fake IDs before and could easily have done it again over the last few days. If Gloria, or whoever she was, got on that plane with a new identity, the authorities may never find her again.

Perhaps Fiona bought the plane ticket. Maybe she bought two.

"Like I said, I have to make a stop first, but then I'd be happy to meet you somewhere."

"Near the airport?" Fiona asked. "Mrs. Wakefield doesn't have much time before her flight."

"Sure." Emily realized she only had a short window to catch them. "There's a Copper Kettle Restaurant not far from the airport. Why don't I meet you there in an hour, in the parking lot?"

Emily overheard Fiona whisper to Gloria. "In an hour at the Copper Kettle parking lot near the airport?" Then

Fiona came back on the line with Emily. "Yes, that would be fine. We'll see you in an hour."

# THE HEART OF LIES

# CHAPTER 26
## The Set Up

EMILY AND MAGGIE RUSHED INTO Ernie's office, finding Colin already there, perched on the corner of Ernie's desk with his arms and ankles crossed. Emily had phoned Colin after speaking to Fiona and had alerted him to the time crunch and shared her plan to ensnare the killer, whichever one it turned out to be.

"We don't have much time." Emily breezed through the door first, carrying both her purse and Gloria's handbag. "Here's the murder weapon." She dug the bloody crystal paperweight out of the older woman's handbag, still wrapped in a white cotton handkerchief, and she slid it into a plastic evidence bag Ernie held open for her.

"I guess luck was on our side." Ernie sealed the bag and marked it with black permanent marker, laying it in a drawer in his desk.

"We still don't know for sure who put it in the purse, but when I reveal the paperweight, the reaction of these women should tell us if it was one of them. Have you got it for me, Ernie?"

He reached into the same drawer where he had placed the other one and pulled Maggie's out. "Sorry about having to take it, Emily. You understand, I was—"

"Just doing your job, Ernie. Yeah, I know."

He handed it to Emily and then locked the evidence drawer.

Emily pulled it out of the bag. "Do you have that ketchup and white hanky I asked for, Ernie?"

"Right here." He handed the items to her and watched with interest, as did Colin and Maggie.

Emily smeared ketchup on the jagged tips of the mountain-shaped paperweight with her finger and set it on the desk in the middle of the hanky to dry. "Colin, can you wire me?"

Colin chuckled at Emily's decoy murder weapon and pushed off the desk, grabbing the box of equipment from behind it. Emily lifted her blouse, with her back to Ernie, and Colin began taping the wire in place.

"Ernie will be in the van listening while you're talking with Fiona and Gloria," Colin said, "waiting for your signal to move in."

"I have the surveillance van out back and I've already briefed a handful of officers on the plan," Ernie explained, fastening his bullet-proof vest. "They'll be in place around the restaurant's parking lot, out of sight, before Fiona and Gloria arrive. As a matter of fact, they should already be on their way over there."

"What about me?" Maggie asked. "I want to come."

"It's too dangerous," Colin warned, continuing to affix the wire to Emily.

When he had to run the wire up through her bra, she slapped his hand away playfully. "I think I can manage the rest of it myself."

She took the mic out of his hand and threaded it under the front of her bra, then taped it to her chest.

"She can keep you and me company in the van," Ernie proposed. "She'll be safe enough."

Colin shot Emily a questioning look.

Emily shrugged and rolled her eyes as she stuck the earbud into her left ear. "I guess it's okay, as long as she's quiet and stays out of the way, but it's not my call. Ernie?"

"I'll be quiet as a church mouse," Maggie promised. "Y'all won't even know I'm there."

"Looks like you're in." Ernie grinned at Maggie.

"Let's load up." Emily pulled the handkerchief around the paperweight, the same way she had found the murder weapon, and stuck it in her own purse.

~*~

"I'm pulling in," Emily said out loud, making sure her microphone was working. An eerie shiver crept up her spine as she anticipated what she was about to do.

As Emily pulled into the Copper Kettle Restaurant's parking lot, she spotted Fiona and Mrs. Wakefield sitting in Fiona's silvery blue sedan. Emily remembered seeing her driving it into the office parking lot a few times.

Glancing around, Emily noticed the restaurant's parking lot was almost empty, grateful there were few patrons in the place in the middle of the afternoon.

"We hear you loud and clear," Ernie replied in her ear. "I'm starting the recording."

Emily swung her white Volvo into a parking space near the sedan. If she had to wrestle one of them to the ground, she wanted to leave an empty space between them for room to maneuver. "I'm getting out."

She climbed out of her car and slung her own purse over her shoulder, carrying Gloria's bag in her hand. As she cautiously approached the women, they got out of the car to meet her. Her heart was thudding so loudly she was certain Ernie could hear the pounding through her microphone. A bead of sweat trickled down her temple and she inhaled deeply, wondering if her plan would work.

*Breathe, Emily, just breathe*

She plastered a friendly smile on her face.

*You can do this.*

"Hi, Fiona, Mrs. Wakefield."

"Oh, Emily, thank you so much for bringing me my purse. I hope it wasn't too far out of your way." Gloria took the bag from Emily. Turning, she set it on the hood of the car. "You're simply a doll, Emily." She dug around inside of the purse as if she was looking for something, slowly at first, then erratically. She spun back to Emily with a pallid, rattled look on her face.

"What's wrong?" Fiona asked at the older woman's odd behavior.

"Is this what you're looking for?" Emily held up the bloody paperweight enrobed in a white cotton handkerchief.

Gloria's eyes grew as big as saucers, then narrowed to a scowl.

"I don't understand. Why did you bring that?" Fiona's eyebrows wrinkled together in obvious surprise. "Isn't that Lucas's paperweight, from the office? And why does it have blood on it?"

Gloria did not answer. She stood stony silent, glaring at Emily.

It was clear to Emily that Gloria was the culprit. "Fiona, this is the murder weapon. I found it in Gloria's purse."

"What?" Fiona screeched and turned to Gloria. "Momma? The murder weapon was in your purse?"

"Momma?" Emily asked. "Gloria is *your* mother?"

"You killed my husband?" Fiona wretched.

"Lucas was your husband?"

"You stupid girl! Shut up!" Gloria ordered between clenched teeth.

"No one was supposed to get killed, Momma, especially not my husband." Angry tears began to flow down Fiona's cheeks.

"You were the mastermind of this whole resort scheme?" Emily asked.

Gloria reached behind her and pulled the gun out of her bag and pointed it at Emily. "No one would suspect an old lady."

"Get ready to move." Emily heard Ernie give the order to his men.

"Not yet," Emily mumbled.

"Hold up, fellas," Ernie ordered.

"What did you say?" Gloria demanded, pushing the muzzle of the gun against Emily's chest.

"I said, not yet—that anyone would suspect an old lady." Emily raised her hands in surrender. "But they will."

"Momma, you killed my husband!" Fiona cried. "How could you?"

"Pull yourself together, girl, if you want to get out of this. Now do as I say. Pop the lid on the trunk," Gloria ordered Fiona.

"It was all her idea," Fiona babbled as she opened the car door and reached for the trunk release. "She planned everything, even having me move here first so *Lucas* could hire me."

"Stop talking, you idiot!" Gloria yelled, as she wagged the gun and motioned for Emily to move to the trunk. "Get in."

"Are you going to kill me like you killed Lucas?" Emily asked, with her hands still raised. Adrenaline was pumping through her veins as she worked the two of them to confess on tape.

"We're moving in." Ernie's voice came through the ear piece.

"No!" Emily erupted, wanting to stop the police from charging just yet.

"Stand down, men," Ernie ordered.

"Let Ernie send the guys in now," Colin snapped into Ernie's mic.

"I'm not doing that." Emily gave Gloria a steely stare, trying to force her hand.

"I'll shoot you right here, then." Gloria glanced around to see if anyone had eyes on her. She pressed the gun against Emily's chest.

"Momma, no!" Fiona shouted.

In a split second, Emily's hands flew down on the gun and she deftly twisted it out of the woman's hand in one smooth motion. Gloria's eyes grew big and she raised both hands. Taking a small step back, she bumped into the car as Emily pointed the gun at her.

"Please, Emily, don't shoot her!" Fiona pleaded.

"Move in, boys." Emily lowered the gun, keeping her eyes on the old girl. "You don't think I'd hand you a purse with a loaded gun in it, do you?"

"Go, go, go!" She heard Ernie give the order. Several police officers raced from behind the shrubs and took Gloria and Fiona into custody, as a dark blue-and-white squad car squealed into the parking lot.

Maggie came running from the van and threw her arms around Emily. "Oh, Em, that was great."

"Good job, Emily." Ernie stepped in with congratulations, her slender hand completely swallowed in his bear claw. "But you had us all plenty worried when the old bat pulled the gun. I wish you'd let us in on the fact the gun was empty."

"Sorry, Ernie, but what would have been the fun in that?" She grinned at him, then glanced around, looking for Colin. She saw him climbing out of the van and moving toward her, wiping the back of his hand over his eyes.

Ernie saw him, too. "He was real concerned about you, Em," he whispered.

Colin stepped up and scooped Emily into his arms. His eyes were moist as he studied her face, then he drew her in so tightly she could hardly breathe. "What were you thinking?"

Maggie peeked up at Ernie and they turned and wandered away.

"I thought I was doing my job," she squeaked.

"Ernie wanted to send in the troops, but you kept saying no. When that woman pulled the gun on you, I thought I was going to lose you."

"I'm okay, see. I'm okay." She gently cupped his face in her hands, meeting his gaze.

He loosened his hold a bit, but kept her firmly in his arms. "Don't you ever pull a stunt like that again."

"I can't promise that." Peering into his misty eyes, she saw genuine concern, forgetting for now her suspicions of him. "What I will do is promise to let you know the whole plan next time. Deal?"

"That's better than nothing, I guess." He lowered his eyes and looked away. His jaw twitched against her palm as her hands still tenderly cupped his face. She brought his gaze back to hers. She kissed him softly and she tasted the saltiness of a tear that had trickled down his cheek.

They stood for a minute clinging to each other, as if the rest of the world had faded away. Hearing a ruckus in the background, they suddenly seemed to remember they weren't alone and stepped apart. A uniformed officer was struggling to help Fiona into the squad car.

"I want a deal!" Fiona hollered from the back of the cruiser. "I'll tell you everything!"

"Shut up, Fiona!" Gloria screamed as Ernie aided her into the back seat on the other side of the vehicle.

Emily and Colin looked at each other. Chuckling, they wandered over to check out their suspects.

Emily approached the side of the cruiser where Gloria sat and she rested her forearm on top of the open car door.

"Just between you and me—no mic this time—why did you have to kill Lucas?"

"I guess it doesn't matter now if I tell you. It was because he and Fiona were going to disappear with all my money."

"You took a man's life because he was stealing your money?" Emily clarified, crouching down to her level.

"Oh, it was more than just that. It wasn't just because he was stealing my money—he was stealing my daughter," Gloria grumbled. "They would have run off and I'd never see her again."

Emily grimaced.

She had seen how her beloved daughter was turning on her, but she noticed Fiona was now listening to what her mother was saying.

"She's not much," Gloria admitted with a note of sadness, "but she's all I have."

Then her voice and her eyes turned steely cold. "No one takes what belongs to me and gets away with it. No one."

# THE HEART OF LIES

# CHAPTER 27
## The Game of Love and Trust

IT DIDN'T TAKE LONG FOR THE MURDER charges against Maggie's son to be dropped, and Camille and Isabel offered to throw a big backyard party at Isabel's house to celebrate. Maggie, of course, accepted. She had been so worried about losing Josh to prison, she decided that every moment was precious.

The night of the party arrived and Emily stood in her somewhat-organized walk-in closet, trying to choose a memorable outfit for the evening. This party would also be a farewell to Colin, who needed to return to San Francisco in the morning, so Emily took special care to look her best.

She slipped into her tight white jeans and pulled a black off-the-shoulder, short-sleeve sweater from the rack and slid it on. "There." She fluffed her tousled blonde curls with her fingers and turned in the full-length mirror to admire her derriere. Gold hoop earrings and a little lipstick and she'd be done.

She checked her watch and realized she still had a few minutes to kill before Colin would arrive to pick her up. Traipsing through the house shoeless, she headed to the breakfast bar to fetch the lipstick out of her purse. While painting on the soft pink lip color, she noticed the stack of mail that she'd brought in earlier. She might as well sort the mail while she waited.

The first envelope was her credit card statement, the second was a misdirected piece of mail—Mr. Terrence Biggens. She marked it with "wrong address" and set it aside. The third envelope was addressed to Evan, from All Security Storage, likely a promotional piece.

She was about to toss it, but there was something about it that made her suspect it might not be junk mail after all. She slid her finger under the flap and ripped the envelope open. Unfolding the paper inside, she glanced over it. It was a letter on company stationery, informing Evan that the advance payments on his storage unit had run out and payment for the next twelve months was due the first of the following month.

Why would he have a storage unit?

*The key!*

Like a light bulb going on in her head, she thought of the brass key. Dare she hope her mystery was solved? She checked the coin purse on the side of her leather wallet to make sure it was still there—it was.

She didn't have time to do anything about it right now, but tomorrow she would definitely go and check it out. She tucked the letter back in the envelope, folded it in half, and shoved it in her bag.

## THE HEART OF LIES

If her stalker broke into the house again while she was gone, she wasn't giving him the address and unit number of the storage place. Whatever was in the unit was obviously something Evan wanted kept secret. And as for Colin, she thought it best not to mention it to him either—not yet anyway—not until she was certain she could trust him.

A sharp rap on the front door brought her running from the kitchen. Seeing the crown of his dark brown hair, she took a calming breath and swung the door wide. Holding it open for him, she struck a sexy pose with one hand on her hip. "Hello, Colin."

His eyes lit up and an enthusiastic smile spread across his face. "Wow, Emily. You look amazing."

He stepped over the threshold, unable to take his eyes off of her. "Babe, you are smokin' hot."

"That's the look I was shooting for," she teased, pushing the door shut.

"Well, you definitely hit your target—three shots to the heart." He groaned, throwing his right hand over the center of his chest and wincing as if he'd been hit.

*He better be the real deal, 'cause this man is definitely stealing my heart.*

She stepped closer and his arms were instantly around her, drawing her into him. He lowered his face to hers, their lips brushing softly together, sending a thrill down her body.

Her off-the-shoulder sweater invited his next kiss there, as his lips tenderly grazed her sensitive skin.

She couldn't stop the little shiver that danced up her spine.

He leaned back, studied her face, as if he were memorizing it. When he closed his eyes, she knew what was coming next and she steadied herself against him as his soft warm lips claimed hers.

"You are such a distraction, Emily."

"Is that a bad thing?"

"I wouldn't say that. It's just that I was going to tell you something when I came in, but when I saw you, everything else flew out of my mind."

"What did you want to tell me?" Emily ran her hands over his broad shoulders, feeling the pulsation of energy streaming between them.

"It may be nothing, but there was a black sedan parked across the street. I'm pretty sure it was a BMW."

Emily ran to the window and peeked out through the blinds. "No one there now."

"It drove off when I swung into your driveway. I wasn't able to see the license plate."

"What about the driver?"

"Tinted windows, but it looked like a woman to me—light skin, dark hair pulled back, sun glasses."

"Isabel drives a black BMW." She hadn't meant to say it out loud.

"Why would it be Isabel?"

"Oh…um, maybe she was coming to see me," Emily covered, "but decided not to bother when you pulled up. She probably figured we wanted some alone time, you know, after everything that's happened."

It was probably best to keep her doubts to herself.

Colin looked puzzled. "Wouldn't Isabel be at her house right now? I mean, the party is at her place tonight."

"Yes, of course, you're right. I don't know why I said that." She tightened her hold around Colin's waist and laid her head on his chest, hiding her face. "The only other person I know with a black BMW was Delia McCall's late husband, but that would be silly to think it was her."

"The car would have passed to her when he died, right?"

"Yes. I think it was owned by her company, so she may still have it, but why would she be following me?"

"We don't even know if it was her, or if it was even the same car. It could have been someone innocently visiting one of your neighbors, couldn't it?"

"I suppose." Emily leaned back and looked up at Colin. "This is your last night here, so let's not talk about it anymore tonight." Emily was determined to shut the thoughts of the black car out of her mind for the evening. She had more urgent things to concentrate on.

~*~

Camille planned the party menu around Josh's favorite foods. He deserved it after all he had been through, thinking he was coming home for a happy wedding and then getting caught in the middle of a murder.

The food was beyond amazing—her rib-eye steaks, baby back ribs, grilled salmon, fresh corn on the cob, homemade sides, juicy watermelon and four different desserts. Maggie and Josh couldn't stop raving.

Emily helped Camille bring the food out to the serving tables on the sprawling stone patio. And as Emily walked through the French doors with a platter of ribs, she noticed Colin standing on the lawn, talking to Alex and Jonathan. He looked in her direction when she stepped out and a warm, bright smile lit up his face. She returned the smile and moved to the serving tables.

As she set the platter down and covered it with foil, Sully had walked up beside her. She turned toward him. The dark circles under his eyes were gone, replaced by the refreshed look that comes with a good night's sleep.

"I want to thank you again for what you did, Emily. I will never in a million years be able to repay your kindness."

Earlier that morning, Emily had gone to the bank and taken a hundred thousand dollars in cash from the safe deposit box. She had delivered it to Sully in secret, to replace what he had borrowed from the city's retirement fund before the auditors showed up.

"I didn't do it for you, Sully." She leaned a hip against the table and crossed her arms, glancing around to make sure no one could overhear them. "You screwed up royally, but your family shouldn't have to pay for your mistakes."

"You're right, I did." He peered over his shoulder, then back at Emily. "My back was against the wall and I chose the easy way out. Or, at least, what I thought would be the easy way."

"I guess you don't have to take all the blame. That Lucas Wakefield was a pretty convincing character."

"I could think of a few more colorful names to call him," he chuckled nervously.

"In all fairness, I should thank you, Sully. If you hadn't been honest with me, we wouldn't have known there was a scam."

Having knowledge about his illegal act and keeping his secret had put her in a difficult position, but she was willing to forgive him for that. "Fiona could have gotten away with millions in investors' deposits."

"So they recovered the money?"

"Yes, the deal Fiona cut included giving up the money. Apparently, when she saw Lucas on the floor of his office she thought he was dead, so she ran. But Josh had only knocked him unconscious. Fiona said she went directly to Lucas's house and used his laptop to transfer all the money from the Paradise Valley Bank to an account they had in the Cayman Islands."

She patted Sully on the shoulder and grinned. "So, you see, it won't take you a million years to repay me," she smiled. "Just until the funds are released. And, thanks to you, all the investors will be getting their money back too."

"I'm relieved to hear that. So, I'm just curious, when did Gloria kill Lucas?"

"According to what she said in her statement, Lucas was crawling up into his chair when she walked in. She could see someone had left him bloody and beaten. They argued over the money and his running off with Fiona, and she said she was so furious that she grabbed the jagged paperweight and cracked him on the head. She believed whoever had beaten him would end up paying for her crime."

"Go figure." He grinned and shook his head.

"When Maggie and I walked in, she was sitting in a chair calling the police. She was sweaty and breathing hard, with blood on her clothes. She'd said she had tried to revive him and we bought it."

"She had a heart attack too, right?"

"Apparently the sweat and hard breathing was from that old woman lifting Lucas out of the chair and dragging him back to the floor. Of course, that's how she got his blood on her, too."

"He had to be at least two hundred pounds."

"She admitted she was calling the police when we walked in only because she'd heard a car door slam outside and someone opening the big wooden doors in front. She was ready in case someone walked in on her. She heard Maggie and I walking in and made it look convincing. It was pretty quick thinking on her part."

"Do you think she faked the heart attack?" he asked.

"Not according to the doctor. A woman her age, having just killed a man and then lifting two hundred and some pounds—it was almost inevitable."

"Well, I better let you get back to what you were doing, Emily. Looks like the food's almost ready. I just wanted to thank you again for the money. It's been deposited and hopefully not missed."

"You're welcome." She watched as he walked back to his waiting wife, seated in a wheelchair at one of the tables, and she wondered if he had shared with her any of what he had done. Probably not. He may have wanted to, but knowing Sully, he'd take it to his grave before he'd burden his wife that way.

Emily glanced over at Colin again, as he continued to shoot the breeze with the guys. She watched him for a few minutes, imagining how wonderful it would be when he moved back to Paradise Valley. They could have lots of get-togethers with their friends. They could be a real couple.

A niggling doubt pricked at her again. She was ready to give him her whole heart, but how could she until she knew for certain he could be trusted? In light of the warning Evan had written in his note, she had to be sure about Colin before she jumped in with both feet.

Emily spotted Ernie refilling his drink at the outdoor bar area. She wandered over to chat with him, thinking it would be an ideal opportunity to find out if Colin truly was who he said he was and put her suspicions to rest.

"Hey, Ernie," she greeted, patting him on the shoulder. "Are you enjoying the party?"

"Can't wait for the baby backs—my favorite." He licked his lips and rubbed his hands together. "Not just that, though, Em. This party was a great idea, celebrating our putting the real killer behind bars and all. Uh, I mean with your help and Colin's, of course."

"You've been a good friend to Colin, almost like a father." Emily rested her hand on Ernie's forearm for a moment.

"Yeah, I've known Colin since he was a kid. His dad and I have been buddies for a long, long time."

Having Ernie confirm their longtime relationship helped put Emily's mind at ease. Now that he was being open with her, maybe she could get him to help her with one more thing. "Since you know our boy so well, Ernie, maybe you can answer something for me."

"Shoot," he said, taking a sip of his drink.

"Why does Colin come unglued when I'm in the throes of solving a case? Is it because of her? Because of Miranda?"

"I suppose it is. When that Gloria woman pulled the gun on you, he just about came out of his skin. I could see the horrified look in his eyes—he was reliving Miranda being gunned down in the line of duty all over again."

Emily nodded her head.

Ernie shook his. "It's going to be a long time before she's out of his head."

"What about his heart? Is Miranda still in his heart, too?"

"You can't just forget someone you were so madly in love with that you were ready to commit your life to them. You should know that, Emily. Will Evan ever totally be out of your head—or out of your heart?"

She paused, thinking about her late husband. "No, you're right."

"It doesn't mean you don't eventually move on and find a new love."

"Do you think Colin loves me?"

"I know he does. That knucklehead just needs time to find the words to say it."

"Foods ready!" Camille shouted across the yard. "Everyone grab a plate and serve yourselves."

"You don't have to tell me twice." Ernie's eyes glowed with anticipation as he bolted from Emily's side.

The crowd was small, just twelve in all—Emily and Colin, Camille and Jonathan, Isabel and Alex, Sully and Carolyn, Ernie and his wife, Maggie, and the guest of honor, Josh.

Alex had set up a couple of long tables on his patio, parallel to each other, which Camille topped with white linens and centerpieces of chunky ivory candles and greenery.

It was a balmy July evening and the sun was beginning to set. Strands of tiny white lights twinkled in the shrubbery and lattice work that surrounded the patio and the yard.

Once everyone filled their plates and took their seats, Alex clinked the side of his wine glass to garner his guests' attention.

"I would like to offer a toast to our guest of honor, Josh." Alex lifted his glass. "We thank you for your brave service to our country, first of all—"

The friends interrupted his speech with a shower of spontaneous applause.

"We are here tonight to celebrate your freedom, Josh," Alex acknowledged as he held his glass out toward Josh, "thanks to Emily, Colin, and Ernie."

Another round of applause broke out.

"Lift your glasses, everyone."

"Here! Here!" the crowd erupted, lifting their glasses and taking a drink.

Josh stood and sincerely thanked everyone for believing in him. "I'm not much for making speeches. My life was uncertain enough after making a couple bone-head decisions." He looked at Maggie. "Sorry, Mom."

She reached up with a sympathetic smile and gave her son's hand a squeeze.

Josh's eyes looked back at his friends. "Anyway, I just want to say I appreciate you all," which drew more applause.

"I hear Colin will be leaving us in the morning, so I especially want to thank him and Emily for the help they gave Detective Kaufman in finding the real killer."

While another wave of applause rang out, Colin leaned over and kissed Emily lightly, which drew whistles from some of the guys.

"Now," he raised his glass, "let's eat before all this good food gets cold!"

The food was consumed and enjoyed. Josh had piled his plate high with some of everything—twice. He patted his stomach and complained he'd have to drop five pounds, which pleased Camille and made his mother laugh.

The sun had long set as the party wound down. As the guests began to leave, Emily and Isabel helped Camille with the cleanup. Maggie offered, but the girls insisted she spend the time with her son.

As Emily and Isabel worked together in the kitchen, scraping dishes and wrapping leftovers, they chatted about their men and the future.

"Hey, did you hear about Maggie's engagement ring?" Isabel chuckled as she finished scrubbing a baking dish.

"No, what?" Emily asked with interest. She grabbed a soft towel and began drying the pans Isabel had already washed.

"Turns out the diamond was a fake."

"Go figure, just like the fiancé."

"Did I tell you Maggie is going to Hawaii anyway?" Isabel tore off a long sheet of plastic wrap. "The honeymoon trip was already paid for—Lucas's parting gift I guess—so she's trying to decide who to take with her. Interested?"

"That's wonderful. I'm glad she's going, but I'm not sure this is the best time for me to go."

Was Isabel trying to get rid of her? Evan's ominous words continued to ripple below the surface of their friendship.

"Besides, don't you think Maggie will feel weird in the honeymoon suite?" Emily asked.

"No, she wouldn't be staying there. She said she was able to change the reservations to a two-bedroom suite for the same price. I think you ought to go. You could use a vacation." Isabel tore another sheet of plastic wrap from the roll and covered a small tray of ribs.

"What about my house?" Emily wondered if she should go off and leave her house exposed.

"What do you mean?"

"Someone keeps breaking in and searching for something. I can't just go off and leave it."

"Would you like me to housesit for you? *Su casa es mi casa*." Isabel stuck the leftover ribs in the refrigerator.

"I'll have to think about it...besides, Maggie hasn't even invited me."

"She will."

Emily hated going through life not trusting anyone, especially Isabel. She missed her old life when she trusted everyone, without question, until they gave her reason not to. Life was so much more fun and gratifying when she could hold her man and her circle of friends close and share everything with them. She needed to get back to *that* life.

"Emily?" Colin stood in the middle of the French doors.

She turned at the sound of her name and smiled at the familiar voice that was so sensual and smooth.

"Your man is calling you." Isabel grinned and elbowed Emily as she dried a glass pan with a soft cloth.

"Could you step out here, please?" He held his hand out to her.

Emily looked to Isabel.

"Go. I can finish up here," Isabel encouraged.

Emily floated over to him, or at least that's how she felt. The warmth from his hand comforted her as he led her through the patio and across the lawn. He stopped in a darkened corner of the yard, where an ornate concrete bench sat among the bushes adorned with twinkle lights.

"Let's sit."

She nodded and sat expectantly on the bench, not knowing what was coming.

He sat close beside her, their bodies touching, still holding her hand.

"I'm leaving in the morning, and I didn't want to wait a second longer to tell you—"

"Are you sure you wouldn't rather have this conversation at my house…in private?"

He tipped his head and shrugged a shoulder. "That would probably be better, but if I don't get these words out, I might chicken out."

"I don't understand. What are—"

He raised his hand for her to stop talking. "You have to stop doing that and let me finish."

She smiled at him and made a gesture as if she was buttoning her lips.

He nodded once and took a deep breath. "Emily Parker, you have torn down my defenses and captured my heart. There is nothing else to say but that I love you—totally and completely."

Pinching her lips closed she looked at him for permission to speak.

He grinned and nodded.

"Oh, Colin," she gasped breathlessly, tears of joy rushing to her eyes. "I love you, too. You don't know how anxiously I've been waiting to hear those words. You could not have said them more perfectly."

He stood to his feet and she followed his lead. His hand gently cradled her cheek, he gazed into her eyes—into her soul. He wove his fingers through her hair and tugged her face toward his. Passion vibrated between them as they stared into each other's eyes.

"I couldn't leave tomorrow without telling you how I felt. I promise you, Emily, I'll move heaven and earth to come back to you."

Her hands embraced the strength of his back as he enveloped her completely. His kiss was so tender, so deep, she thought she would faint from the deluge of emotions flooding her body. He scooped a muscular arm beneath her knees and literally swept her off her bare feet.

Emily fixed her watery eyes on him as he carried her in his arms. She searched for the words to tell him she would wait for him, but her mind was swirling so deliriously that it made her dizzy. No words would come. All she could do was drape her arms around his neck and kiss him again.

"My heart is yours," he declared. "Please don't break it."

## THE END

*Thank you so much for reading my book,*
***The Heart of Lies.***
*I hope you enjoyed it very much.*

*Debra Burroughs*

The highest compliment an author can get is to receive a great review, especially if the review is posted on Amazon.com.

Keep Reading for a Preview of
***The Scent of Lies***

## THE HEART OF LIES

### *The Scent of Lies - Excerpt*

# PROLOGUE

*Life has a way of not turning out the way you had planned, of taking you down roads you had no intention of ever going. Moving in unexpected twists and turns, some bends in the road make you stronger, while others can destroy you.*

\*\*\*

The housekeeper gasped and split the air with a horrifying, ear-piercing scream as she burst in on the mister and misses. She discovered the wife, clothed in a creamy satin robe, with her dark wavy hair floating around her shoulders, kneeling beside her husband's almost lifeless body, which lay on the plush living room floor.

The wife stared wide-eyed at the bloody kitchen knife in her hand.

"Help me," the man whispered almost imperceptibly, terror shimmering in his eyes, trying to grab hold of her wrist.

"Ricardo," she cried, shaking her head violently. "No! This can't be happening."

"Delia..." he gasped.

"Call nine-one-one, Marcela!" the misses ordered.

"Marcela," the man hissed with his last breath.

"Oh, my God, Miss Delia!" Marcela stood paralyzed.

"For heaven's sake, Marcela, go call the police!" the wife screeched. "I think my husband is dead!"

## The Scent of Lies - Excerpt

# CHAPTER ONE
## Friends, Husbands, and Lovers

"BABE, IT'S TIME TO GET UP," Emily Parker muttered sweetly.

She had awakened to the brilliant morning light streaming in through her bedroom window and sleepily stretched her arm out to her husband's side of the bed, searching for his warmth. At the sensation of the crisply cold sheets, her hand recoiled. Flipping back the covers, she sat up and shook her head. After all this time, she still caught herself reaching out for him.

It was late on a lazy Saturday morning. Sleeping in was so unlike her, but after tossing restlessly in the night, with imaginings of her late husband floating in and out of her mind, she hadn't drifted off to sleep until the wee hours of the morning.

Now, after a quick shower, she stood in the middle of her overflowing walk-in closet, looking for the perfect outfit to wear for her celebratory lunch with her best friends. She surveyed the racks of clothes, unable to make up her mind. She glanced at his side of the closet. Everything was exactly as Evan had left it that final morning six months ago. Still, she had not yet been able to bring herself to get rid of his things—she had her reasons.

From time to time she would drape herself in one of his shirts or sweaters just to smell his scent and to feel him near. Today would be one of those times.

Compelled as she was by her dreams, her need to feel close to him won out over her need to hurry, and she buried her nose in a navy blue hooded sweatshirt hanging on the rack. Breathing in the lingering trace of his rugged masculinity brought him vividly to her mind. She could not help herself—she still missed his crooked smile, the warmth of his strong arms wrapped around her and how glorious he made her feel when they made sweet love.

Emily pulled it off the hanger and shrugged it on, hoping for some emotional comfort. Then she zipped it up and stuck her hands in the pockets, surprised to feel the crackling of paper in one of them. She pulled out a small folded note. Her curiosity piqued, she opened it. In blue ink, the name Delia and a phone number was scrawled in the cursive penmanship of a woman.

*Who is Delia?* She frowned at the note. Was she a client, an informant, a friend? A lover? As fast as the thought about this female possibly being Evan's lover popped into her head, she pushed it right out again. She'd always had complete trust in him. They had been absolutely happy, until the horrible night he was killed.

## The Scent of Lies - Excerpt

He'd never given her any reason to suspect he had ever been unfaithful to her. *I'm just being silly.*

Her cell phone beeped a reminder and she realized she had spent far too long wallowing in Evan's clothes. Now she really needed to hurry and get dressed for the lunch date with her girlfriends. They were celebrating five years from the day they all first met and began what had grown into a close circle of friends. If she was late, they'd never let her hear the end of it.

She grabbed a pair of white slacks that she knew would show off her slim figure and added a silk turquoise blouse that everyone said set off her dazzling greenish-blue eyes and her head of tousled honey-blonde curls. Emily stepped into her trendy Espadrilles, grabbed her oversized leather purse, and flew out the door.

The girls had chosen the Blue Moon Café—the current hotspot in Paradise Valley—because of the nouveau-gourmet menu and outdoor patio with a breathtaking view of the river. Emily pulled her white Volvo sedan into the crowded parking lot. As she approached the front door, she spotted her party seated under a large blue umbrella at a table on the patio. It was a good choice. They could enjoy the breezy spring air and the sound of the rushing water flowing by while they toasted their anniversary.

Emily made her way through the bustling restaurant, lively with laughter and conversation, and as she stepped out onto the sunny patio, the girls were chatting away.

"Hello, ladies." She eased the empty chair out and tucked herself into the group.

"Emily, you're late," Camille Hawthorne pointed out. Camille was like a mother hen to the girls, being a bit older than the others, having a daughter in high school and a son in college. Her looks would not give her age away, though, and she wore her fiery red hair in a cropped and spiky style. But her husband, Jonathan, a sales executive for a local corporation, was the only one who could get away with calling her *Red*.

"I know, I know. I'm sorry. I got a little distracted and lost track of the time," Emily apologized as she scooted her chair closer to the table.

"We were just concerned, Em. You're never late," Isabel Martinez added, tossing her long dark curls over her shoulder. As an FBI financial analyst, Isabel was matter-of-fact and to the point. Usually dressed in a business suit, she appeared relaxed in her jeans and designer t-shirt.

"Well, all y'all know, I'm the one who's always late," Maggie Sullivan admitted in her fading Texas accent, twirling a strand of long blonde hair around her finger. Truthfully, Maggie had a bad habit of being late for almost everything, except for appointments with her clients. As a fitness trainer, she was obsessive when it came to two things—her looks and her business. Emily always thought she resembled a blonde Barbie doll.

"You said it, not me," Isabel replied to Maggie, while looking over the menu.

"Is everything all right?" Camille leaned over and asked Emily in her caring, maternal way.

## The Scent of Lies - Excerpt

"Yes, I'm fine." Emily placed her napkin in her lap. "I was standing in my closet trying to decide what to wear and—"

"Yes, I've been known to stand there for half an hour trying to figure out what to put on," Camille interrupted.

"Well, it wasn't just that." Emily's gaze lowered briefly. "I couldn't make up my mind so my eyes wandered over to Evan's clothes hanging there, calling to me. I just had this overwhelming desire to be close to him."

"Oh, I see. Well, that's understandable." Camille grabbed hold of Emily's hand, giving it a light squeeze.

"It probably sounds silly," Emily turned to Camille, "but I smelled one of his sweatshirts and it brought a rush of memories back. So I put it on. The lingering scent of his clothes—it's like he's still there with me. I miss him so much, Cam." She felt herself being pulled back into the moment and her hand fluttered to her chest as her eyes gazed out over the water. "It made me remember how I felt when he held me, when he kissed me...when he made love to me."

"Oh my, Emily!" Camille giggled nervously, fanning herself with her napkin, as her face warmed to the tones in her red hair.

"The time just slipped away," Emily said apologetically. Coming back to the present, she looked down at her menu, a blush of embarrassment heating her cheeks.

"You'll never get over him if you don't start letting go. It's been six months, hon. Don't you think you should start packing up his things so you can at least begin to move on with your life?" Camille asked. "Evan was a wonderful man, Em, really he was, but he's been gone for a while now. You're still here and you deserve to be happy." Camille looked around the table for support. "Don't you agree, girls?"

"Yes, Em," Maggie agreed, "it is time you start havin' some fun again, girl."

"Maybe she's not ready." Isabel came to Emily's defense. "Six months isn't that long, really."

Emily looked over at Isabel and gave her a smile of appreciation. "What I'm ready for is food." She was also ready to change the subject. Her gaze flew around the busy patio. "Where's our waitress?"

A young woman appeared at their table just in time to rescue her, pad and pen in hand. "Hi, I'm Katie. What can I get for you ladies?"

"I'll have the sea bass." Emily jumped in first.

"That sounds good," Camille agreed, closing her menu and looking up at the young woman. "How is that prepared?"

"Uh, sautéed, I think," she replied sheepishly. "Sorry, I'm new here."

"Don't pay any attention to her," Isabel said to the waitress, frowning at her fiery-haired friend. "She's a chef. Can you tell? I'm sure however it's cooked will be fine."

"I guess you're right, Isabel," Camille conceded. "I will have the sea bass."

## The Scent of Lies - Excerpt

"Just a garden salad for me, please, Balsamic vinaigrette on the side," Maggie ordered. "I have to watch my girlish figure, y' know." She patted her flat tummy.

At thirty-six, Maggie was obviously proud that she still possessed the slender figure she'd had when she was a twenty-two-year-old starlet in Hollywood. As a young single mother, she had moved there from Texas with her little boy, trying to get her big break. Unfortunately, her big break never materialized. So, leaving her deadbeat husband behind, she and her son moved north to Idaho, where her brother and his family lived. She'd worked hard, learned all she could about fitness and training, eventually opening her own business as a personal trainer.

"Hmmm," Isabel tapped her finger against her lips. "I'll have the Kobe beef burger, and I'd like the seasoned oven fries with that."

"Isabel, that's a ton of fat and calories," Maggie pointed out.

"I know, but it tastes so good. Besides, I ordered it just to bug you," Isabel teased.

Maggie grimaced. Isabel carried a few extra pounds and often promised Maggie she'd work to take them off when she had time, but she never seemed to find the time.

"You are what you eat, Isabel," Maggie told her for the thousandth time.

"Well, maybe I should eat a skinny person, then." Isabel flashed a mischievous smile. "But I don't see that on the menu."

"There's just no point talkin' to you about it." Maggie rolled her eyes and shook her head.

"Exactly."

The waitress collected the menus. "Thank you, ladies. I'll be back shortly with your food."

Emily took a sip of her ice water. "So, what's new in your world, Camille?"

"Oh, I have the most exciting news!" Her face lit up and her hands flitted about. "You know that big candle business that's expanding and building all those new warehouses and offices down by the railroad tracks?"

"You mean Heaven Scent?" Isabel offered.

"Yes, that one. They're also expanding into a new line of bath products and they're having a big launch party. Guess who they hired to plan and cater the event?" Camille wore a smug grin.

"Hmmm, let me think." Isabel tapped her chin mockingly.

"Me, you silly." Camille patted Isabel's arm. "Oh, I'm so thrilled!"

"Wow, that's a big job. Kudos," Maggie said.

"Yes, Camille, that's fantastic," Emily chimed in. "Congratulations!"

"Thank you all. It's going to be fabulous." Camille declared, smiling broadly. "But enough about me, what's going on with the rest of you?" She glanced from face to face.

"I'm happy to report my fitness trainin' business is goin' well. Oh, and I just have to tell y'all that I have the most gorgeous, delicious new client. He's tall, dark and oh-so-handsome," Maggie gushed.

## The Scent of Lies - Excerpt

"Sounds like you'd like him to be more than a client, Maggie." Isabel raised a questioning brow.

"Maybe." She giggled.

"He's not married, is he?" Isabel asked suspiciously

"I don't think so. He doesn't wear a wedding ring and he hasn't mentioned a wife."

"It's best to make sure, Maggie, before you start getting all dreamy over him," Camille warned.

"Yes, Mama," Maggie deferred sarcastically.

"Well, I'm working on a big case," Isabel said. "Do you remember the man who was arrested for killing that family in eastern Oregon, George Semanski? The FBI is building a case against him, and he'll be going to trial in a few months. I'm headed out of town in the next few weeks as part of the work I'm doing on it."

"Oh my gosh, Isabel," Maggie exclaimed.

"Why is the FBI involved?" Emily asked.

"Because after killing the family, Semanski kidnapped the neighbor's kid—or I should say he *allegedly* kidnapped the neighbor's kid—who happened to be at the house during the murders and took him across state lines, which makes it an FBI matter," Isabel explained.

"That makes sense." Maggie nodded.

"What about you, Emily?" Camille asked.

"Me? I guess my real estate business is doing *okay*." The word okay carried a hint of uncertainty.

"Not great?" Camille asked, sticking out her bottom lip sympathetically.

"More like limping along," Emily answered. "I have a young couple I'll be showing homes to later this afternoon. I'm *really* hoping they buy today, because Lord knows I could certainly use the commission right now. A couple of my deals are set to close in the next few weeks—fingers crossed—but there are not nearly as many as there use to be."

"Are you still paying the lease on Evan's old office?" Isabel asked.

"Yes, I'm on the hook for another year, unfortunately. And because it is such an old building, subleasing is almost impossible. The building is practically vacant as it is."

"Ouch," Isabel responded.

The server returned with a plate in each hand and another server followed with the rest of the food, setting the plates down in front of each of the women.

"Mmmm, it smells delicious." Isabel took a whiff of her burger and fries.

"Yes, it does, and everything looks great too. Thank you, miss," Camille told the young waitress.

"I'll be back to check on you ladies a little later. Enjoy." Katie moved on to another table.

As soon as she left, Emily gently clinked her knife against her water glass a few times to bring her friends' attention to her.

"First, before we dig into our lunches, I want to say thank you all for picking this lovely restaurant for our celebration. I'm so enjoying the sunshine and the river view," Emily began, and all the other women nodded their agreement.

## The Scent of Lies - Excerpt

"Secondly, in honor of celebrating the five-year anniversary of the day we met and began our friendship, I would like to make a toast." Emily raised her glass. The other women picked up their glasses, as well. "I want thank each of you for being there for me when I needed you most this last year, after Evan died, and for us all being there for each other through the ups and downs of our lives. You are the best friends any woman could have, and I love you all!"

"Here's to all of us!" Camille chimed in and they all took a sip of their drinks. "Thank you, Emily. That was so sweet." She patted Emily on the leg. "Now girls, why don't we take a walk down memory lane?"

"What do you mean?" Emily asked, as she picked up her fork to dig into her fish.

"It's been a long time since the special day we're honoring today. I thought it would be fun to talk about it. Do you girls remember that day we first met?" Camille glanced around the table. "And why you were there?"

"Of course," Isabel answered, munching on one of her oven fries. "You were holding a cooking class at your catering shop and we came to learn how to cook."

"You were all such newbies," Camille chuckled, picking up a forkful of sea bass. She had just opened her catering and event-planning business in a small warehouse space and had offered a series of cooking classes to start bringing in money and to meet potential new clients. Her idea worked brilliantly and it pushed her business forward to success. Those classes also brought this circle of women together and they had grown to become best friends.

"I remember that I took the class to learn how to cook somethin' other than my mama's down-home recipes," Maggie recalled, sprinkling a little dressing on her salad. "I had hopes of impressin' and snaggin' me a successful man, but it hasn't quite worked out that way." Maggie offered a mock pout. She was still single, much to her chagrin. But her little boy was now grown and had recently enlisted in the Marines, and she was financially independent and providing for just herself.

"Evan and I were newly married," Emily recalled, "and I wanted to learn to cook for his sake. I was the worst cook ever, and you really helped me, Camille. Of course, I was so bad it wouldn't have taken much to make me better," Emily admitted, which drew laughter from the girls.

"And what about you, Isabel?" Camille asked.

Isabel set her burger down and cleared her throat while she wiped her mouth with her napkin. "Alex wanted me to take the class. He loves to cook and he's quite good at it. With him being a lawyer and me working at the FBI, we both work pretty long hours. I took the class for him, so we could have fun cooking and creating dishes together on the weekends. It's hard to believe it was five years," she patted her tummy, "and fifteen pounds ago." A nervous giggle escaped her lips.

"Hey, wasn't there another woman in that first class with us?" Maggie asked.

"Yes, Abby something?" Emily said.

## The Scent of Lies - Excerpt

"Abby Randall," Isabel replied. Her memory was sharp and clear. As a financial analyst, she had a habit of paying close attention to details.

"Yes, poor Abby," Camille said.

"What do you mean, poor Abby?" Emily and Maggie said in unison, then turned and grinned at each other.

"Oh, you haven't heard?" Camille sat up straight and leaned forward.

"Heard what?" Maggie's interest appeared to be piqued, obviously expecting a tidbit of juicy gossip.

"Now, don't tell anyone you heard it from me, but she and Bob are getting a divorce." Camille leaned back a little, as if to let the information sink in.

"Divorced? Abby and Bob always seemed so happy," Emily commented. "I ran into them a few times around town, at a restaurant or at the store. They seemed like things were going well. I wonder what happened."

"Well, I'm not one to gossip, but I ran into her one day at the mall and we chatted for a few minutes," Camille explained, picking at her sea bass. "Abby had taken classes from me several times, so I probably knew her better than any of you. She told me she thought they were blissfully happy and everything was going along beautifully. They have three children, you know, a nice home, and lots of friends—she said their life was perfect. Then one day, out of the blue, Bob told her he had fallen in love with another woman and he wanted a divorce. I'm sure it just broke that poor woman's heart."

"How can that happen?" Emily asked. "I mean, how can you think everything is perfect, and then out of the blue your husband doesn't love you anymore?" At the mention of another woman, her mind went to the note she'd found in Evan's pocket just an hour or so earlier. She shook her head to get rid of her burning desire to know who Delia could be.

"Abby said he traveled a lot for work, so he obviously did whatever he wanted to while he was away," Camille surmised, "and then pretended to be the perfect husband and father while he was home. I guess he just got tired of pretending."

She paused and her expression became sullen. "Now that I think about it, my Jonathan travels a lot for work too. You girls don't think that could happen to us, do you?" Camille's upbeat and carefree tone turned serious and she sounded genuinely worried.

"No, Camille," Maggie replied, putting her hand over Camille's. "You need to stop talkin' like that."

"My word, you and Jonathan are perfect together. I don't believe for a moment he would do that to you, or your children," Isabel told her. "Please, Camille, just kick that horrible thought out of your head right now."

"I agree, Camille. That's just plain crazy talk," Maggie added.

Emily didn't say anything. She was caught up in her own thoughts, wondering if something like that could have happened to her and Evan. Like poor, unsuspecting Abby, Emily had thought she and Evan were blissfully happy too, but now she was having doubts. And if it could happen to her and Evan, it could also happen to Camille and Jonathan, couldn't it?

## The Scent of Lies - Excerpt

Even in the refreshing spring breeze, sitting in the open and expansive outdoors, Emily felt like she was suffocating under all the talk about unfaithful husbands, and she felt compelled to cut and run. "I'm sorry to cut this lunch short, ladies." Emily abruptly stood, pulled a twenty dollar bill out of her wallet, and laid it on the table.

"But you've hardly touched your lunch," Camille said in surprise.

"I need to meet those clients I was telling you about. I'll talk to you all soon."

Looking stunned and speechless, Maggie, Camille, and Isabel stared in silence as Emily dashed a quick glance behind her then hurried away.

# THE HEART OF LIES

**THE HEART OF LIES**

The Scent of Lies - Excerpt

# CHAPTER TWO
## A Ring of Deception

EMILY REGRETTED HAVING TO LIE to her friends, but she simply had to get out of there. All that talk about *seemingly* happy marriages and *possibly* unfaithful men was more than she could stomach. After that conversation, she was even more driven to discover who this Delia woman was.

At least it was true that she did have an appointment to show homes later that afternoon, but since she had a couple of hours to kill before then, she'd decided to head over to Evan's old office. One way or another, for her own peace of mind, she had to find out if her late husband had been cheating on her.

Emily pushed open one of the large wooden doors and entered the lobby of the historic gray-stone building that sat on Main Street in the heart of Paradise Valley, a quaint, picturesque town situated just to the north of Boise,

Idaho. After walking down a short hallway, she stood before the door to her late husband's office. The opaque window in the door still bore the lettering Evan Parker, Private Investigator.

Fidgeting with the key in the old keyhole, it finally gave in and unlocked. She pulled in a deep breath to steady herself as she entered, standing still for a moment, surveying the room. She had not been to this office since Evan was killed in it. The murder had gone unsolved, and she had been left to wrestle with the unknown.

Heart-wrenching memories came flooding back to her, and she was momentarily paralyzed by them. Evan had been found shot to death here, in the corner by the file cabinets, a single gunshot to the back of his head. The local police had no suspects and no prospects.

There had been a fat stack of cash with a rubber band around it found in a locked drawer of his desk, totaling five thousand dollars. Since the money was still there, the authorities figured it wasn't a robbery, but it did cause them to wonder why he would have that much cash with him. Emily wondered too—on more than one occasion.

Since Evan had been shot at fairly close range, with no sign of a struggle, the police assumed the killer must have been someone he knew. They had questioned every one of his clients after finding their names when they searched his computer and the file folders in the cabinet.

The police had even investigated Emily to rule her out. Fortunately, she was having dinner with the girls at a restaurant when it happened, so she was almost in the clear. There was always the possibility, the detective said, that she'd hired it done. Maybe her paid killer, the

## The Scent of Lies - Excerpt

detective suggested, was someone posing as a new client that just hadn't made it into Evan's records yet.

In time, the police decided Emily probably had nothing to do with her husband's murder. So, with no real clues, old Joe Tolliver, the town's only detective, eventually gave up and filed it away as a cold case. The pile of cash was eventually released to Emily.

It wasn't that Paradise Valley could not afford to hire another detective, because it had grown into a largely affluent community. In the last ten years or so, it had become known for its million-dollar homes built along the Boise River, and there were an ever-increasing number of five- and ten-acre horse property subdivisions gobbling up the surrounding farmland.

The reason for having only one detective was simply that the mayor and city council members saw no need to waste the taxpayers' money. Paradise Valley hadn't had a murder in more than twenty years—until Evan was killed.

*Focus*, Emily ordered herself, remembering why she was there. Her mission was to find out who this woman, Delia, was.

Sitting down at Evan's old metal desk, she rummaged through it, searching for anything that had this woman's name on it. She came up with nothing. Then she went through all the folders in the file cabinet. Again nothing. She checked the calendar in his computer and even did a total search of the hard-drive for the name—still nothing.

Her eyes moistened and her throat tightened a little when she noticed the framed photo on the desk. It was a picture of her and Evan, smiling and snuggling in happier days. Picking it up, she lovingly traced his face with her finger. Her heart missed his sandy brown hair and piercing blue eyes.

Emily spied the cross-directory phone book on top of the file cabinet and gently set the picture down. She grabbed the directory and flipped it open on the desk. Digging around in her purse, she found the slip of paper that showed Delia's phone number. She laid it down next to the book.

Scanning the pages as she ran her index finger across them, she located the number in the directory and read the name Delia McCall. The name sounded vaguely familiar. "Delia McCall," she muttered several times, but she couldn't place it. So she decided to be brave and dial the number. She needed to know this woman's connection to her husband.

The phone on the desk had been disconnected long ago, so she made the call from her cell phone.

"Hello." The woman's voice was low and sultry.

"Is this Delia?" Emily asked nervously

"It is. Who is this?"

"This is Delia McCall?" Emily asked again, her heart thudding in her chest.

"Yes. Who is this?" the woman insisted.

"This is Emily Parker, Evan Parker's wife."

"Oh, Emily, yes, Evan had mentioned you." Delia's voice changed to a lighter tone.

"Evan mentioned me?" Emily was stunned by her comment. She wondered why her husband would be talking to this woman about her.

"Yes, several times."

## The Scent of Lies - Excerpt

"I have to know, Ms. McCall, what was your relationship with my husband?" Emily held her breath for the answer.

Delia stuttered and stammered, obviously caught off guard. Was she hiding something?

"Well?" Emily pressed, irritated by the woman's evasiveness. If it had simply been a business relationship, why would she not just come out and say it? She decided to ask what she was really wondering. "Were you having an affair with my husband?"

We hope you enjoyed that excerpt from
### The Scent of Lies
A Paradise Valley Mystery, Book One

*Available on Amazon.com
in eBook and Paperback*

Turn the page for an excerpt of
### Three Days in Seattle

## *Three Days in Seattle - Excerpt*

# PROLOGUE

WHITNEY BEGAN TO STIR from a deep sleep, waking to find herself in pitch-black darkness, her hands and feet bound. She tried to move, but she couldn't. Yanking against the ropes proved useless, as the bonds were fastened to something solid.

Her head began to pound and her breath was coming in short gasps, but she couldn't get much air. Something was over her mouth—duct tape, maybe? She didn't know or care, she just needed air.

She struggled to scream, but the only sound she could make was a high-pitched moan.

*Where am I? What's happening to me?* Murky thoughts slogged through her disoriented mind. *Maybe I'm dreaming*, she thought. *Wake up, wake up, wake up!* But it was not a dream.

The sound of something scraping the floor made her freeze. She tried to listen, hear if someone or something was coming, but her heart thudding in her ears made it hard to concentrate.

A door creaked open, and she blinked as the harsh light hit her eyes. Was someone coming to rescue her? Or was it her captor? She decided not to risk it and shut her eyes, going limp, and hoping her pounding heart would not give her away.

## Three Days in Seattle - Excerpt

# CHAPTER ONE

"FORGET IT, NIGEL! It's been a very long day. I'll finish up in the morning. I just need to soak in the tub for a while and get to bed. I will call you first thing tomorrow, I promise." Kate McAllister clicked off her cell phone and set it on the bathroom vanity, exhausted after her hectic photo shoot in the Hollywood Hills ran late into the evening.

The warm water in the claw-foot tub was beckoning her. She was anticipating being enveloped by its warmth, letting it soothe away the stress of the day. Sticking one painted toe in the water, she checked the temperature before getting in. *Perfect*, she sighed softly.

As she was about to drop her fluffy white robe to the floor and step into the bath, the cell phone shrilled on the vanity behind her. "Shoot," she muttered under her breath. "If that's Nigel again, I'm going to kill him."

A slight frown creased her brow as she turned and glanced at the Caller ID. She recognized the area code was for Seattle, where her baby sister Whitney lived, but if it were her sister, the phone would have shown her name and not *Unknown Caller*.

Peering up at the wall clock, she saw the time was ten-forty-five pm. *Why would someone I don't know be calling me this late?* Tension began creeping up the back of her neck. *No one calls this late just to chat.* She reluctantly picked up the phone.

"Hello?"

"Kate, this is Suki. I'm sorry to call you so late." The woman on the other end of the line rattled on, "But, I, well, I need to—"

"Whoa. Slow down. You said your name is Suki?" Kate questioned, raising an eyebrow.

"Yes, you know, Whitney's roommate."

"Oh, yes, sorry. I didn't recognize your name. Now, slow down and tell me – what's wrong, Suki?"

"Whitney's gone missing."

"What? When?" Panic began to set in. Kate's thoughts began flying in a thousand different directions, like a flock of sparrows spooked by the threat of danger. Gathering her thoughts, she tried to focus. Ordinarily, she connected with Whitney every day or two, but she had been so busy with work lately that Kate was ashamed to admit she did not notice when she hadn't heard from her sister recently.

"She's been missing since last night. Well, no, today. I mean, well, I didn't realize until this morning that she hadn't come home last night."

"Maybe she just stayed overnight at a friend's house. She is twenty-four years old. She can stay out all night if

## Three Days in Seattle - Excerpt

she wants." Kate hoped that was all it was. The thought her sister could really be missing made her feel sick in the pit of her stomach.

"No, no, I don't think so, really. I think she would have told me so. We try to keep each other safe that way, you know. I have such a bad feeling about this, Kate. I think you should come to Seattle right away."

"You mean, like right now?" This news was all so unexpected. Frantic thoughts swirling in Kate's mind made it hard to process.

"Well, yeah. I mean, as soon as you can, of course."

"So, what do the police say?" Kate asked, searching for a voice of reason.

"Police?"

"Yes, Suki. You did call them, didn't you?" Incredulous that her sister might be in danger and the police had not yet been informed, Kate's eyes widened as she stared blankly at the phone. *Are you kidding me?* Her heart began beating hard against her chest, sending pulsing blood painfully racing to her head.

"I'm sorry, Kate, don't get mad. I think you have to wait twenty-four hours before you can report someone missing, don't you?"

"How should I know, Suki? I would have called them to find out, not just assumed." A muscle twitched in Kate's jaw.

"You're right, you're right. I'm sorry."

"I will call them as soon as we get off the phone. I want to talk to the police myself before I come running up there." *Suki had all day to call me, why did she wait until now? Was she hoping Whitney would eventually show up? Something doesn't feel right.*

Perhaps Whitney was just staying over with a new boyfriend that Suki didn't know about. Or maybe she went with some girlfriends for a long weekend. *Suki is probably just overreacting.* Kate clung to that thought to give her a sense of security.

On the other hand, if her sister really were missing, of course she'd drop everything and hop on the first flight to Seattle. She felt uneasy just cancelling work and reorganizing her life on the whim of this woman she barely knew. Kate had photo shoots in the Los Angeles area lined up all week, people depending on her, so she wanted to be sure it was warranted.

"Kate. Your sister is missing! You really need to come as soon as possible," Suki pressed. "Surely, you don't have anything to do that's more important than this, do you?"

Kate recognized the guilt card being played. Her late mother had been a master at it.

"No, of course not. Nothing's more important than finding my sister, if she really *is* missing. However, I am going to call the police first and see what they say, even though you may be right about the twenty-four hour thing."

"Then you'll come?"

As much as Kate hated the thought of upending her whole world overnight, she had to consider seriously the possibility that Suki might be right. If Whitney needed her, she had no choice but to go to Seattle on the first flight she could get.

## Three Days in Seattle - Excerpt

"Yes, yes, I'll come. After I talk to the police, I'll check for flights out of L.A. tomorrow." Kate would have to wait until the morning to change her work schedule. "I appreciate you letting me know, Suki. I'll be in touch."

***

Suki hung up from her conversation with Kate and immediately made another call.

"Hullo," a young man answered.

"It's done."

# THE HEART OF LIES

**THE HEART OF LIES**

**Three Days in Seattle - Excerpt**

# CHAPTER TWO

"HEY, LADY! YOU'RE UP," a young male's voice came from behind her.

"What?" Startled, Kate looked around.

"You're up, over there at the counter." The impatient teenager pointed to the airline ticket counter.

His voice had jerked her out of a daze. She'd been standing in the long, slow-moving passenger line, replaying her situation and the unproductive conversation with the Seattle Police. She hadn't been able to get beyond talking to the officer at the front desk because Whitney had not been missing long enough. He hadn't told her anything of value one way or the other, except that if she was really concerned, she should come as soon as possible. Of course she was concerned. She loved her sister. How dare he suggest otherwise.

It was because of that bond, that if there were any chance Whitney actually *was* missing, Kate would drop everything and go. She had arranged to fly to Seattle on the next available flight.

Unfortunately, getting to Seattle was not so easy. Engine trouble on her connecting flight from Salt Lake City had forced the plane down in Boise, where she had to spend the night and get a new boarding pass for her last-minute change in flights.

Embarrassed when she realized she was holding up the line, her face reddened and she rushed to the counter.

"I'm in a huge hurry, ma'am," Kate said, slapping her driver's license down on the counter a little harder than she'd intended. "Do you think you could get my boarding pass really fast?"

The ticket agent glared at her, then moved like a snail. Kate was sure she must have offended the woman. Glancing up at the monitor on the wall, it showed that her Horizon flight to Seattle was departing in twenty minutes, but she was stuck at the ticket counter in this crowded Boise airport, awaiting the re-issue of her boarding pass.

Kate checked her watch for the umpteenth time, feeling her heart thumping in her chest. *Come on, come on, come on, lady! I have a plane to catch!* She tapped a staccato beat with the heel of her shoe.

Finally, the ticket agent offered up her pass. Kate grabbed it, tossed her long blonde hair over her shoulder and turned abruptly to run for the security gate.

*Splat!*

Kate normally considered herself a controlled, refined, twenty-eight-year-old woman. But here she was, sprawled out face first on the hard floor, having tripped over a child's rolling backpack that she neglected to see in her haste. A manly, well-groomed hand reached down and helped her up. Mortified, her cheeks flushed a bright red.

The helpful hand belonged to an attractive man who looked to be in his early thirties. Kate could not help noticing his deep green eyes, thick brown hair and the broad shoulders filling out his fleece pullover.

"Are you okay?" His voice was warm and deep.

"Yes," she replied, a nervous giggle escaping her lips.

"All, except my pride. Thanks for the help."

Her cheeks flushed hot as she scrambled to gather up her purse and coat and made a beeline for the security gate.

I hope you enjoyed that short excerpt from
my fast-paced Romantic Suspense novel,

## *"Three Days in Seattle"*.

It is available on Amazon.com
in eBook and paperback.

*Debra Burroughs*

# THE HEART OF LIES

LOOK FOR

# **THE CHAIN OF LIES**
A Paradise Valley Mystery: Book Three

It is available on Amazon.com
in eBook and paperback.

# THE HEART OF LIES

# ABOUT THE AUTHOR

Debra Burroughs writes with intensity and power. Her characters are rich and her stories of romance, suspense and mystery are highly entertaining. She can often be found sitting in front of her computer in her home in the Pacific Northwest, dreaming up new stories and developing interesting characters for her next book.

If you are looking for stories that will touch your heart and leave you wanting more, dive into one of her captivating books.

www.DebraBurroughsBooks.com